Lucy's Dilemma

Lucy's Dilemma

Sasha Fenton

Stellium Ltd

Published 2015 by Stellium Ltd
22 Second Avenue, Camels Head
Plymouth, Devon PL2 2EQ
Tel: 01752 367 300   Fax: 01752 350 453
email: stelliumpub@gmail.com   web: www.stelliumpub.com

Sasha Fenton has asserted her moral
right to be identified as the author of this work
in accordance with sections 77 & 78 of the
Copyright, Designs and Patents Act 1988 (as amended)

British Library Cataloguing in Publication Data:
A catalogue record of this book is available from the British
Library

ISBN: 978-0-9575783-2-6
Kindle ebook ISBN: 978-0-9575783-3-3
Cover design by Jan Budkowski

Typesetting by Zambezi Publishing Ltd
Printed in the UK by Lightning Source UK Ltd

The characters, names, stories and events in this book are fictitious products
of the author's imagination. Apart from some historical facts, any resemblance to
actual events, locations, or persons, living or dead, is purely coincidental.

About the Author

Sasha Fenton became a professional dancer, actor, singer and acrobat at the age of twelve, "retired" at twenty to live a suburban life as a wife and mother. She then became a professional astrologer, palmist and Tarot Reader, spending the next three decades giving consultations.

To date, Sasha has also been a prolific writer, with 129 books to her name, international sales of over 6.5 million copies, and translations into fourteen languages. She has written many astrology columns and thousands of articles on mind, body and spirit subjects for various magazines and newspapers.

Interspersed with regular radio and television broadcasts, Sasha has somehow managed to find time to serve on the Executive Council of the Writers' Guild of Great Britain, as Chair and Treasurer for the Advisory Panel on Astrological Education (APAE), and as President and Secretary of the British Astrological and Psychic Society.

Writing fiction has always been on Sasha's mind, and now that she has finally started, she finds herself thoroughly enjoying the process, as a totally new literary direction.

Sasha is married with two children, four lovely grandchildren and one small dog. She was born in London, but now lives in Plymouth. As hobbies, she has a knack for languages, can fly a plane, play golf, dance the tango and catch trout on a fly. She grows veggies and makes excellent chicken soup! However, she can't knit and she's hopeless with mobile phones.

Acknowledgements

Thanks to my husband, Jan Budkowski, and my daughter, Helen Quintiliani, for checking the manuscript, making useful suggestions and for their support and encouragement. Also to Riccardo Quintiliani, for his help with Italian wording.

Thanks to the spirits of the following larger than life characters: Apollonius, Anne Christie, Jonathan Dee, Dimitros, Tony Fenton, Frances Shulman and the utterly gorgeous Sir Thomas Hatherleigh himself - all of whose help has been invaluable in so many ways...

And a warm thank you to "Arms of Old", near Hatherleigh in Devon, for teaching Jan and me how to use bows and arrows. Their expertise has helped me immensely, and given me a lasting fondness for the English Long Bow.

Contact Sasha at:
www.stelliumpub.com
email: stelliumpub@gmail.com

Contents

Part Two

Characters in the Story

NAME	AGE	ROLE
CHARACTERS IN PART ONE		
Emson Barotse	46	PPS to Frances Shulman
Baz Baverstock	39	Margie's husband, Thomas's deputy at TUDOR
Margie Baverstock	35	Sophie's friend, astrologer, psychic
Shelley Baverstock	8	Baz and Margie's daughter
Taylor Baverstock	5	Baz and Margie's son
Aunt Bessie	52	Carlo's "aunty" at Hatherleigh Farm
Bessie's friend and others	Various	They help out at Hatherleigh Farm
Riva Blake	22	Lucy's friend
Alec Blitz	32	Dashing Mossad agent
Harry Byers	Baby	Thomas's nephew
Katherine Byers	36	Thomas's sister
Robert Byers	6	Thomas's nephew
Steven Byers	41	Thomas's brother-in-law
Simon Carlisle	51	Prime Minister
Sir David Cromwell	49	Director of TUDOR
Lady Helen Cromwell	48	Wife of Sir David
Jack Duquesne	27	Baz's junior, fun guy, flirt
Fred	79	Works in Carlo's kitchen garden
Sophie Hatherleigh	33	Wife of Thomas Hatherleigh
Thomas Hatherleigh	38	Deputy Director of TUDOR
Jackson	38	Farm Manager
Julie, Emma, Jessica, Ryan, Jason	Early twenties	All work at TUDOR

Characters in the Story

NAME	AGE	ROLE
CHARACTERS IN PART ONE		
Val Lynch	55	Margie's Mum
Gavin Mason	34	Sophie's ex
Raj Patel	29	Technical & science expert
Lucy Sanders	22	Techie, works at TUDOR
Frances Shulman	54	Home Secretary
Uncle Silas	Old	Sophie's late uncle, inventor of the Project
Jill Standish	46	Sir David's secretary
Kelly Vance	23	Baz's junior, friend of Jack
Wilf, Jane Frieda & their family	Middle aged	Servants at Austin Friars
NEW CHARACTERS IN PART TWO		
General Andrei Balabolin	72	Retired KGB officer
General Valeri Balabolin	48	Andrei's son, Head of Russian Commonwealth Security Office
Irina Grodzinska	37	Polish security officer
Sir Charles (Carlo) Hatherleigh	38	Thomas's country cousin
Douglas "Smiley" Kitteridge	68	Retired MI6 executive
Janessa Patel	30	Wife of Raj Patel

Prologue

The World is a book, and those who do not travel read only a page

In Sophie's Inheritance, we learn that after the death of her parents and a nasty divorce, Sophie Mason only had her much loved, aged Uncle Silas left, but then he died, leaving her two unexpected legacies. The first was a massive fortune, and the second a contraption that he called 'The Project', which he insisted was a machine that would travel through time and space. Towards the end of his life, Sophie had humoured her uncle by helping him work on the Project, but she didn't share his belief about its abilities.

In 1540, Sir Thomas Hatherleigh was a respected Director of *'The Office of State Security for England and Wales'*, serving under Henry the Eighth's First Minister, Thomas Cromwell. When Cromwell falls from favour, Thomas also finds himself headed for the Tower, even though he'd done nothing to deserve his fate.

One day, Sophie decides to use the Project to rescue Thomas, intending to drop him back in his own time, but in a safer situation - all of which leads to a series of unexpected events.

So, now you can read the next episode in the Tudorland series…

Part One

Chapter One

Family is the most important thing in the world
PRINCESS DIANA

BAZ'S NEW JOB

'Daddy's home!' yelled Shelley.

The two children jumped into their father's arms and soon he was carrying them into the kitchen.

'I won't be able to do this much longer,' he laughed, 'you're getting too heavy.'

The rich, meaty aroma of beef casserole filled the kitchen and reminded Baz that he was ready for his dinner. Although he'd come home late, he knew it would be a while before the meal was ready, so he changed out of his work clothes and read to the children before tucking them in. An hour or so later, when the children were asleep and he'd eaten enough to take the edge off his hunger, he felt relaxed enough to give Margie his news, but even so, his tone was slightly tentative.

'I've been offered a new job and a promotion, so it'll mean more money, due to the higher rank.'

'That's good! Or at least I suppose it's good - you don't look too sure about it.'

'The thing is, it's not police work as I've known it; it will be intelligence and counter intelligence work.'

'What, you mean James Bond spookery and all that?' Margie was beginning to see why Baz was edgy.

'Not exactly. The overseas spying department is MI6, while I'd work for a branch of internal security that prevents terrorists, spies and others from doing damage to *this* country, though there might be some travel on occasion. There are several organisations that deal with counter terrorism and a branch that is purely devoted to protecting the Royal Family, but this is a new department that's only recently been set up and it has a broader brief than just terrorism. Needless to say, I'd have to sign the Official Secrets Act and I wouldn't be able to discuss the work with you.'

'That's fair enough, Baz, although if there was any real danger, I'd see it coming and I'd warn you. Official Secrets Acts aren't much of a barrier to a psychic.'

Baz shrugged and smiled at that.

Margie went on, 'the main thing is how *you* feel about the job. I mean, is it something you really fancy?'

'To be honest I think it is, Margie. It'd be a challenge. This is a completely new department, so I'll be able to grow my own team, while I could always transfer back to the normal police later if I was unhappy. I think it'll be all right. Sir David Cromwell's been asked to head up the new department; I've met him a couple of times and he's a good man. He has a reputation for toughness, but he seems fair, and I've never heard anything really negative about him. The main thing is that he's competent, and as you know, the one thing I really hate is working for a prat.'

'Yeah, I know that gets you down,' said Margie thoughtfully.

'They've asked me to bring across anyone I want from the nick, so I've asked Jack Duquesne, because knowing I'd have him at my back gives me some comfort, and there are some young techs who can cope with the fancy computing stuff that I'll want to take with me. My old governor will be a bit miffed at the idea of losing Jack and some of the others, but he's got a backlog of officers who could do with moving up the ladder, so I expect he'll cope.'

'What's the new department to be called, Baz?'

'Well, the official name for the new department *was* going to be some convoluted collection of letters and numbers, but Sir David insisted on an acronym of *'Terrorism and Unprecedented Danger to Our Realm'*, the initials of which spell out TUDOR!'

Margie choked on her fruit squash and upset the glass all over the table, then when she finally managed to catch her breath, she exclaimed in true Londoner fashion, 'Do wot!'

Tearing off a few sheets of kitchen towel and mopping up the squash, Margie muttered, 'Bloody Norah, Baz. Sir David Cromwell *and* TUDOR. You should add Tommy Thumbscrews to that lot and you'll have a department fit to put the fear of God up *any* potential enemy.'

'It could come to that, Margie. It could come to that...'

'Something's up, isn't it? I know you can't say anything, but I can feel it in my water. That's the problem with being psychic. Mum says my weirdness comes from the Irish side of my family, but I wouldn't have put my West Indian granddad and his ancient crone of a mother beyond doing a bit of Voodoo to bugger up their enemies if they thought it necessary.'

'You know doll, we might need a bit of magic ourselves before long, and your remote viewing skills could come in handy.'

'You'll have a data department, with access to GCHQ, Vicap, Interpol, CyberSearch and the rest, so you're hardly going to need my skills.'

'Margie, I have a feeling that I'm gonna need *everything* I can lay my hands on, but I won't really know until I get there.'

* * *

Meanwhile, Margie had a problem of her own that she hadn't yet mentioned, and now she decided to get it off her chest.

'Baz, I'm worried about Mum.'

'Why, what's up with Val?' asked Baz.

'The doctor has told her there's something amiss with her uterus or her ovaries or something, and until she's had some tests done we don't know exactly what it is.'

'Any psychic vibes, Margie?'

'I personally doubt that it's cancer, but I get the feeling that she'll need an operation, though I'm just too close to the situation to be sure, Baz. She needs to get tests done - and quickly.'

'Tell Val to book herself in with a private surgeon and we'll pick up the bill.'

Margie sighed with relief. 'I'm so glad you said that. She'll refuse the help of course, but I'll push her to accept because by the time the NHS gets around to doing anything... well, it could turn into a real problem.'

'Get on to Val now and tell her to make the arrangements pronto. I can't have you both tearing your hair out, and even if the news is bad, Margie, it's better to deal with it sooner rather than later.'

* * *

After they'd cleared up and Baz had taken the newspaper into the sitting room, Margie rang her mother. Val told her daughter that she didn't want to be a financial burden, but Margie lost her temper and told Val to make the arrangements pronto or she'd frog-march her to the doctor's and do it for her.

After the conversation, Margie reported back to Baz. 'She's going to talk to the doctor tomorrow about private options. To be honest, Baz, despite her grizzling, I think she's relieved.'

'The silly cow could have asked us for help, but I understand where she's coming from,' sighed Baz. 'She's getting older and she wants to be as independent as possible, financially and otherwise, but this isn't the time for heroics.'

He took Margie's soft hand into his own. 'I do hope she'll be all right, love,' he said softly, 'I'm very fond of your mum, you know that.'

'I know, I know.' Margie sighed deeply. 'We can only hope and pray until we know more.'

'Why don't you go along to the hospital with her, Margie? I can take some time off to stay here with the children if needs be. I'm very close to telling my boss that I'm taking the new job anyway, so I won't be doing much more than finishing up paperwork and passing things across to others for a while.'

'I might need you here for a day or two at that, Baz. Thanks for offering.'

Baz had a brain wave. 'Why not ask Tom and Sophie to give you a hand? I'm sure they'd be delighted to take the monsters to the zoo or something. In fact, it might be good for the kids to stay with them for a while.'

'Yeah, the kids'd like that. I'll talk to Soph tomorrow and see how she's fixed.'

'Look love, your Tarot cards are on the shelf there, why don't you sit with me and toss out a card or two. It might ease your mind.'

Margie grabbed her cards, sat down, took them out of their box and slowly shuffled them. She decided to use the cards as an oracle, so she spread them out face down and pushed them around in a circle until she felt it was time to stop. Selecting three cards at random, Margie slowly turned them over. The first card was the *'Three of Swords'*, confirming her feeling that an operation was in the offing for her mother. The second card was the *'Four of Swords'*, which traditionally represents recovery from wounds obtained in a battle, but in our modern world, it represents rest and recovery from a stressful time or from illness. The third card was *'Strength'*, which also signifies recovery, and as a Major Arcana card, it represented a good outlook.

Baz was right, the oracle had made Margie feel a little easier, but nothing would really settle her jumpy stomach until her mum had seen the specialist.

Chapter Two

TUDORS

Any sufficiently advanced technology is indistinguishable from magic

ARTHUR C. CLARKE

When her abundant dark auburn hair had lost its glow and turned to salt and pepper ugliness, Frances Shulman had taken to dying her mop a bright carroty red, and while this did nothing for her looks, it matched her hot-temper perfectly, and on this particular morning, she was fuming. Her beautifully booted and suited Permanent Private Secretary, Emson Barotse, was at her side as usual, awaiting instructions while stifling a small sigh. He could see his day was starting badly.

'Emson, it appears that those arseholes at Five, Special and Counter Terrorism haven't heard anything yet.'

'Heard anything about what, Madam?'

'I've just had a strange phone call from Johnny over at Six, and it seems that some new organisation called *'The Sword of Kublai Khan'* or some such thing is at work. The bastards have set their sights on the UK because they see us as a softer target than the US and we represent a good place in which to show off their strength.' Looking over her glasses at Emson, Mrs Shulman went on. 'Johnny's had a call from Israel from a Mossad chap called Alec Blitz, and this Blitz bloke told Johnny some garbage about this new group intending to blow up Westminster Abbey. Literally trying their hands at a modern day gunpowder plot while William and Kate are christening their latest baby.'

'Mossad? They're a bit gung-ho though, aren't they, Madam?' said Barotse warily. 'What does Johnny make of it?'

'Well, he seems to trust this Blitz fellow and he thinks there's something to the story. Look Emson, get on to Cromwell at that new outfit he's set up and see if there's anything *they* can do, and tell them to get on to it quickly.'

Emson brushed a miniscule piece of fluff from his perfect dark blue sleeve. 'This is sounding like something from Hollywood, Madam.'

'Regardless of your un-esteemed opinion, we haven't got time to waste, so talk to Cromwell and tell him to sort it out. That's what the bugger's paid for isn't it? Give him the Blitz connection and tell him to get on with it.'

* * *

Sir David Cromwell looked every inch the powerful Director with his square, aristocratic CEO's face, carefully trimmed light brown hair and close shave. He was normally to be found seated at a rosewood executive desk in his spacious office in the government department called *'Terrorism and Unprecedented Danger to Our Realm'*, now better known by its acronym, 'TUDOR'. However, today he was seated at the head of the oversized teak desk in the newly installed boardroom on the eleventh floor of the Millbank building on the banks of the Thames. Seated round the table were Baz Baverstock, Jack Duquesne, the computer whiz, Raj Patel, and a new young operative called

Kelly Vance. On Sir David's left hand side, sat his elegant secretary, Jill Standish.

Sir David was fiddling with his Mont Blanc pen. Truth to tell, he used a common or garden ballpoint most of the time, but the Mont Blanc gave him comfort when a problem claimed his attention. Those who worked for him called the pen his 'security blanket', but only when they were sure their boss was out of earshot. Cromwell knew this perfectly well, just as he knew everything that went on in his world, but he let it pass as a reasonable piece of banter. Jill Standish glanced at Sir David's serious expression as he proceeded to open the meeting.

'Emson Barotse from the Home Secretary's office called me early this morning and asked if I would get on to Johnny Thorne at MI6; when I spoke to Johnny, he suggested that I contact a chap called Alec Blitz in Mossad, and he kindly gave me Blitz's direct number. The story Blitz has to tell is hard to credit; apparently, he's received a heads-up from the upper echelons of Hezbollah, and they got the story from the upper echelons of Al Qaeda. It was *they* who wanted the tale to be passed on to Mossad and thence to us - or to someone like us in the UK.'

Sir David looked around the table at the astonished faces of his crew as he went on. 'Believe it or not, the Hezbollah man told Blitz about a new group of hotheads who are intent on making a name for themselves. They want to create the kind of havoc - and here I quote - "That would bring the name of all decent Arab terrorists into disrepute and bring shame down on all their heads." The Hezbollah bloke heard a whisper that this lot aren't Arabs, and neither are they Iranians, Pakistanis or anything else that we are accustomed to, so they are thumbing their noses at all that lot as well as at the Western Democracies.

Mossad doesn't know exactly who these jokers are, but thinks they might be a combination of something from the borders of China and Russia, along with some Argentineans. Anyway, whoever they are, Hezbollah and Al Qaeda don't want to be blamed for World War Three breaking out if these idiots actually get away with something, and they don't want the State Secretary for havoc in the White House to jump on the story. They say that if this reaches her ears on a day when her HRT isn't kicking in properly, the whole Middle East could find itself being nuked.'

The assembled group gaped at Sir David and Jack Duquesne even went as far as discreetly to scrape an ear out with his little finger, in case a sudden build-up of wax was affecting his hearing.

Baz asked, 'Have we any real idea about the nature of this group or exactly what they have in mind?'

'The word in the desert is that they intend to disrupt the christening of the Duke and Duchess's new baby by blowing up Westminster Abbey and murdering the Royal party, among other things.'

A gasp went around the table.

Sir David looked sour. 'They seem to be planning a simultaneous attack, or perhaps a series of linked attacks, on various sites, while at the same time, recreating the 1605 Gunpowder Plot, but under the Abbey this time, rather than under the Houses of Parliament.'

'The whole point of using the Abbey for these occasions is that nothing can reach it,' said Baz. 'There's no tube tunnel nearby and there's nothing else down there either. The Royal Protection squad checks the crypt, so how can anything hope to get down there?'

'Well, as I see it, the first thing we have to do is to find out what *is* under the Abbey, even if it isn't actually marked on maps and so forth. What about sewers? That famous sewer designer, Bazalgette, must have dug something under there, surely? After all, the Abbey must have a loo and whatnot?'

'Yeah, of course,' said Baz, 'but my guess is that those will be checked, and we can find out easily enough.'

Sir David was fiddling with his pen again. 'Look, let's all work on finding out as much as we can and we'll meet back here at eight hundred hours tomorrow.'

* * *

At eight on the Friday morning, the TUDOR team members regrouped and reported their findings. Raj had pulled out all the stops and rung someone from the Corporation of London to ask if he could take a look at the archives, but when he mentioned the Abbey, the curator suggested that the Museum of London would be more use because Westminster was outside the old City boundaries. He also suggested the Thames Watermen as a resource, because they kept archives of the area in and around the Thames.

Raj dispatched Jack to the Museum of London, along with an enthusiastic junior who could record any useful conversation and ask any questions that Jack might not think of. Raj discovered that an Act of Parliament had formed the Thames Waterman's Company in 1514 to afford safe passage to travellers who hitherto had been at the mercy of cutthroats and robbers, but its archives only ran from the late 1600s. He thought it worth a try though, because the Company would have records of the ancient watergates that were used by boatmen when picking up and dropping passengers at riverside destinations. It was possible that these indentations into the Thames' banks might once have led to hitherto unknown pathways and passages.

He sent Kelly and another junior on that mission, while two more youngsters were despatched on a rare jaunt away from the office to visit the Maritime Museum in Greenwich. He also suggested that Kelly try the Westminster City Archives at the Library in Victoria Street when she'd finished with the Watermen.

* * *

Despite all this effort, none of them located a direct line into the crypt, although Jack and Kelly had picked up whispers about an ancient tunnel which may have started life as a culvert or even a tributary of the Thames. Rumour had it that it had been dug in Tudor times to enable monks to escape when Henry the Eighth was dissolving the monasteries. None of this was making much sense though, because Sir David knew the Abbey had already been old in the fifteen hundreds, and it hadn't been destroyed during the Reformation, but nevertheless, he decided that he wanted this line of thinking pursued.

'Get on to Simon Scharma and Simon Sebag Montefiore, Raj, and see if they know anything about this.'

'Yes sir, but I think it was David Starkey who wrote a book on Henry the Eighth,' replied Raj.

'Well, get on to that sarcastic sod too, if it'll help.' Sir David had a habit of pulling his ear when he was thinking, so by now he was giving the lobe a good tug. 'Find that *Time Team* lot from the telly with that Tony thingy and that scruffy professor, Phil Harding and whatnot. They use those geophysical machines to locate things, so who knows, they might come up with something.'

Sir David looked pensive for a moment, sighed and said, 'What we really need is a bloody *time machine*, then we could go back and find someone who lived in London in the

1500s and ask them about tunnels. As far as I know, there was a great expansion of building in the area during the late fourteen and early fifteen hundreds, after the country recovered from the Black Death and the mess caused by the Wars of the Roses. So, if a tunnel had been built during Henry the Eighth's time, someone from that era would have known about it.'

Sir David chewed his lip and fiddled with his Mont Blanc, while Baz cleared his throat.

'I might be able to help you there, Sir.'

Sir David glared at Baz. 'You're telling me you're a history expert?'

'No, Sir.'

'You're telling me you've got a time machine lurking in your back garden?'

Baz shifted in his seat, now certain that he was on the point of throwing a perfectly good career out of the window. He swallowed and decided to roll the dice. His throat was so dry that he actually croaked. 'Such machine does exist, and it's called *The Project*. It's a time and space machine, because it can travel to different times, but also to different places. It's... ah... lurking...'

Baz started to dry up.

Sir David was getting red in the face. 'Well, get on with it man!' he shouted. 'Where's the bloody thing lurking - if it exists at all, that is - *and* if you haven't gone raving *mad*!'

The others were all staring at Baz open mouthed. Now almost gabbling, Baz tried again. 'It's in my wife's friend's garden shed, Sir.'

'You mean to tell me that your wife's best friend just happens to own a time machine?'

'Yes Sir, I do.'

Sir David's face was moving from red to purple. 'Are you *insane*!' he roared.

'No Sir.'

Now Sir David spoke dangerously quietly. 'What the fuck is this all about?'

Baz asked if he could have a glass of water, and as Jack was the nearest, he poured the water and passed it to Baz. Once Baz had taken a few sips, he told the team the story, starting right at the beginning with Sophie and her uncle, her first attempts with the Project, and how the safety rings worked if the time traveller got into trouble and needed a quick ride home. Finally, he gave a brief explanation about Thomas Hatherleigh and even about Katherine and Steven Byers and their son.

At this point Jack jumped in. 'I can actually believe this, boss, and I don't think Baz is bonkers at all.' He looked at the astonished faces around the table. 'You see, there was a really funny incident at Tom and Sophie's wedding, and something niggled away at the back of my mind at the time. I forgot about it then, but now it's starting to make sense.'

Sir David looked at Jack and said wearily, 'Well, I wish it'd make sense to me.' He turned to his secretary and asked her to organise coffee for them all. 'Go on Jack, You'd better tell us what's on your mind.' Jill Standish suddenly looked very down in the mouth, so Sir David spoke to her. 'If you're frightened of missing something, Jill, you can use the boardroom phone to order coffee.' She brightened immediately and walked over to the side-board to make the call.

Jack told his story. 'As Baz said, Sophie is his wife's best friend and they've been friends since before she and Baz met, so naturally, when Sophie was getting married, she invited Baz and Margie to the wedding. I wasn't part of the story at the time, so I wasn't there – well not to start with anyway. As it happened, it was a second wedding for both of them, because Tom was a widower and Sophie was divorced, so they did the deed at the Register Office with his rellies and a few friends. It turns out that Sophie's previous husband was a major drunk and a druggie, as well as being a great dollop of dough that's gone completely to pot. Somehow, he'd got wind of the wedding and the news sent him ape-shit. After the ceremony, the wedding party came out of the Register Office and one or two of them started to take a photo or two to mark the occasion, and under normal circumstances, that would have been the end of it.'

Jack turned to Baz. 'Remind me Baz, what was the ex's name?'

'Gavin Mason.'

'That's right, Gavin. The slob had brought along a couple of dozen eggs to chuck at the bride and so forth, but Sophie ducked and missed getting smeared while Baz's wife Darcy Bussell'd out of the way when the eggs came flying in her direction. After all that, Baz and Tom raced across the pavement and grabbed Gavin.

'The stretch of pavement outside the Register Office is rather wide, so the lads must have bolted across it at a rate of knots, and they grabbed the gorilla and rushed him back over the pavement and pinned him up against the Register Office wall. As I heard the story later from a rather lovely blonde called Marianne, who happened to be a guest at the wedding, it was Tom who got hold of Gavin and pinioned him with Baz helping him. Then Tom's brother-in-law, Steven and another guest helped to keep the drunken idiot pinned to the wall while Baz yelled at Margie to call the nick and get some uniforms round.'

Jack looked around the room and saw that he had everyone's undivided attention.

'Well, I couldn't miss out on the fun, could I? So I hitched a ride in the squad car, and once they'd taken Gavin away, I stayed on to pay my compliments to the bride, groom and everyone else.'

'Including the blonde with the nice tits,' interjected Baz.

'Well, of course,' said Jack.

'Who you ended up donating one to,' said Baz, lifting an eyebrow.

'Naturellement, mon brave,' countered Jack.

'Get on with it, you oversexed Casanova!' Sir David was almost beside himself, but also extremely intrigued.

Jack went on. 'It's only now that I can see it. You see, it was Tom who had fat Gavin in a classic arm lock. Looking back, I can see that if Tom had had cuffs on him, he'd have cuffed the sod in no time flat. Quite frankly, I'm not sure I'd want to be on the wrong side of him.'

Baz said, 'You're absolutely right, Jack. I thought nothing of it at the time, but he is quick and effective. He's clearly been a rozzer in the past - it stands out a mile.'

Jack took Baz's glass and helped himself to a sip of his friend's water.

'I went back to the nick to finish my shift and I caught up with the wedding group later at Tom and Sophie's flat. I have to tell you, there's something *about* the bloke. He has a kind of restrained power. He's friendly enough, but he's quiet. He's an observer who misses nothing, and he asks more questions than he answers.' Jack took another drink. 'If you were to ask my opinion, Boss, I'd say that Thomas Hatherleigh is ex-army, ex-cop or an ex-spook - and at a very high level at that.'

After another drink from Baz's glass, Jack continued with his observations. 'Tom made himself out to be Hidalian; you may remember that the Government allowed Hidalian asylum seekers to come in and take a fast track to citizenship when that nasty little war was going on in their country. It had something to do with an ancient alliance and the fact that Hidalians helped us out in the two World Wars. It crossed my mind even then that he might have been Stasi or whatever they have over there, but when I think of it now, he's nothing like any of the Hidalians I've come across. He doesn't even *talk* like them, and neither do his sister and brother-in-law. They have a rather formal and oldy-worldy way of speaking. They don't say thee, thou, and whatnot, but they definitely don't sound modern. Anyway, at one point, we got chatting about my name being French and we switched to speaking French for a bit. His French is absolutely word perfect, but it's strangely old-fashioned, like something out of a Zola novel... or even older... if you get my drift.'

Jack turned to Baz. 'You said that Tom had been very quick off the mark when he went after Gavin. I saw the tail end of that and to be honest, Baz, I had the feeling that Tom wouldn't have stopped at merely cuffing the bugger if we hadn't been there.' Jack looked thoughtful and then speaking as much to himself as to the others said, 'I can't say I've much to base this on, but I don't think Tom is from Hidalia at all and I don't even think he's from our era... I think he's Elizabethan or medieval or something.'

Turning to Baz, Sir David asked, 'You're also suggesting that this Thomas Hatherleigh has moved forward in time from Tudor England?' Sir David's eyebrows were threatening to join his receding hairline.

'Yes, I do. And his sister and brother-in-law too.'

'Just a minute, just a minute, let me think.' Sir David was thoroughly tetchy, but also unusually excited. 'I know a bit about the Tudor court, because my great, great, great, Christ knows how many times removed, grandpa was Henry's First Minister.'

'You mean, *Thomas* Cromwell?' asked Baz.

'Yes. I've read a lot about him and his work. He was a bugger to those who he saw as a threat to the crown, but kind to his friends and family. Apparently, in 1534, everyone was told to swear an oath to the effect that Henry was now the head of the church in England and Wales and that the Pope was out of the picture. After a thousand years of Roman Catholicism, not everyone could live with something that radical, so on Henry's behalf, Cromwell had a couple of archbishops executed for refusing to take the oath, and when it came to dealing with a bunch of recalcitrant Carthusian monks, Cromwell locked them up and let them starve to death. He was intensely loyal to his king, but he was said to be a lot like Stalin.'

A knock on the door announced the arrival of coffee, along with a large plate of biscuits. Raj removed the water bottles and glasses and put them on a side table, while the young lady who'd brought in the coffee put it down on the boardroom table. Sir David helped himself to a bourbon cream and a couple of rich teas while Jill handed him a coffee.

A thoughtful look passed over Sir David's face, while he studied a biscuit. 'Come to think of it, I seem to remember reading about a guy called Hatherleigh who ran the security service of the day. He reported to Cromwell, but when Henry decided to arrest Cromwell and execute him, this Hatherleigh chap got wind of it and managed to escape to Flanders. The usual thing for a subordinate who worked for a boss who was in trouble in those days was to denounce the boss in very black terms and rush to join some other faction, as it was only by working for the right boss in the right faction that one could hope to survive. Maybe this Hatherleigh bloke didn't feel like playing turncoat, or perhaps he got denounced in his own right in some way, I don't know which. The weird thing is that there was some doubt as to whether he ever actually *reached* Flanders, because history tells us that he simply disappeared - and that he was never heard of again. Kind of like the Lord Lucan of his day.'

Sir David fiddled with his pen and muttered quietly, 'However, why the fuck are we discussing all this ancient history when we've got more than enough of our own problems right here and now?'

Baz rushed to get his words out before his courage deserted him for good. 'You're quite right, Boss. The reason Thomas Hatherleigh *didn't* reach Flanders is because he's living on the other side of the Thames and working at the CAB.'

The TUDOR crew gazed at Baz in open-mouthed amazement, while Sir David was still considering the possibility that his second in command was completely off his rocker.

Baz said, 'If you like, I'll ask him to come over and you can quiz him about Tudor London yourself.'

In the absence of anything else that looked remotely useful, Sir David decided that he might as well meet this Hatherleigh chap. 'Well, I guess you'd better send for him, Baz. You never know…'

Chapter Three

FRIDAY NIGHT CURRY

Sometimes I wonder if men and women really suit each other. Perhaps they should live next door and just visit now and then

KATHERINE HEPBURN

Lucy Sanders sipped her gin and tonic while dipping pieces of poppadom into mango chutney.

Her friend Riva smiled at her. 'The chutney's always good here and so's the raita, but I've always wondered why Indian restaurants insist on serving that lime pickle. It tastes like fiery cabbage in washing up liquid.'

'When did you last taste washing up liquid, Reev?' laughed Lucy.

'Well, you know what I mean.'

The waiter loaded up a heated metal platform with dishes of rice, lamb and chicken, along with several chapattis.

'How're we going to manage this lot?' asked Riva.

'We will, love. We always do.'

'Sadly, you're right, which is why my waistline will never be sylph-like.'

When the waiter had gone and the girls had piled up their plates, Lucy asked Riva something she'd always wanted to know.

'How did you get your name, Reev?'

'Well, you've heard of Riva del Garda?'

'The Italian resort?'

Riva nodded.

'Yeah. Mum took me there on a holiday when I was a kid,' said Lucy, 'it's a pretty place.'

'Well, my parents went there a year or so after they were married, and they conceived me there.'

'So they named you after the place, like the Beckham's did with Brooklyn?'

'Exactly so.'

Once they'd made inroads into the curry, Riva decided to return the compliment and ask Lucy something she'd always wondered about.

'How did you come to meet Chris, and why on earth did you stay with him for so long? I mean, he was pleasant enough, but I could never understand that relationship.'

'It's a long story, Reev.'

'This is a big curry, Loo, so we've plenty of time.'

Lucy ran a hand through her russet waves while taking a moment to think. She'd never talked openly about her life, but her friendship with Riva had turned out to be a good one, so she felt it was time to open the shutters. After a moment's thought, Lucy made a start.

'It all starts with Mum and Dad, really. They met when they were in their early twenties and married because Patrick was on the way.'

'Patrick's your older brother, eh?'

Lucy gave a nod while munching on a particularly tasty piece of chicken. 'Both Mum and Dad are nice people as individuals, but they're no good with each other, so they split and Mum brought Patrick up on her own. Dad always gave her as much money as he could, and he'd take

Patrick off her hands for a few days from time to time. She also had help from the two sets of grandparents.'

'Was your Dad a womaniser?'

'And how! He was very good looking, with laughing eyes, reddish brown wavy hair and a lovely smile. Women wouldn't leave him alone, and he didn't discourage them. That was the main reason for the break-up.'

Riva agreed that a man with a roving eye wasn't great husband material.

'When Patrick was about fourteen, Dad was down on his luck and needed somewhere to stay, so Mum took him in for a while, and she promptly fell pregnant again - this time with me. She actually considered a termination, but Dad wasn't keen, and when Patrick got to hear of it, he made a great fuss, yelling that he couldn't bear the idea of Mum "killing his brother or sister", so there I was.'

Lucy helped herself to some rice while still mentally back in the past. 'Dad continued to help financially and Patrick did what he could, even taking me to college with him on occasion. He said having a smiley baby in a pushchair helped him pull the girls!' Lucy smiled at the thought, then went on with her story.

'Mum didn't have as much parental help with me as she'd had with Patrick, because her parents had moved to Spain, and Dad's father was dead, but Dad's mum was still around, and she helped out by looking after me from time to time. She was a lovely lady.'

'Did your mum have boyfriends?' asked Riva.

Lucy nodded. 'There were one or two, but the first one to move in with us was Bernard. He's not a bad bloke in himself, but he has three young children from his previous marriage and they stayed with us a lot of the time. When I wasn't around, the two girls would help themselves to my makeup and my clothes, while his son was a rude, mouthy, noisy, dirty brat of about ten who did all he could to make my life difficult.'

'Christ!'

'That wasn't the worst part, though. Dad was living with his latest squeeze, and the woman had three daughters who were older than me; whenever I stayed at their home, they treated me like rubbish and tormented me. Their favourite trick was to chuck nail polish on my clothes.'

'Ouch,' said Riva looking at Lucy in horror, 'you just can't get that stuff off.'

'That was why they did it. It wasn't as though I could afford to replace the stuff, so I often ended up having to wear ruined jeans and my school uniform with their bloody polish on it. I gave up on the idea of owning anything other than school uniforms from then on, because bloody Bernard's kids would help themselves to anything nice and the other lot would destroy it. In the event, even my school stuff was often covered with shit of one kind or another.'

'Euch!' exclaimed Riva.

Riva remembered something from her own school days.

'Schoolteachers can be amazingly thick, Lucy. I had a friend who had to take care of her sick mother and mentally handicapped brother. There was very little money in the house and she gave what there was in the way of treats to her brother. She admitted to me that she was often scruffy, with clothes that were too small, worn out and sometimes less than clean. She was also often very tired and hungry, but the real problem came at Christmas. The rich kids routinely gave each other presents and their parents made a point of buying expensive gifts for the teachers to butter them up, while my friend could only give them a home-made Christmas card. All that brought opprobrium down on her head, and her schoolwork was marked down so that she was made to feel a fool. The teachers often talked to her as though she was a troublemaker or something!

'Did she give up, Reev?'

'For a while she did, but once she had children of her own, she started going to evening classes and she caught up, eventually getting a degree in geography of all things.'

'Well, if you ever meet up with your old friend again, please tell her that Lucy Sanders is glad for her,' said Lucy with real warmth.

Realising that as far as school had been concerned, she had been fairly lucky, Lucy said, 'I had one or two teachers who looked down on me, but most saw my potential, so I guess I was lucky in that respect, at least.'

'Yeah, but having rotten kids to deal with at home must have been bloody awful,' said Riva.

Lucy came back to the present. 'On one occasion, Dad's step-daughters trashed my laptop, and if I hadn't just backed up all my work a couple days earlier, I'd have lost two years of school work.'

'Christ, Loo! Didn't your dad say something to them?'

'Yeah, he did. And he bought me a new laptop, but they just waited until he wasn't looking before messing me about again, and however much you try to ignore it, relentless hatred and name calling gets you down. I eventually came to the inevitable conclusion that I couldn't live with either of my parents. I couldn't bear the idea of going into care and living with some kiddy-fiddler who takes children in for payment, so even though I was still only fifteen, I asked Dad if he would rent a flat for me.'

'And did he?'

'Property wasn't as stupidly expensive as it is now and Dad had some money hidden away that his girlfriend didn't know about, so he bought me a flat, and it's the one I'm still living in now. It was in his name until I passed my finals, and then he made it over to me. Perhaps he felt guilty, or maybe dishing out that kind of largesse made him feel good. I didn't ask, but needless to say, I was immensely grateful. Patrick had moved in with his girlfriend by then, so he didn't have much money to spare, but he sent something towards furniture, while the grandparents also pitched in. I trawled second hand shops and soon made myself a nice refuge. I made it a rule from day one that only my parents and Patrick and his girlfriend could come to the flat. Strangely enough, I didn't feel as lonesome on my own as I'd done when living with my so-called family.'

'Christ, Loo, I didn't realise it'd been that bad.'

'Well, it could have been worse, Reev. Nobody hit me or groped me, and until I was fifteen, I had a bedroom to myself. Neither of my parents really had time nor space for me in their lives, and nor did anyone else either. Perhaps it was lucky for them that I worked hard at school and didn't give them any trouble, but I wasn't being good to make their lives easy. It was just that I realised that if I could get good qualifications, I would get a good job and then I wouldn't need to ask them for anything.'

'I completely get it, Loo: if you can stand on your own feet, nobody can hurt you, can they? But then you met Chris. How did that happen?'

'Soon after moving into the flat, I started looking for something to do, and I found weekend work at a garden centre. The bloke paid me off the books until I was sixteen, and then I became "official". Anyway, one day Chris came in with a friend who was looking for plants and stuff, and we got chatting. A week later, he came back and asked me out for a drink. Chris had just taken a job in a new art gallery and the pay wasn't good, so he needed a flat share. I didn't have to worry about rent, but I still needed to find the council tax, utilities and all the rest of it, so I suggested that he move in with me and contribute to the bills, and the arrangement worked well for both of us.'

'So he was more of a flat-mate than a boyfriend.'

'Well, yes... but we also liked each other. Remember, I was still only sixteen and I was putting a great deal of energy into my studies, along with running the flat and working part time, so I guess I just didn't have the time or energy to go out and look for boyfriends. Living with Chris was a lot like living with a brother, and I was used to that after growing up with Patrick.'

Riva looked directly at her friend. 'You were having sex with him though, weren't you?'

Lucy gazed sightlessly across the room while her mind turned back to the day Chris came to her bed.

'We'd been to a party with some of his friends and we both got a bit tipsy, and when we got back to the flat, Chris wanted to make love. I was happy to be loved... and I guess I was curious about sex.'

'What was it like?' asked Riva. 'Was he any good?'

'Well, I've nothing to compare it with, but the truth is that I found it disappointing. I thought there'd be an explosion of passion or something, but I didn't feel much of anything really.'

Riva began to realise the extent of her friend's loneliness and inner sadness. She helped herself to some more lamb while trying to imagine what Chris had been like as a lover.

'Well, what did Chris do?' asked Riva quietly. 'I mean, did he turn nasty or something?' Riva twirled a blond strand and stared intently at Lucy. 'You know, I always thought he was a bit wet, and I even wondered whether he was gay or something. How old was he anyway?'

'Chris was almost six years older than me, so he was nearly twenty-one when we first met. Looking back, I'm sure he was on the way to becoming gay, but I don't think he was a very sexy man - either way, if you see what I mean.' said Lucy equally quietly.

Riva's eyebrows went up and she actually stopped eating.

'I think that living with me made Chris appear straight to others, which even in these enlightened days can be useful. I just accepted things as they were, and while it's true that we did make love once more after that – again after we'd been drinking a bit – that was it. He'd never shared my bed or my bedroom at nights, so we just left it at that. Later, when my life started to get a little easier, I began to want more.'

Lucy leaned in closely to Riva and checked the other tables, ensuring she wouldn't be overheard. 'One day, I looked at a medical site on the 'Net and checked out the measurements for male equipment. I discovered that every part of Chris's crown jewels was grossly undersized, so I think he must have lacked the requisite amount of hormone or something.'

Riva's eyebrows now shot up so far that they threatened to leave her face, while she struggled to keep her mouth from falling open.

'I mean, the pictures on the 'Net looked the same shape as Chris's equipment, but in a bigger version, if you get my meaning - a lot bigger, really. Put it this way, the stuff on the 'Net resembled turkey giblets, while Chris's man-bits looked more like pigeon's giblets.'

This was too much for Riva, who now completely lost it, stuffing her napkin into her mouth to prevent herself from making a scene. It took her time to get her breath back, but when she could speak again, she asked Lucy how the relationship ended.

'I was in my second year at university when Chris was suddenly offered a dream job in Canada. I was glad for him, but it left me up the creek financially so to speak, so I borrowed a bit from Patrick and got a small student loan to see me through. I'd kept my weekend job at the garden centre going, and while waiting for my results to come through, I also found office work as a temp during the week, and that helped me repay Patrick.'

Riva thought Patrick selfish for expecting his kid sister to repay him, but she kept her opinion to herself.

'Chris sent me an email telling me he was happy in Canada, and that was the last I heard of him.' Speaking as much to herself as to Riva, Lucy said, 'It's eight months since he left; and it's gone so quickly.'

'You'd like to find someone nice now, though, wouldn't you?' asked Riva.

'Yeah, of course I would,' nodded Lucy. 'But I don't know where to start looking.'

'Men turn up in the strangest places, Loo, and who knows where the next one will be – for either of us, that is. After all, I've had a few boyfriends, but I haven't met Mr. Right yet – only "Mr. Alright for Now", from time to time, so let's hope there's someone nice out there for both of us.' Riva gave her friend a wicked grin and said, 'And let's hope the men we meet have something better than shrivelled pigeon giblets to offer us.'

The two girls ended their meal giggling so hard that several of the other diners turned to stare at them.

Chapter Four

SIR DAVID MEETS THOMAS

The darkest places in hell are reserved for those who maintain their neutrality in times of moral crisis

DANTE ALIGHEIRI

Baz's call caught Thomas at an early meeting, but when Baz said it was important, Thomas concluded the meeting and told the others to ask his assistant, Teresa, for anything they needed.

He put the office phone back to his ear. 'Are you all right Baz? Is something wrong with Margie or the kids?'

'They're fine, Tom, but something's blown up at work that you can help us with - and it's very urgent indeed. Can you get your arse over to Millbank for a meeting?'

'Of course. Do you want me to come right away?'

'Like yesterday, Tom. Look, jump in a cab. I can indent for the fare money and all that, just get here ASAP.'

'Don't worry about the cab fare, Baz. Who do I ask for?'

'Just ask reception for TUDOR and give my name. They'll buzz me and I'll come down.'

'Okay, see you soon.'

* * *

Thomas arrived at Millbank forty-five minutes later and he was working his way through the reception's security and getting a pass made up while the receptionist rung through to Baz. A few minutes later, Baz walked briskly out of a lift, greeted Thomas and then led the way to the bank of lifts. On the way up to the boardroom, Baz commented that he'd never told Thomas his governor's name, but that it was Sir David Cromwell.

'TUDOR? Cromwell?' queried Thomas.

'Indeed. TUDOR stands for *'Terrorism and Unprecedented Danger to Our Realm'*. It's the name of this particular counter terrorism organisation and our governor is a direct descendant of your Thomas Cromwell, so he's into all things Tudor, if you see what I mean.'

Thomas lifted an eyebrow but there wasn't time for questions, because they were soon striding into the TUDOR boardroom. Several pairs of eyes gazed at Thomas with intense interest, while Baz made the introductions and showed Thomas to a seat. What they saw was a tall, elegant, dark haired, good-looking man with amazing blue eyes. He might have been good to look at, but he didn't look especially out of the ordinary.

Sir David came straight to the point. *'The Project,'* he said.

'Ah,' replied Thomas quietly.

'Are you who Baz says you are?'

Thomas took a moment to gather his thoughts and then in a measured tone, addressed Sir David directly.

'I am Sir Thomas Hatherleigh, late of the *'Office of State Security for England and Wales'*, reporting to Sir Thomas Cromwell. I was dubbed a Knight several years ago in Tudorland, after a period of time spent working for King Henry in the Holy Land. Habit makes it hard for me to say exactly what the nature of my service was, despite the fact that as far as you are concerned, it happened almost five hundred years ago. Let us say that certain enemies of the crown and of this country were… eliminated as a result of my investigations.'

The silence in the room was profound. Thomas went on. 'Am I right in thinking that Thomas Cromwell was your ancestor, Sir?'

Sir David nodded slightly.

'Sir Thomas Cromwell became the Earl of Essex not too long before he was arrested. Perhaps it was hubris on his part or perhaps Henry allowed it to go through as a means of calming any fears your ancestor may have been harbouring as to his future. Perhaps King Henry liked him one day and disliked him the next: he was quite capable of that.'

'What was your position in the *Office of State Security?*'

'I was the Director.'

There was a general intake of breath.

'My job would now be considered a cross between Director of MI5, MI6, the Police and that of Home Secretary. I was also directly involved in interrogation at times.'

After giving the others a moment to absorb the astounding information, Thomas started again.

'Sir Thomas Cromwell was King Henry's First Minister, so he was the only person who stood between the crown and me, but I didn't envy your ancestor, because it was clear to those of us who knew him, that King Henry's behaviour was becoming less stable by the day. I have since learned that King Henry later wished he hadn't listened to tittle-tattle and that he bitterly regretted executing Cromwell, but by then it was too late. As far as I was concerned, I could have saved my own skin by denouncing Sir Thomas and joining some other faction - Northumberland, for example - but I hated the idea. And who would trust a turncoat anyway? My obduracy and my difficult position became my death sentence, but then Sophie read about me and realised that there was no recorded ending to my life, which apparently made it possible for her to remove me from my perilous situation. Her original idea was that after a few days, she would return me to some other part of the country, or perhaps to Flanders where I might make some kind of fresh start. However, in the event, I stayed here in New London, and my sister and her family have since joined me.'

Jill poured a cup of coffee for Thomas and handed it to him with a couple of packets of sugar. She gave him a pleasant smile and Thomas thanked her.

'My position was very senior in today's terms, but you have to remember that the population of England only numbered 2.7 million, with another quarter of a million in Wales. Ireland was administered as a separate colony, and Scotland was a hostile foreign country that usually allied itself to France. The Scots tried many times to attack or undermine England before and during my time in Tudorland, but the English also attacked the Scots many times. In addition, we had to plough a careful path between France, Burgundy, the Holy Roman Empire, Brittany, Gascony, the Pope and occasionally even what you would call the countries of the Middle East.'

Thomas looked directly at Sir David and asked, 'Is that enough for you, Sir?'

Sir David lifted a shoulder, nodded and said that it certainly was. He stared at his pad, pursed his lips and fiddled with his 'comfort pen'. Then he looked straight at Thomas and said, 'I don't know how to ask this of someone who doesn't work for our modern security service, but I feel I have no choice. Would you be prepared to take a trip back to your Tudor time for us if it would help us avert a major disaster? One that directly threatens our own Royal Family, that is?'

'Of course. When do you want me to go?'

Ten minutes later, Sir David was telling Thomas the reason for the potential expedition. 'We've had some very clear intel that a mixed group of Parmian trouble makers have decided to show the West how clever they are, so these jokers have joined a group of Argentineans who have decided to pay us back for keeping them out of the Falkland Islands in 1982. Apparently, it's the Argies who are in charge of the operation, the idea of which is to blow up Westminster Abbey at the very moment when the Duke and Duchess of Cambridge are christening their baby.'

Sir David pursed his lips and waited a moment before going on. 'The Duke refuses to move the christening to another venue or to change the date as he says that would send the terrorists the wrong signal, so the problem has landed in our lap, so to speak. Unfortunately, we can't find any record of tunnels that run right under the Abbey, but there is a rumour hanging around that a tunnel *was* dug during Henry the Eighth's reign when the monasteries were being dissolved. From the little that we have managed to glean from history books and the Internet, it seems that this particular tunnel would have been constructed around 1540 to 1541.'

'Well, Sir David,' said Thomas. 'I left in June 1540 and if there'd been any tunnelling going on then, I'd have known about it, so your timing is probably right. Apparently, the harassing of monks and nuns and the disso-lutions got much worse *after* Cromwell was executed. Despite what people think, there was no *carte blanche* state-sponsored torturing when Cromwell was in charge, and every incident of torture that occurred during his time required a royal warrant. After Cromwell died, things changed for the worse and tyranny became embedded.'

Thomas went on to explain how the Project worked, and when Sir David realised that they could stay in Tudorland as long as they wanted, but only appear to be away from New London for less than twenty minutes, he suggested that they all go - apart from Raj, who would coordinate the operation from Millbank.

Baz looked puzzled. He asked, 'How will we New Londoners manage in such a strange environment?'

'You've no need to worry, Baz, I'll show you all you need to know,' responded Thomas.

Jack wondered what Tudor girls were like, while Kelly wondered how she would cope with the clothes and being a woman in such a masculine era.

Jack told them about a novel that he'd recently read where people were sent back to fourteenth century France. The book ruled that they weren't allowed to take pistols with them as it would be anachronistic, paradoxical and that such weapons would muck up history.

Sir David told him they would definitely be tooled up, regardless of anachronisms, paradoxes or history, because their security came first. They'd also take water, medicines and anything else they needed for health and safety.

Kelly started to feel a little more confident.

Chapter Five

PLANNING THE TRIP

You can't connect the dots looking forward; you can only connect them looking backwards. So, you have to trust that the dots will somehow connect in your future. You have to trust in something - your gut, destiny, life, karma, whatever. This approach has never let me down, and it has made all the difference in my life

STEVE JOBS

Thomas asked if he could have an hour to ponder the problem, as there was a lot to take into consideration, so Jill Standish found him a desk in the large outer office and equipped him with paper, pens, pencils and a ruler. She also gave him the Official Secrets Act to read and sign. His mobile needed recharging, so he asked if he could have another phone *pro tem*. Jill got one of the lads to plug in a landline for him while she found a charger that fitted Thomas's mobile and set it on a side table to recharge. She fetched a coat rack and a hanger and hung his suit jacket up neatly.

By eleven o'clock, they were all back in the boardroom. The men had discarded their jackets and ties and Kelly had dumped her cardigan. The familiarity of the situation made old habits kick in, so Thomas soon found himself taking control of the meeting.

'Firstly, I want to speak to my brother-in-law, Steven, because he worked for the Exchequer and he'll have more idea of who to contact with regard to building work. Once we start to make enquiries, other names are bound to bubble up, so we may get a line on who did any digging around the site and why it was carried out. Steven's a good guy and he won't talk to anyone outside our circle about any of this - after all, when you think about it, we've managed to get through over a year without anyone knowing we're from Tudor times, and keeping quiet about something like this will be nothing in comparison.

The others nodded at this comment.

'I will need Steven to come back with me to Tudorland to see whether his house or mine are still available to us, because we will need a base. The two houses are side by side in Austin Friars, which is near Moorgate and Bishopsgate. Steven and I brought our caches of Tudor money and gold with us from Tudorland, but we'll need to take them back with us along with even more money so that we can finance whatever we'd need at the Tudorland end. There were no banks in England in those days, only vaults under jewellery shops or safe places in people's houses - as was the case with mine, assuming we can still get in there.'

The others looked thoughtful as they took in the serious implications of having to operate in such an unsophisticated time.

'We will need a supply of gold in small lumps, but no modern jewellery, because hallmarks and gems cut in the modern style will bring too much attention to bear. We also need to schedule our arrival some time *after* the date of Cromwell's execution and at a time when my disappearance was old news, so to speak. King Henry never had a problem with me as such, but there are criminals who would love to even a few scores with me, so we need to avoid drawing too much attention to ourselves. Your history books tell me that King Henry executed Thomas Cromwell on July 28 1540, so I suggest we consider early November as our start date, because the dust will have settled by then.'

'What do we wear?' asked Jack.

'Well that's my next issue,' said Thomas. 'I still have the clothes I was wearing when Sophie first rescued me, although they are no longer in good condition. When we lifted Katherine and Steven out during an outbreak of plague, Sophie advised us against bringing any unnecessary clothing with them for fear of contamination, so they came across in their undergarments and we burned those and mine upon their arrival.'

'Christ, I hadn't thought of plague,' said Sir David, shuddering.

'Well,' said Thomas, 'that is another good reason for landing in Tudorland in November, because the sweating sickness and other diseases diminish in cooler weather.'

Sir David took over. 'Who else wants to go?'

Baz and Jack immediately volunteered, as did Kelly.

Jill Standish coughed discreetly.

'What is it, Jill?' asked Sir David.

'I can get in touch with '*Angels*' in Shaftsbury Avenue. They provide the clothes for films and TV, so I can take the lads and Kelly along today if you like, but Thomas had better come with us to ensure the outfits look right.'

Sir David gave her a nod. 'Good idea.' Sir David asked Thomas if he could take time off from his job. Thomas told him that he'd already been on the phone to his bosses and explained that there was a family emergency and that he'd be out of the office for at least a week.

Baz said, 'What about weapons? I will definitely want my pistol with me.' He turned to Thomas. 'Tommo, can I wear a pistol rig under a cape or something?'

'You'll wear a doublet, which is like a fitted windbreaker, but you will also wear a short cloak over the doublet, so your pistol will be easy to reach while still being out of sight.'

'That's a blessing. It means that Jack and I can be tooled up. What about you, Tommo?'

'I wouldn't know what to do with a pistol if I had one, but I'll have a sword.' He turned to Jill. 'Also, even though the others can't use a sword, they'll need to wear them because a gentleman without a sword would stick out a mile. Everyone will need a dagger - if only to eat with - and that also goes for Kelly.'

Jill thought for a moment. 'Angels keep swords I'm sure, so you can pick out whatever is suitable, along with scabbards, belts and so on. We can supply you with knives from the armoury here.'

Sir David asked Thomas, 'Will Kelly be useful to you or would a woman be in the way in Tudorland?'

'I'd like to take Kelly along with us if that's all right with her.' He turned to Kelly. 'As a woman, you will be able to go into places without raising suspicion, because nobody will believe you could do anything useful. There's no women's lib in Tudorland.'

'That's fine. I'll do whatever's necessary,' said Kelly.

'You can keep a pistol in a velvet belly-bag or you can wear a rig under a cloak.' Thomas turned back to Sir David. 'The Project is small. It's based on an old Peugeot 206 estate, so we'll need several trips to take all of us and whatever gear we need. I'm going to need Sophie to ferry the Project back and forth, and I know she'll want to be in control of it in case something goes wrong with it. The

Project is getting old, so it may develop glitches if someone else uses it, and frankly, we don't need that.'

Sir David said, 'Jesus Christ. The sooner we can bring the machine in here and clone it the better.' Addressing Raj, Sir David said, 'I bet you and your techies would love that job, eh?'

'You're right there, Boss.' Said Raj, starting to drool at the thought of it.

'Anything else, Tom? You don't mind being called Tom, do you?'

'Not at all. Everyone calls me Tom, both here and in Tudorland.' Thomas consulted his list. 'As far as you are concerned, we'll be away from New London for less than half an hour, but we'll actually live in Tudorland for several days, so I've drawn up a basic survival list. We'll need broad-spectrum antibiotics, such as streptomycin or tetra-cycline in case of trouble, plus basics such pain killers, wound dressings and the kind of thing a soldier on active service would have access to.'

Raj jumped in. 'I can get drugs and army packs, includ-ing water purification tablets. Would there be room in the Project for bottled water?'

'Yes, and perhaps you could get us some teabags, instant coffee and soft drinks?'

He turned to the rest of the group and said. 'Life without servants would be too hard, and it wouldn't leave us time for what we need to accomplish if we have to take care of everything ourselves. Bear in mind that we don't have tap water, so someone has to get it up from the well and filter it for use and someone has to take the dirty water away again. We'll take modern toiletries and loo rolls and I suggest we wear our modern underwear, because it's more comfortable than Tudor under-clothing. The servants will think it weird, but we can use the Hidalian stunt in reverse,

47

telling anyone who cares to know that you come from Hidalia, as that will explain your peculiarities.'

'Thank God for Hidalia,' muttered Baz.

'Indeed, Baz. By the way, do you know of any small explosives we could use? I don't know if we'll need them, but I'd rather be prepared.'

'Semtex,' replied Baz. 'It's like soft plastic, so you cut whatever size piece you want and stick a detonator into it. The lads know how to use it. Also hand grenades. They have a pin that you pull out, after which, you have a minute or two to chuck the thing as far as you can in the direction of the enemy before they blow up.'

Thomas nodded. 'Now, obviously I need to talk to Sophie, Steven and Margie about all this, so how about getting them in here today? Steven might even come up with ideas I haven't thought of. He worked in the Exchequer and he's a bright lad.'

Sir David nodded. 'They'll all have to sign the Official Secrets Act, but I can't see that being a problem. As you said yourself, it pales into insignificance against the secrets you've all had to keep for the past year. By the way, I'm coming with you - to Tudorland, that is.'

The others stared open mouthed at their boss.

Sir David stared his team down. 'I've done my time in the field! I'm fit and I want to go.' A peevish note crept into his voice. 'After all, this was *my* ancestor's time and place, and I'd love the opportunity of seeing it.'

Thomas took his time answering, and then he looked directly into Sir David's eyes. 'I understand precisely what you are saying, but if you come along, I must still insist on taking total charge of the operation myself. In short, I must go back to my old position and status and you will have to act as my junior. When we return to New London, we will revert to you being the head of TUDOR and me to a CAB line manager once again.'

Sir David agreed instantly. 'No problem,' he said.

'I also suggest that you use some other name while you are in Tudorland.'

'Good point. My mother's name was Wilson, so for the time being, I'll become plain David Wilson.' Sir David bit his lip and fiddled with his Mont Blanc, 'Will you take your knighthood back again?'

'I must. I may need to contact some of my old staff and such spies and trustworthy informers as I can find, and they all know me as Sir Thomas.'

'I'll leave it to Raj and the others to keep their ear to the ground for the threats to the secondary targets while we get on with the main business of the day. And so, Sir Thomas, I am now recruited as plain David Wilson.'

'Indeed you are.'

Kelly spoke up now. 'You know we always have an operational name for a raid, so what about something Tudor... how about *'Operation Beefeater'*?'

Sir David smiled. 'Operation Beefeater it is!'

He picked up is Mont Blanc and then put it down again in a gesture of finality. 'Right, lads and lasses,' he said, 'Phone your relatives and get them here and then we'll take a trip to *Angels*.'

Now, for the first time, Sir David smiled at the intrepid team.

* * *

Several miles to the north-west of Millbank, Lucy Sanders had finished making notes for her forthcoming finals before downing an egg and oven-chip supper. Now she was settling down to watch the television. The TV guide didn't have anything that she wanted to watch, so she turned to the small collection of boot-sale DVDs that she'd bought herself for just such occasions. One was a four-DVD set, with each disc containing ten episodes of an old TV series that she had missed. The series was "The Tudors", and it started with Catherine of Aragon fastening a ribbon to a jousting lance that the young Henry VIII was about to use to demolish an unfortunate opponent.

Chapter Six

OPERATION BEEFEATER

*I feel very adventurous. There are so many doors to be
opened, and I'm not afraid to look behind them*

ELIZABETH TAYLOR

Thomas phoned Sophie and asked her to come to Baz's
office right away, and to bring Steven and Margie with
her. Margie said she'd dump the kids on Kate and pick Steven
up, so they should all get to the office by two o'clock. She
asked Thomas what was going on, but he told her that she'd
find out soon enough.

When they arrived at Millbank, the receptionist called
Baz on the intercom, while preparing passes for the new
arrivals. Baz came down, gave Margie and Sophie a kiss,
shook hands with Steven and led them all to the lifts and
then through the TUDOR reception to the outer office,
where they all read and signed the Official Secrets Act. Jill
made a note to get more copies in, as she was beginning to
run low.

Once that was done, Baz led them into the boardroom.
Sir David had endured a certain amount of stick when he'd
insisted on having such an oversized table installed, but
nobody was criticising him now. Jill had phoned a friend in
another organisation in the building and commandeered

half a dozen extra seats. Her friend said they could keep them, and she'd indent for new ones later.

Raj asked Julie to organise sandwiches, biscuits and cakes, but when Steven told him about Sophie's diabetes, he changed the order to granary sandwiches, fruit, cracker biscuits, a selection of cheese, tomatoes and washed celery, along with sugar-free soft drinks, saying it was time they all ate a better quality of food in the office anyway.

The gang trooped in and Margie apologised for the fact that they were all sporting jeans and casual clothing, reasoning that it sounded as though it was more important to get to the office quickly than worry about their appearance. Sir David said they were just fine as they were, and thanked them for coming in so quickly. Taking the meeting, he told the newcomers exactly what was going on, and as expected, the family group all blew out their cheeks and whistled.

Steven said, 'Well you'd better recruit me as well, because I'm not leaving a job of such a delicate nature to this collection of undisciplined pirates. They'll need a steadying hand, *and* they'll also need me to get them into the right departments in the Tudorland ministry.'

Thomas asked Steven if he was sure about this, and he got a flea in his ear in return. Steven pointed out that in Tudor times, Westminster Abbey was known as the Cathedral of St. Peter, and that the actual abbey part of it had closed due to the dissolution, but that it hadn't been destroyed. King Henry had re-designated St. Peters as a cathedral as a 'King's Peculiar', as was the case with several other places that King Henry had chosen to keep intact.

Sophie said, 'I'll ferry you and all the stuff back and forth, and collect you all at the end. The Project is old and a bit cranky, so I daren't let anyone else use it. By the way, what about getting a roof rack and pod from Halfords. That would give us more space for goods, wouldn't it?' While the team were agreeing that this was a good idea, Sophie asked if she could borrow a techie to help her test-run the computers before they set off and Raj nearly leapt into her arms at the chance!

Margie said, 'Kate's got a nanny at the moment, because her baby's only three months old, so it won't be hard for her to keep my kids for a while. I'll drop their nightclothes and toys over there, and then I can go on to Morrisons for food and supplies. It would be useful if you could all give me lists of what you want, and I could do with some help if you've got anyone you can spare.' Thinking for a while, she said, 'Someone will have to go to Halfords for the rack and pod and we'll need help getting it fixed to the Project.'

Sir David assigned a junior to go with Margie, while dispatching a lad to sort out the rack and pod. Turning to Jill, he said, 'We need to get down to Angels pretty quickly for the costumes, so can you speed things up by phoning ahead and telling them what we want? That way, they might start looking stuff out for us?'

Jill nodded and made notes.

'Raj, I think you should go with Sophie so you've got time to buy parts if there's a problem.' Looking at them both, he said, 'Remember to keep the receipts and we'll reimburse you later.'

Raj and Sophie nodded.

Margie bent forward to talk to Sir David. 'Can Steven's wife Kate run liaison for the family team, then if there's something we need, I can get it quickly and meet Sophie back at the Project? Perhaps you could courier a copy of the Official Secrets Act over to Kate for her to sign and return.'

'Good thinking. Jill will run liaison here, because I suspect that Raj will be busy with Sophie. Make sure every one of us has everyone else's phone numbers.'

Raj, Sophie and Margie got on their way, while Steven, Baz, Jack, Kelly, Thomas and plain David, as he now was, climbed into a taxi.

* * *

When the crew arrived at Angels, Thomas decided that his old outfit was too battered to use again, so everybody ended up buying two new outfits each. This turned out to be easier than they thought, because the costumes from the old BBC series called "The Tudors" had been stored there, so there were loads of absolutely ravishing outfits for them to choose from. Thomas explained that they should avoid certain colours and designs, because not all modern colours or materials existed before the advent of modern cloths and chemical dyes.

When they looked at themselves, they saw themselves transformed. The men sporting doublets and knee length riding breeches rather than puffy Tudor trunks, but also hose, knee boots and cloaks, wide belts that were folded over in front, with swords in scabbards that swayed just behind their left hips. Thomas and Steven immediately felt at home in the their new outfits, while the others turned this way and that in front of mirrors and tried to get used to the unusual feel of the Tudor clothing. Kelly adapted pretty quickly, because like most women, she had occasionally worn ball gowns, and her Tudor dresses weren't that much different.

Thomas opted for his signature black with slashes of white, while Steven chose deep brown with a lace trim for one outfit and green with white slashes for another. Sir David went for grey with white embroidery and a fur collar for one costume and plum with pink slashes for another. Baz looked terrific in bottle green slashed with white, and just as good in a second outfit of light brown with cream embroidery. Jack looked amazing in black slashed with burnt orange, while choosing a ridiculously impractical shade of pale sand and a cloak with a fox collar for his second costume. Each of the men chose two pairs of Tudor boots, and their outfits were topped off with feathered velvet caps that Thomas called bonnets.

Kelly chose one dress in dark green brocade and a second in various shades of pink. They had all decided against Tudor underwear, but Kelly's dresses had tight bodices that left no room for a bra. The green one had pleated muslin inset into the chest area, but the pink one was low at the front with a high ruffled collar at the back. A couple of jewelled moon shaped head-dresses completed the outfits, while Kelly's wavy brown hair, freed for once from its usual barrettes and elastic bands swished down her back below the headdress. When she tried on the somewhat revealing pink dress, Jack looked appreciatively at her and she poked her tongue at him in return. The sight of her tongue made the irrepressible Jack risk a clip round the ear by gazing at her mouth and licking his lips. Despite the banter, Kelly knew the pink outfit made her look really pretty, and as always, she forgave Jack for being his usual saucy self.

Kelly decided to use her own walking shoes with the green dress, but she bought a pair of pink leather shoes with a low heel to wear with the dressy outfit. The men even found embroidered and lace trimmed linen handker-chiefs to tuck into their doublets, along with leather purses of a suitable design.

Kelly looked at herself in the long mirror. This outfit looked so different from her usual kick-ass working outfit of black cargos and sweats or her office trouser suit, that she couldn't help admitting to herself that it was a real treat to see herself looking so feminine for once. Then a lad arrived from the office with six sheathed daggers for them to attach to their belts.

* * *

By ten that night, the team was gathered in Thomas and Sophie's garden workshop. Sophie and Raj had indeed found some faults with the Project and they had carried out some emergency programming. Now the car was ready and the pod was fully loaded for the first trip. They all agreed that Thomas and Steven should go first, to check that their households were still available to them, so Steven squeezed himself into the back seat with some of their gear and Thomas climbed into the front passenger seat. Raj checked the batteries and helped Sophie check the laptop. When he gave her a thumbs-up, she punched in the now familiar coordinates of time, place and old-style date, and then pressed the enter key. The Project shimmered and disappeared, but ten minutes later, it was back with Sophie in the driving seat on her own.

The three young Tudors filled the Project and the pod with more kit, while David and Jack stuffed as much as they could into the car's interior before squeezing into the car themselves. Once more, the Project disappeared, but ten minutes later, it was back and ready to transport Baz, Kelly and the last of their equipment. Baz gave Margie a kiss, climbed in with Kelly, and then once again the Project disappeared.

When Sophie and the Project arrived back at the Mews, Margie asked if Sophie had managed to get them into Thomas's old home; Sophie nodded and said she'd left them in Thomas's old office.

* * *

The Tudors had chosen to arrive in Tudorland in the dead of night, so when Thomas climbed out of the Project, he switched on his torch. He was mightily relieved that his office hadn't changed. He found some candles and lit them while Steven stepped out and started to unload the equipment, Thomas hugged Sophie and waved her off before crawling under his desk and stowing the team's valuables in his hidey-hole. Then he took a quick tour of the house. It was empty, although the great hall and the back rooms where his clerks had once worked were now full of planks, sheets of wood and carpentry tools.

When Thomas returned to the office, Steven went next door to see what he could discover. He walked out of Thomas's back door and across the gardens at the rear of the two houses while digging his old key out of his belt purse, hoping it still worked. It did. So now, Steven stepped into a hallway and approached the stairs, but then he was almost felled in his tracks by a hard blow that caught him across his midriff.

A female voice called out, 'Stop, Wilf, it's Mister Steven!' Steven's rotund housekeeper, Janie, held a candle up to his face.

An equally rotund Wilf put down the length of wood and gazed at Steven in wonderment. 'Goodness, Sir, I'm so sorry I hit you. Are you back from Flanders?'

Steven struggled to get his breath before hissing, 'Yes Wilf, I am.'

Janie spoke up, 'Can I suggest we go into the kitchen, so that I can put on some oil lamps and get us some ale. I could do with a draft after that shock, and I'm sure you could both do with one as well.'

* * *

Wilf looked a little uncomfortable; then he cleared his throat and said, 'You see, Sir, my Alfred has started mending shoes and boots for people in the back rooms of this house and he also has a carpentry business in Sir Thomas's house. We didn't want to abandon the houses, so when neither of you came back, we thought it better for us to start some kind of business.' Wilf still looked embarrassed, but he went on gamely. 'Anyway, that's better for us than looking for work in service, as we might not be as lucky with another family as we'd been with yours, so it means we're still here and using the houses, but doing so as though they were our own.'

'Don't worry, Wilf, that's fine. Look, I don't have much time at the moment, but I will be here with Sir Thomas and some other friends for a few days. If Sir Thomas's house is habitable, we'll stay there, and once we've gone, you can keep my house for good. I'm pretty sure Sir Thomas will be happy for you to have his as well, and that will give you and your family permanent security, won't it? We may come back for an occasional visit if you are happy to see us from time to time, but the houses will remain yours from now on.'

'It'll be a relief to know where we stand, and it will be really good for all of us to have such excellent houses,' said Wilf.

'Meanwhile can you look after us as you did before - for a few days, anyway? There are five men and one woman. I'll pay you as much as I can,' said Steven.

'Don't bother about paying us, Mister Steven. If you're giving us your house and Sir Thomas's house, I guess that's payment enough for ten lifetimes,' answered Wilf.

Janie jumped in. 'How's Mistress Katherine? Is she all right? And what about young Robert?'

'They're both fine, Robert's at school and we now have another son who we've called Harry.'

'Oh, that's wonderful! I'm so glad to hear it. Please give them our love when you see them, won't you Sir.'

Steven smiled at Janie and said gently, 'You don't have to call me Sir, now.'

'It's force of habit. Anything else would feel wrong for you and for Sir Thomas and for your friends.'

Steven swigged down the rest of his ale and stood up. 'I'll bring Sir Thomas and the others through to meet you. They're all foreigners, so they speak English in a very strange way, so I expect it will be a while before you can all understand each other properly. They're all good people though, and we're all here on the King's business and for the defence of the realm.'

'I don't doubt that for a moment,' said Wilf.

Chapter Seven

BEEFEATER TUDORS

*Do not go where the path may lead, go instead where
there is no path, and leave a trail*

RALPH WALDO EMERSON

Thomas greeted Wilf and Janie and introduced the team while Janie poured tankards of Wilf's home made ale and put a platter of pound cake on the table. When Steven told Thomas about the houses and the deal he'd struck with his own home, Thomas immediately agreed to pass his home over to Wilf and Janie as well. Janie told him that his own household servants had moved on to other employment soon after he left. He'd never felt the same about them as they all did about Wilf, Janie and their children, so he was happy with the arrangement, especially now that he knew they'd always be welcome if they ever needed to come back to Austin Friars on "business" again.

Janie made a start on the practicalities.

'The young lady had better sleep in our house while the men sleep in Sir Thomas's. In theory, you could have your old room back, Mister Steven, but Wilf and I are using it now, so it makes sense for us to make up beds for all the men next door.

'I'll need help with the heavy work, so I'll speak to my sister. She inherited a bit of money from her late husband, so when her last job came to an end, she decided not to rush into taking another and we work well together. I'm sure she'll be happy to join me here and I know she'll want to help out, Mr Steven. My lads will also give a hand and we can pay them something ourselves. The only problem is that the great halls in both houses aren't in a good enough condition for dining at the moment, so perhaps you can dine in the kitchen. Would that be all right?'

'Of course it will,' said Steven. 'I'll give you some money towards the extra food even so, Janie, because while properties make you a wealthy family, they won't cover the short-term food bill. We don't need anything special, but there will be six extra mouths for breakfast and dinner.'

'Thank you, Sir. I will be glad to accept a little for that. As you say, meat and vittals cost money these days.'

Janie woke her daughter and told her to give her a hand with making up the beds. Janie showed Kelly to a bed in Elaine's room, while Thomas took back his old room next door and gave David a room for himself on the same floor. They suggested that Baz and Jack share what had been the large guest room on the floor above.

When Wilf saw how tall the men were, he pulled the mattresses off the two small double beds and laid them side-by-side on the floor, laying another mattress sideways across the bottom of them. This way, each man had a sleeping space that was large enough to accommodate him in comfort. Jack helped Wilf carry the two bedsteads out of the room and to stack them in the passageway. Wilf said his sons would move the bedsteads out of the hall the following morning.

He apologised for the fact that the men would have to sleep on the floor, but they waved his apologies aside and said they'd be fine. With several good feather beds covering the mattresses and more on top, their host and hostess had managed to cobble together warmth and comfort for the men. Will told them he'd arrange for them to have fires in the room the next day and to keep them lit for the duration of their stay. After storing everything else in a spare room, the two households fell into a grateful sleep.

The TUDOR team rose next morning to the sound of Tudorland waking up. Horses clip-clopped along the road and carts clanked and rumbled along, while hawkers shouted and church bells rang. One of Janie's sons and her daughter brought jugs of hot water and cloths so the team could wash, and they assured their young helpers that they would leave any remaining toiletries for them when they left.

It struck the New Londoners that doing a tourist trip to an old house on a day out was one thing, but living in one was another. The timbers creaked and the house seemed alive in a way that modern dwellings weren't. It also struck the New Londoners that these Austin Friars dwellings were large and well-appointed houses by anyone's standards, and they started to grasp the positions of wealth and status that Thomas, Steven, and their families had occupied in their Tudorland days.

In the kitchen, Janie made a large pot of porridge, apologising profusely because she didn't have anything fancier on hand for her distinguished guests, but they were all perfectly happy with porridge. She reached into a cupboard and took down a stone pot containing honey for them to drizzle into the porridge and she put out a plate of thick slices of seedy bread and another stone pot containing butter. Thomas insisted that Janie and her family join them at the table and that they should no longer consider themselves lower orders, but they said they preferred to stay in their familiar roles. Janie apologised again, this time for feeding them in her kitchen rather than in the dining room, but she stopped apologising when they all loudly insisted that they much preferred eating in the warm kitchen to a cold and formal dining room. The New Londoners weren't used to chemical-free newly baked bread, stone ground porridge oats and freshly churned, creamy butter, let alone such wonderful honey, and Kelly began to wonder whether five hundred years of progress was all it was cracked up to be.

To drink, Janie offered them ale or fresh milk. She said she was sorry for offering them milk, which Tudorland folk considered fit only for children or low class people, but Kelly drooled at the sight of the full-cream milk and happily accepted a stoneware mug of it, saying that she was very happy to be considered low class. The men opted for pewter pots of the typically low alcohol Tudor ale. Steven took Janie on one side and asked her if the outbreak of plague that so worried Kate had affected anyone in her family.

'Thank you for asking, Mr Steven. We were lucky this time, because the sickness remained in the dock area before fizzling out.'

'I'm glad you escaped, Janie. Kate was already deter-mined to move to Hidalia anyway, and that outbreak was last straw. I think the sudden deaths of Anne and Joseph weighed on her mind, and she feared the same thing hap-pening to Robbie. Life in Hidalia brings its own problems, but plague isn't one of them, and neither is the Sweating Sickness, so that eases Kate's mind.'

When Jack spotted the ravishing fair-haired sixteen-year-old Elaine, his mouth fell open, but Thomas noticed Jack's interest and decided to cut him off at the pass.

'If you so much as touch Elaine or give her one moment's encouragement, I'll have you flogged. Remember, you're a commoner here and I'm a peer of the realm, and I can do anything I like with you. *Her* only way forward in this world is to find a decent husband, and she won't be able to do that if her virginity goes west; she'd have a problem even if her reputation is compromised. In fact, it might be an idea for Janie to send young Elaine to her sister's house for the duration.'

Jack was shocked. He'd never been told to lay off a woman in such terms before, and he began to see that this world ran to very different rules to those of New London. In an unaccustomedly humble tone he apologised and said, 'Please don't send her away. I won't give her any encouragement.'

'Good. Just keep it in your codpiece for once and you'll be fine.'

When they had eaten and drunk their fill, Kelly helped Janie to clear the table and Baz set Janie's heaviest waterpot onto the fire to heat for the washing up. Janie protested at all this help from 'the quality', but Baz grinned at her and told her they'd be happy to help out until her family came in to give her a hand. Janie's middle-aged heart melted and she smiled at the tall, open-faced, good-hearted Baz.

When they all trudged into Thomas's office for a meeting, Janie despatched her sons, Alfred and young Godfrey, to set chairs round Thomas's 'boardroom' table. When the lads spotted the ballpoint pens and notepads their eyes lit up, and Thomas assured them they would leave all the gear behind when they left. Then Thomas made a start.

'Steven and I have had a chat, and we think the best thing is to recreate the problem that we have in New London, so we will pretend there is a gunpowder plot being planned for what you call Westminster Abbey and Steven and I call St Peter's Cathedral. If anyone asks what we're doing, we can use that as a raison d'être.'

The others agreed that it was a sensible plan, so Thomas went on. 'Steven, I suggest that you take David with you to the treasury and see if you can find someone with knowledge of the layout of buildings in the area of the Abbey, while I'll take Baz with me and see if I can locate any of my old informants.' Turning to Kelly and Jack, he said, 'I think you should go to St Peter's, look around and familiarise yourselves with the area. Join in if there's a service, and walk around the outside as well as the inside. You've got your London A-Z haven't you, Jack?'

'I've also got the 1553 London map.'

'I hope you won't meet any trouble, but you should both be tooled up.'

They showed Thomas their holster rigs, and Thomas nodded and went on, 'I have some money here for each of you. It should be more than enough for a few days. Keep a little in the drawstring purses that you have on your belts and put the rest in these bags inside your clothes.' He handed the men modern plastic pencil cases to slide under their doublets, while Kelly showed Thomas her hidden travel belt that had a zipped compartment in the back of it. She kept a few pennies in a drawstring belt purse as well. 'You'll notice that the street layout hasn't changed much in five hundred years, so you should be able to find your way around easily enough, but there's no trustworthy public transport. We could hire horses to ride about on, but you're probably better off on foot, although you'll be very tired by the time you're finished.'

* * *

'We've also got a long walk ahead of us, so we'd better get going,' Steven told David as they stepped out of the house.

'We're going to the treasury building, aren't we?' asked David.

'That's right. It's in Whitehall.'

'Well, where else would it be,' laughed David, taking care to avoid the stinking flow of water in the middle of the road. 'Will it matter that it's Saturday? I mean, won't everything be closed?'

'No, things only close on a Sunday in Tudorland.'

When Steven had worked for the Exchequer, he'd worked partly from home and partly in Whitehall, so he was familiar with the route. When they reached the main road, David noticed that the buildings on either side weren't the stone ones that existed in New London, but typically Tudor buildings with lots of wood and plaster. He was reminded of *The Wig and Pen Club* near the law courts in New London.

He felt hugely excited to be in the place that he'd read so much about, but just as Baz had commented earlier, he could see that reading about a place and living in it were two different things. After all, who could recreate the noise and stink of medieval London and the appearance of the people? He'd always thought ordinary people would be clothed in brownish rags, but the people were brightly dressed, with colourful patches here and there where garments had been mended.

* * *

The doorman at the Exchequer had the big stomach, florid complexion and bulbous nose of a big drinker, but he was sober enough now, and he greeted Steven warmly.

'Mister Byers, are you returning to us, by any chance?'

'No, Cooper,' said Steven, 'I'm only visiting, but I need some intelligence on a different matter to my usual work and you might be just the man to point me in the right direction. It's well known that your head is full of extraneous information and you may be able to save me valuable time.' Steven looked up and down the passageway outside the doorman's little office, pretending that he wanted to avoid being overheard.

'Look, come into my office, Sir; there isn't much space, but it is private.

'I'm obliged to you, Cooper.' The three men squeezed into the small space and closed the door. There wasn't room for them to sit, so they stood around Cooper's table. The story Steven told Cooper was pure fiction, but he reckoned it would do the trick.

'As you probably suspected, I moved to Hidalia with my family and with Sir Thomas, after he was falsely condemned.'

The doorman gave Steven a solemn nod.

'Recently Sir Thomas ran into a man who told him he'd heard a story about a plot to blow up the Cathedral of St. Peter while King Henry is giving thanks to Our Lord for allowing him yet another year of his reign. The story seemed far-fetched, but Sir Thomas decided to investigate it, and I'm giving him a hand. The gentleman with me is Mr David Wilson. He's Hidalian, but his English is quite good. He is a good friend and he has offered his help us in this dangerous affair.'

'Goodness me, Sir, that's a real problem. How is this blowing up supposed to be achieved?'

'Good question, Cooper. Apparently, the idea is to move gunpowder into the crypt, and as no conspirator could stroll through the Cathedral with a keg of gunpowder under his arm, there has to be a tunnel somewhere and we need to find it.'

'Now, that's a poser sir.' Cooper looked up to the ceiling for inspiration. 'I would try asking the Worshipful Company of Masons for help, Mr Byers. They're based at the Guildhall. They know more about church building than anybody in the country and they would know if any-thing is going on. If the tunnel is illegal, they might be able to send people to look in the buildings around the Cathedral and see if they can spot any digging going on. Another idea might be the Company of Watermen and Lightermen, as they know all the watergates and any tunnels that might run inland.'

'Cooper, you're a genius!' exclaimed Steven.

Cooper actually blushed at the accolade.

'Do the City masons operate outside the City walls?'

'My cousin's a master mason *and* a member of the Guild, and I know from him that they certainly do work beyond the City boundary. I'm not sure how far they go - I think the limit is seven miles from the City, but that would certainly include Westminster.'

'Thank you Cooper, you've done your country a major service. May God bless you.'

Steven dug a few pence out of his leather drawstring purse and gave them to the doorkeeper for his trouble. Cooper touched the rim of his cap and nodded.

Once they'd left the building, Steven said, 'That man's going to be full of himself now, I'll wager.'

David smiled in agreement.

Steven and David walked eastwards until Steven suggested they stop at an alehouse for a bite, and as David was more than ready for some lunch, they stepped into the Three Feathers. There was a bar along one side, which made the dwelling look like something out of a cowboy film, but without the typically Victorian wall mirror behind the bar. The remainder of the room was filled with tables and several people sitting about and eating. Steven ordered what he called 'small ale' and a wedge of game pie for each of them. Amazingly, the pie came with what the publican called *herbs*, which turned out to be boiled carrots and beetroot. David pronounced everything absolutely delicious. After their meal, they walked to the

Guildhall and now David was in for another surprise. Indeed, he stared in amazement.

'Steven, I thought this would be another old lath and plaster type of building, but it's not much different to our New London Guildhall. Indeed, I can actually recognise it as part of the modern building. Without other tall buildings all around it, it stands out and it looks far grander than it does in New London. I've been inside on many occasions for formal dinners, but I've never really thought of it in connection with the actual Guilds, although that's obviously what it's all about. I must look into it when we get back to New London, it'll be fascinating to learn more.'

As it happened, they didn't have much luck at the Guildhall, but they *did* find someone who gave them names of three building companies that may have worked on repairs and renewals at the Cathedral. The early winter light was fading, so as there were no street lamps in Tudorland and only the occasional 'flare torch' sticking out of a wall here and there, they decided to head back to Austin Friars and call it a day.

* * *

Lucy Sanders was home alone and relishing the peace after a hectic day in the garden centre. She wasn't in the mood to work on her thesis, so she fished out the Tudor DVDs, to see what Henry and his court were up to, from the point where she'd left off previously. This episode showed Henry feeling aggrieved when his wife's Spanish relatives made it clear that his role was to become their poodle, a situation that soon became exacerbated by his first meeting with Anne Boleyn.

As Lucy put it to herself, 'This was a situation that needed to be read "between the *loins*".'

Chapter Eight

REPORTING BACK

Setting goals is the first step in turning the invisible into the visible

TONY ROBBINS

By the time Steven and David reached the house, the others were also trickling in. They were grateful for the fact that the house had indoor water closets and even more grateful to leave their dirty boots in the special boot tray in the hall and shove their feet into New London flip flops and slippers.

Baz, Jack and Kelly collected cartons of long-life semi-skimmed milk, a super-large pack of PG Tips, bags of sugar and a gallon container of still water, while Baz found the box filled with mugs and teaspoons. In the kitchen, Jack helped Kelly pour the water into the kettle and he set it on a trivet over the fire, while Kelly put a large box of Fox's biscuits on the table.

Janie and her sister Frieda watched all the activity with great interest, and immediately agreed to try a mug of the unusual beverage. After the TUDOR team had downed a mug or two of tea and done their best to polish off the biscuits, stoutly aided in this endeavour by Janie and her equally tubby sister, they felt refreshed and ready to return to Thomas's office for a debriefing session.

Thomas turned to Kelly. 'How did you and Jack do?'

'We decided against walking all the way to Westminster, so we walked down to London Bridge and hired a Thames Waterman to row us up-river,' responded Kelly.

This brought a chorus of 'Jammy sods, sneaks, and lazy lowlifes' from the others.

'Funny you should mention the Watermen,' said Kelly, 'because we asked our crew if they'd heard anything, and they said there was definitely something odd going on in a watergate up river from St. Peter's, as he called it. We'll take a look at it tomorrow.'

Jack chirped up. 'Kel and I walked around inside the church and we saw the area of the Cathedral that the royal family is most likely to use during the christening. One thing that surprised me though was the age of the building.'

Thomas nodded, 'It's very old. William the Conqueror was crowned there in 1066, and the building was *old* even then!'

Like David, who had been surprised by the Guildhall, the youngsters also began to appreciate the durability and age of so many familiar British buildings and institutions.

Then Jack really captured the team's attention. 'You know, Kel and I snuck into the crypt. It's a vast space with many areas, but we paced it out and slowly worked our way towards the bit directly below the Christening area. I'd taken a torch with me just in case, and that allowed us to creep around in the crypt, so to speak.'

'Good thinking,' said Thomas with a smile.

'We didn't see a tunnel as such, but we did notice a spot in the right area where some of the stones in the wall appeared to have been disturbed, and there were fresh looking pieces of stone and dust on the ground.'

They pulled out their mobiles, so they could show the others photos.

Jack remarked that it had cost them three Tudor pence for the upstream journey, but only one and a half for the same journey downstream. He said the Waterman had told them that the price changed according to the tide and whether they had to row up or down river. Steven and Thomas smiled at Kelly and Jack's surprised response to something that was so familiar to them.

On the face of things, Thomas and Baz hadn't got too far, but they had discovered some useful snippets.

Baz said, 'Tommo took us to an insalubrious dock area that made Dickens's descriptions of London's underworld look like a classy tea-party. It reminded me of some of the stories Val's mum used to tell about her West Indian husband's early experiences of trying to cope with life in the East End of London when he first came over from Jamaica.'

'We discovered that the intifada that King Henry had announced against the monasteries is now much worse than it was when Thomas Cromwell was running things, mainly because Henry is running through the country's money thoughtlessly, and looking to the monasteries for additional funding. There's a veritable pogrom being perpetrated on any monks and nuns who're stupid enough to try to continue their established way of life. In some places, they're hiding out in various parts of their churches. We think that's probably the case with St. Peters, because several brave monks are trying to keep up the work of helping the poor and whatnot, but it's becoming increasingly dangerous. Adding the data together, it's very likely that someone *is* digging an escape tunnel against the day when the remaining monks will need to get away.'

Jack suddenly came to see that it was one thing to study these events as part of a university course, and quite another to live among people who were suffering as a result of them. He realised the reformation must have felt like the precursor to the holocaust for those who were destined to live through it.

* * *

The next morning, team Beefeater enjoyed a superb breakfast of freshly cut ham, eggs, bread and tea. Janie and Frieda decreed that only they were to be trusted with the serious business of tea making, and they'd ordered in extra milk for the team, carefully instructing the churn lad to bring them some of the less creamy milk for the tea. They lined the mugs up on the counters, each with its precious tea-bag installed in it, and they'd found some lovely handmade sugar bowls for the table with spoons sitting in the sugar. They gave the team strict instructions only to use the sugar spoons for the purpose of putting sugar into their mugs, and other spoons to actually stir the tea, because sugar was too rare and delicate a commodity to be spoiled by a wet spoon.

It was really weird for the New Londoners to see cheapo white sugar and bog-standard teabags as rare and precious commodities, but they then considered the cost in human lives it had once taken to bring such merchandise to Britain. Clipper crews coping with storms and the ghastly slave trade brought the New Londoners to the conclusion that tea, coffee and sugar were very precious commodities indeed, which they would never again take for granted.

After breakfast, Thomas gave the team some good news.

'Today is Sunday and nothing is open in the City apart from churches, so I suggest that while the weather is dry and not too cold, you take a walk around and get a feel for the city. Bear in mind that there are thieves and pickpockets

73

around, so always travel in twos, keep your weapons handy and keep your wits about you.

'As for me, I'm going to church, and you might want to do the same. There are still some Catholic churches open if any of you happen to be Catholic, and there are plenty of Protestant ones with services in English, so take your pick and enjoy the experience. It will be good for your soul.'

David said, 'I have a feeling St. Mary's in Cheapside is a Catholic church, and I would love to go to Mass there.'

'You're a Catholic?' said Jack with some surprise.

'Very lapsed,' admitted David, 'I couldn't take communion without going to confession, and it would take me all day to own up to all the sins I've committed since I last confessed, but I would love to hear the mass in Latin.'

'Would that be the Bow Bells church?' asked Kelly. 'My dad was born in the City Road hospital, which had once been within the sound of Bow Bells, and that made him a bona fide cockney.'

David looked thoughtful. 'The City was burned out in the Great Fire of London in 1666, but when a church is destroyed, another is usually built on the same site. The St Mary-le-Bow that's on the site now is a Christopher Wren job, but there would have been a church there before.'

Steven spoke up. 'I think the church you're talking about is called St. Mary de Arcubus, and its name comes from the fact that the doors and windows are bow-shaped arcs rather than tall and pointy Gothic ones.'

David confirmed that the Wren church also had bow-shaped arches.

Kelly asked David if she could accompany him to mass at St Mary's, and David said he'd be delighted to escort her. Thomas said he'd also like to go to mass, even though he was even more lapsed than David, having become a Protestant while working for Thomas

74

Cromwell, so the three of them opted to walk to Cheapside. Thomas realised that it was a relief for him to have migrated to New London where he could go to a different denomination of church every Sunday if he chose.

Baz, Jack and Steven chose to attend the service at Steven's local Protestant church, and then take a walk through the city and across London Bridge. Steven said that the Southwark area operated under different rules from the City, so they'd be able to find a tavern or eating house open there on a Sunday. Thomas, David and Kelly also decided to head over the river once they'd been to church. Steven said he'd have a word with Janie and Frieda and tell them to expect them back for dinner in the evening.

They all had a wonderful day. The Latin made the mass more dramatic, fascinating and uplifting for David, while Kelly just loved being there to see it all. Thomas felt relieved at being able to thank God for saving him from Henry's axe, for giving him a wonderful wife and such great friends. He wanted God and all the saints to know that he was happy, and for them to receive his most heartfelt thanks. He lit a candle to St. Jude, the patron saint of lost causes, because his cause had once been so very lost.

Steven, Baz and Jack also enjoyed their church service, although Baz and Jack said afterwards that they had missed the familiar Protestant hymns. It took them by surprise to realise that the hymns they knew so well hadn't come into existence until two or three centuries *after* the Tudor era. Jack had been delighted to hear the minister and congregation reciting his favourite 'I lift up my eyes to the hills' psalm, even though the wording was a little different from the familiar King James's bible version.

Dinner that night was a convivial affair and their two cooks had clearly gone to a lot of trouble. Janie served some surprisingly fresh fish, followed by a rack of venison.

There were no potatoes, but a little rice and plenty of freshly baked bread, with the evening's herbs being carrots and parsnips with a little butter and some chopped coriander. Kelly asked how come the Tudors used an Indian herb like coriander, and David explained that the English had developed a taste for eastern herbs and spices during the Crusades, and that these had found their way into the medieval diet. Earlier in the day, Janie had dispatched Alfred and Godfrey to buy jugs of French wine, which was dark red and very fresh, like Beaujolais.

In the absence of television, the group fell back on the entertainments of older times, so with a few drinks inside them, Baz, Jack and Kelly decided to serenade the group with school hymns and Christmas carols. They discovered that David could sing *'Silent Night'* in English and German, while Jack remembered all the words to everything, and he had a really good, light tenor voice. Then Jack told them a strange story about a glorious hymn that he had always loved.

'The words of this hymn come from a weird poem about a group of Vedic priests in India, who go into a forest and drink themselves stupid on a brew that they call Soma. The brew must have been concocted from something hallucinogenic, and the idea was for them to have some kind of religious experience, to get in touch with the spirit world and to discover the reality of God. The poem says they took the wrong approach, because this wasn't the Christian approach. The first and last of the verses of the hymn go like this:'

'Dear Lord and Father of mankind,
Forgive our foolish ways:
Reclothe us in our rightful mind,
In purer lives Thy service find,
In deeper reverence, praise,

In deeper reverence, praise.

'Then the last verse:

'Breathe through the heats of our desire
Thy coolness and thy balm;
Let sense be dumb, let flesh retire;
Speak through the earthquake, wind and fire,
O still, small voice of calm
O still, small voice of calm.'

Kelly raised an eyebrow at Jack, 'Are you going to let your senses become dumb and let any part of your flesh retire, Jacko?'

'Not likely, Kel. I can't let a world full of beautiful girls go untouched, can I, but I love hymns and I get their sentiments.'

Steven said, 'You don't seem to have much trouble with the 'thee and thy' language either, do you Jack?'

'None at all, Sir.'

Kelly said, 'Do you know, Jacko, I've always thought you something of a throwback, and I'm now wondering whether you've had a previous life – perhaps in Elizabethan times. I guess those days are only about forty years after this era, and I can just see you wading through all those bored-to-death daughters of West Indies functionaries in the time of the privateers.'

With a sudden presentiment, Kelly felt the room cool while ghosts from some other time began to gather in the strange atmosphere. 'I wouldn't be surprised to hear that you'd hitched a ride on the Project and visited the Elizabethan era, Jack.'

'I might just do that one of these days, Kel. Yes, I might,' answered Jack.

David closed their unusual evening by recalling a prayer from his childhood.

'If you can stand to hear a Jesuit prayer in such a determinedly protestant country as this now is, here goes…'

'Dearest Lord,
Teach me to be generous;
Teach me to serve You as You deserve;
To give and not to count the cost,
To fight and not to heed the wounds,
To toil and not to seek for rest,
To labour and not to ask for reward
Save that of knowing I am doing Your Will.'

They all said a hearty amen to that.

Chapter Nine

FOOTPADS

Champions keep playing until they get it right
BILLY JEAN KING

'I'd like David to accompany me today,' said Thomas, 'and I suggest that the rest of you go to the Guildhall with Steven and follow up on the masonry companies. David and I will join you tomorrow and knock off the rest, and hopefully, by the time we get back tonight, we should all be somewhat further forward.'

Then Thomas doled out some more cash and bade the crew good hunting.

* * *

Thomas and David crossed the Bridge to Southwark and headed for a tavern, where Thomas asked the pot man whether he'd seen any of his old contacts. The pot man was unresponsive until Thomas gave him a few coins, whereupon he directed Thomas to a tavern called *"The Rooster."*

At the Rooster, a huge man with a cauliflower ear and a monstrous scar down one side of his face greeted Thomas like an old friend. Thomas introduced his friend as Samuel, and as he spoke to him - and despite the archaic language - David recognised a bog-standard copper's fishing expedition. Then, to his utter amazement, Thomas's great troll of a friend told them that he had actually heard of a genuine plot to blow up St. Peters! Apparently, a group of terrorists had been seen ferrying kegs of gunpowder up river to Westminster!

This was unbelievable! The Beefeater team had dreamed up the story to give them a credible reason for their search, but now it looked as though there really *was* a Tudor gunpowder plot for them to uncover, alongside the New London one. Thomas asked Samuel whether he'd heard anything about a tunnel leading to the crypt of St. Peters. Samuel shook his head, but suggested that Thomas and his Hidalian friend get lost for a while and meet him back at The Rooster when the church bells rang two o'clock.

Thomas didn't think it was a great idea for them to hang around in such a dangerous area, so he suggested they make their way back over the bridge. They hadn't gone far when two rough looking men wielding knives appeared in front of them, and neither Thomas nor David were surprised to find another filthy wretch appear behind them because this was a classic ambush tactic. The footpad behind them looked like an emaciated teenager, so Thomas drew his sword and went after him first, yelling at David to shoot the other two. The young lad ran off, but when Thomas turned back to help David, his mouth fell open. David hadn't drawn his pistol at all, but was happily fighting off both footpads with a sword - and doing a credible job of it! Thomas leaned against the nearest wall and casually crossed one leg over the other, grinning while he watched the performance.

Thomas noticed that David wasn't wielding a Tudor sword, but something of a design he'd never seen before. He noticed that David's fencing was stylish, but despite the unusual delicacy of his footwork and his fancy style of swordsmanship, he was doing very nicely. Of course, David had taken on knaves with knives rather than experts with swords, but it was clear that he was having a thoroughly good time.

Suddenly David brought his sword down in a sharp chopping action onto one of the men's shoulders, then wheeling round and stabbing the other in the chest. Neither wound was fatal, but both were enough to bring the fight to an end, so the men ran off, while David's face was a picture of joyful triumph.

'What the hell was that all about?' asked a grinning Thomas.

'I used to fence for a hobby - French rules and all that stuff - so I thought I'd give it a go. When you fence for sport, you obviously don't want to hurt anybody, so it was a nice change to be able to draw a little blood.'

Thomas held out his hand to David. 'Can I take a look at your weapon?'

'It's a sabre. You can do fancier stuff with foils or épées, but this is a heavy weapon that slices as well as stabs. I think it started life as a cavalry weapon, and there's a curved version that works well when slashing downwards from a mounted position.'

'Let's cross the river and find a bit of open ground. I'd love to try your sabre?'

'Why not? We can have a practice fight with each other's weapons. It'll be interesting.'

Once over the river, they found a grassy space and swapped swords. It was a weird experience for Thomas to take instruction from David on something he'd done all his life, but he was happy to learn the new tricks, so he practised David's techniques of what he called 'right of way', which meant threatening an opponent by holding the sword out in front of him, then defending by blocking with a clash of swords and preventing the opposing sword from reaching his body. The final part of the sequence was to beat the other player's sword aside and lull the opponent into a false sense of security so that he moved forward too quickly and impaled himself on the weapon, while the swordsman quickly punched it forward again. The fancy footwork took a bit of getting used to, but Thomas had to admit that it did the trick. In his turn, David struggled with the heavy medieval sword, eventually getting the hang of it well enough, and coming to the conclusion that all those Robin Hood films were wrong: the main purpose for the heavy sword is to slash at the opponent any way you can, rather than thrust and parry with any measure of elegance.

Back on the bridge, the men bought themselves a lunch of bread and cheese and ate while leaning over the parapet. The river was very busy and it was fascinating to watch, though the smell coming off it wasn't pleasant. Soon enough, they strolled back to the Rooster where Big Samuel greeted them with a wry look.

'Sorry you had a bit of trouble, Tom. I guess the idiots took you for a pair of fops. If I'd got to them first, I'd have told them to leave you alone because I know you can look after yourself, though I heard that it was your Hidalian friend here who did the damage. Good for him.'

'Crikey,' said David, 'news gets around quickly.'

Samuel said, 'It certainly does. Now, while we're on the subject of news, I have some for you. I had to grease a few palms to get it, so…?'

Thomas immediately drew a handful of shillings out of his leather purse and handed them over.

'I didn't spend anything like that much,' said Samuel.

Thomas gestured to Samuel to keep the money.

'Listen. There *is* a tunnel coming into St Peter's, and the story goes that it's monks who are digging it, but a group of blaggards plan to take it over when it's finished. Apparently, King Henry isn't waiting for his anniversary to give thanks - he wants to do it on Christmas Eve, so that's when the place is due to go up. I've heard that gunpowder is being stored at the back of a watergate further up-stream, and the idea is to move it down into the tunnel under cover of darkness. Word is that the tunnel is almost through to the crypt by now.

Thomas was thoughtful. 'God's teeth, Samuel. I wonder who's behind the plot.'

'Apparently, it's Catholic Spaniards who were angry at the way Henry treated Catherine of Aragon, and now they're upset at the way he's treating the monasteries.'

Thomas thanked Samuel and wished him and his family well. While walking back to Austin Friars, Thomas and David discussed the work Thomas had done in Tudorland, and the work that David was now engaged upon in New London. It became obvious that Thomas's work at the Security Office and David's at TUDOR were amazingly similar. Both had suffered from political pressure from above, and both had to push their junior operatives to perform while protecting them from unnecessary harm. They realised that terrorists are much the same in any era, and it's only the means they use that's different. They agreed that life at the top can be lonely and it's always dif-ficult, and they also discovered that they had now formed a firm and enduring friendship.

* * *

That evening, the others were astounded to hear Thomas laughingly relate his and David's adventures, and tell of their fencing session by the riverside. Then Thomas related the astonishing news about the Tudorland gunpowder plot and the monk's tunnel.

'Our original idea of a tunnel leading to St Peters from the back of a watergate was wrong, but there *is* a watergate upstream that is being used to store the terrorists' gunpowder before moved it into place for detonation.'

'So now we have two gunpowder plots to solve in one go,' said Baz.

'Apparently,' said David, 'and amazingly, it's Spaniards of one kind or another who are behind both.'

Jack now looked a bit peeved, so Thomas asked him what was up.

Jack complained, 'Do we really need to do Fat Henry's dirty work for him? After all, Tom, he was going to chop your head off, wasn't he?'

'Well Jack,' answered Thomas, 'King Henry may be a pain in the arse, but as a Knight, I've sworn an oath of fealty to the Crown - and I see that as loyalty to the *office* of the Crown rather than to whoever's wearing it. I can't back down on that now, even though it's hardly appropriate when one considers that my life is in New London, but while we're here, we might as well sort this mess out anyway. It will be good practice for us.'

Jack grudgingly saw the point.

Steven and Baz reported that they had visited three masonry firms, and while the first knew nothing, the others had told them a similar story to the one Thomas and David had heard.

Kelly and Jack had got nowhere with their first two masonry companies, but then they'd struck gold. It turned out that one of the men they talked to had a cousin who was a monk at St. Peter's, and when Jack told him about the gunpowder plot, the mason feared his cousin would get caught up in the mess. The mason decided to ask his cousin to show the team the tunnel the following day. He told them that this was emphasising the conclusion to which he'd already come, namely that his monastic cousin would be wise to leave London for good - and perhaps even leave the country for the time being.

* * *

By now, Lucy was sitting her final exams at university, and relaxing by working her way through the story of Henry VIII and Anne Boleyn.

Chapter Ten

COURT CAPERS

Politics have no relation to morals
NICCOLO MACHIAVELLI

Tuesday morning dawned cold and dry, so the team made their way to Blackfriars, where the mason repeated his story about the tunnel and added another vital piece of information. He told them that the entrance to the tunnel was on the south eastern edge of a piece of land called Tothill, which is to the west of St. Peter's.

The group walked on through Whitefriars, but then Kelly asked them to stop because she wanted to investigate a shop she had noticed. She went into the shop and came out a few moments later with several small cloth bundles. As soon as the team had found a convenient wall to perch on, Kelly unwrapped one of the bundles and showed the others some strange, green things. Another bundle revealed two nutcrackers.

'These are cobnuts,' she explained, 'and the only place I've ever seen them is in Waitrose. They may be related to hazelnuts, because they look similar on the outside, but the kernels are white and they feel damp. When we were kids, we used to call them "wet nuts" because of their clammy feel. She handed a few nuts to David and told him to peel off the green covering and then crack open the nut.

David and Baz inspected the strange white, damp kernels before trying their unusual snack and washing the nuts down with cans of Coca Cola from Jack's backpack. They agreed that the unusual treat was very tasty.

* * *

The Whitefriars mason was a short man with a strong, muscular frame that resulted from many years spent lifting and shifting stones around. He introduced himself as William and told Thomas that he owned a small business specialising in a fancy kind of stone carving. He offered to accompany Thomas to the Cathedral, leaving his manager in charge.

'I suggest we take boats upriver, and when we reach St. Peter's, you'd better wait outside while I find my cousin.'

When they arrived, William disappeared into the cathedral, emerging soon after with a man clad in a plain, ordinary doublet. William introduced him as Brother Nicholas.

'Nicholas no longer wears his habit, as it would be dangerous for him,' said William quietly.

Brother Nicholas led them away from the cathedral to a spot in a small, nearby wood, where they saw that the earth had been disturbed and that fresh earth had been scattered around. Pointing to the earth, he said, 'This came out of the tunnel, and we spread it around to avoid drawing attention to the tunnel.'

'This reminds me of *'The Great Escape'* with Steve McQueen,' said Baz.

David joined in. 'There was an even earlier film based on a book called *'The Wooden Horse'*. It was written by Eric Williams, who I think was one of the actual prisoners of war in the Stalag. They also needed to get rid of the soil without drawing attention to the tunnelling, but another problem was of finding ways of preventing the tunnel from collapsing on them - also lack of fresh air, I think.'

William and Brother Nicholas didn't understand the team's references to films and books, but they nodded their heads enthusiastically at the problems that David had outlined.

'Those are the very adversities that we encountered. We spread the soil around in the woods as you said, but we were also very lucky to come across a Cornishman who understands mining, and he advised us to line the tunnel with wood and use tree trunks to prop up the overhead planks. We put in air vents and disguised the outlets by planting bushes around them, and we've hung oil lamps along the way.'

Jack asked, 'Can we go through the tunnel?'

Brother Nicholas nodded, and suggested that Steven and Jack accompany William and himself through the tunnel while the rest make their way to the Cathedral and slip into the crypt. Jack took off his backpack and gave it to Kelly to tuck under her cloak.

William opened a leather sack and took out four lamps, each of which held a fat candle. 'Brother Nicholas will take the lead and I will take the rear.'

They found a lighted oil lamp a few metres inside the tunnel and they took the light from that for their lamps. The journey through the tunnel was unnerving and claustrophobic, but within an hour, they reached the wall of the crypt, much of which had been gouged out with just a thin facing of stones remaining in place. Brother Nicholas carefully drew out a smallish stone and peered through the hole. It became clear that several stones had been taken out and then replaced so that a casual observer wouldn't notice - assuming anyone would feel inclined to go into the dark crypt in the first place. Brother Nicholas called softly through the hole, and Thomas answered him. Thomas and David helped to push out another couple of stones and soon there was enough room for everyone to clamber through.

'Well, well, well,' said Baz.

The New Londoners could see that if the tunnel had existed in Tudor times, some part of it could be reconstructed in New London - and for the same evil purpose. It would be impossible to find the original Tothill entrance in New London because the woods were long gone, but there was a fair chance that they'd find the Abbey end of it.

Nicholas, William, Jack and Steven brushed off as much dirt as they could from their clothes and the team split up, emerging carefully from the crypt, strolling through the church and drifting out through the main door. The team reconvened by the riverbank.

Thomas spoke urgently to Brother Nicholas. 'You and your companions must leave St. Peter's. There is a plot afoot to harm the King and once this gets out, his troopers will take anyone who can be accused of involvement. There's no point in you and your companions being implicated in a plot that has nothing to do with you, so I suggest that you leave immediately and continue doing God's work elsewhere.'

Brother Nicholas nodded sadly, saying that he took their point, while William hugged his cousin, knowing this was the last he'd ever see of him.

* * *

At their usual after-dinner meeting, Thomas said that he needed to visit the Privy Council to warn the authorities of the plot and he asked Steven to go with him. The others said they'd spend the rest of the day heating water for a good wash, and they offered to heat up water for Steven and Thomas so they could enjoy a decent wash on their return.

Steven's helpful Whitehall doorman told them the court was sitting at Tower of London, along with the Privy Council. Ever since Thomas's near brush with the axe-man, he wasn't keen on revisiting the Tower, but he knew it couldn't be helped, so he decided to put a brave face on it.

At the Tower, Thomas and Steven spoke to one or two trusted Councillors and it wasn't long before the news reached King Henry's ears. The King sent an order to Thomas and Steven that they should ask a court clerk to produce a written report for him. He also ordered the whole team, including the four 'Hidalians', to attend upon him the next day.

* * *

The team spent the evening bathing, and Elaine helped Kelly to wash her hair. The young girl was over the moon when Kelly told her to keep the remaining shampoo and conditioner for herself. When Thomas and Steven returned, they rested their aching muscles in two heavenly tin baths in front of a fire in Steven's room.

The next morning, Janie suggested that they ride down to the boat station rather than mess up their decent clothes and boots in the mucky streets, so she despatched Alfred and Godfrey to the livery stables to pick up suitable mounts, telling the lads to hire an additional couple of mounts for themselves, so that they could go with the team as far as the river and bring all the horses back to the stables once the team had embarked.

Kelly was disconcerted when she saw she had to ride sidesaddle but she found it easier than she thought, especially as she would only be ambling along. David knew how to ride, but Baz had never fancied horse riding, so he was unenthusiastic, but he soon discovered that it was easy to sit on the docile London mounts while they trundled slowly through the city. Soon the riders relaxed and watched the world go swaying by, and even Baz agreed that the experience was better than he thought it would be. When they reached the riverside, they hailed a large rowing boat with two oarsmen to take them down-river, to the Tower.

On arrival at court in the Tower, the team waited in an anteroom until they were ushered into the King's presence. Jack sauntered in if he owned the place, surreptitiously checking out the court ladies as he went. The ladies in their turn, along with every other member of the court, watched the team with curiosity. When they reached the throne, Thomas and Steven executed a deep Tudor bow, while David, Baz and Jack gave a typically modern British bow with their feet together and heads dipping slowly forward. To Kelly's surprise, her childhood ballet lessons kicked in, so she held out her skirts, took a confident step to the left and swept her right foot behind her as she bobbed into a deep ballet curtsey. When they stood up, they were faced with a large man on a gilded throne, while a second throne held a very pretty young girl, who turned out to be Catherine Howard.

King Henry was a big man with a big personality. At six feet four, he towered over everyone at court, and even among the team, only Baz equalled him in height. Henry was dressed in a deep red velvet doublet and trunk hose. His outfit was dotted with jewels, threaded with gold lace and slashed to allow patches of white silk to show through. Kelly could feel the attraction emanating from this powerful and vigorous forty-nine year old, and she suddenly understood how he would affect the women

91

around him, even without the obvious charisma of being an absolute dictator. King Henry was still in good shape and his weight didn't look out of place on his large frame; while she knew from history that Henry would eventually lose the obesity battle, at this point in time, his fondness for sports was keeping his girth in check. The men in the team couldn't help but feel awed, and that even extended to Thomas, despite the fact that he'd met King Henry several times before.

The King's voice was lighter than they thought it would be, but it was warm. He spoke to Thomas first, using the confusing royal 'we'.

'Sir Thomas Hatherleigh, it's good to meet thee again. We're glad thy life was spared, because without your intervention, ours would now be in danger, as would that of our dear wife.' Henry patted his wife's miniature hand.

Kelly couldn't help wondering how such a little girl managed to have sex with such a lot of man, and it occurred to her that even sitting astride him would be awkward, but she brushed these thoughts aside while focusing on what Henry was saying.

'Please introduce us to thy team. We understand they are Hidalians, is that not so? It was so wise of you to select a team from our Hidalian allies than to link with an English faction who might denounce thee and tell lies about thee once again, as did your previous superior, Sir Thomas. After all, you nearly lost your life as a result of Cromwell's treachery, is not that so?'

Thomas let the stupendous suggestion that it was Thomas Cromwell who'd consigned him to the axe-man pass on the basis that it was never a great idea to disagree with a tyrant. It crossed Thomas's mind that he was bloody glad to be out of this slippery world, and that Sophie had done him a massive favour by rescuing him. Thomas quickly recovered his poise and went on to make the introductions, starting with his brother-in-law, Steven. Henry greeted Steven and then politely asked the 'Hidalians' a few questions about their country. In the magical way that Kings manage to achieve, Henry actually knew quite a bit about Hidalia, saying that he'd heard it was mountainous and very pretty. He also said he'd heard there was good hunting there. David assured him that there was and that the fishing was also good in 'his' country.

'You will be interested to know that we have some intelligence for thee,' said Henry. 'We sent our troopers to the watergate up-stream from St. Peter's at your suggestion, and the troopers discovered several sacks of gunpowder secreted within. After a little interrogation, the captives were happy to tell us about the rest of their gang. They admitted that it would have been stupid to leave the powder in such a place for any length of time, as it would become damp and useless. Indeed, they told our men the watergate hiding place was purely temporary. They then described how it would be moved to lie beneath us at St Peters and to be ignited at the opportune time, so now we can safely say that all's well that ends well, eh?'

Kelly shuddered a little at the King's casual way of telling them that the men had been 'happy' to tell the king's interrogators about the plot and that they had been equally 'happy' to give their friends away. It seemed likely that the men had been thoroughly tortured before making these revelations, leading her to consider the stupidity of taking on someone like King Henry in his own bailiwick.

'We're very glad to hear that you are safe now, Sire,' said Thomas, working hard to keep his voice even. 'This is such good news.'

King Henry went on, 'It appeareth that the gang members were mainly those who do not like the fact that we are in the process of banishing Popery and superstition from our land, and while some were English, others were Spaniards from the Holy Roman Empire. We've caught most of them, but one man, Jose Lopez, had already left for Spain, and it's said he was the ringleader. If he shows his face back in England, we will have him arrested and brought to the Tower. It was a dastardly plot, and we are relieved that it is all over - and so quickly and neatly done!' Henry regarded the team, while little Queen Catherine smiled broadly at them. 'And now Sir Thomas, we wish to honour thee and thy people for your help in this matter.'

A page approached Henry with a cushion in his arms and a shiny sword lying across it. Thomas felt his blood run cold, but he kept his face impassive. Another approached Henry with a much smaller cushion, and the King took something out of his doublet pocket and placed it on the cushion.

'Sir Thomas, thou art already a Knight, since we honoured thee following thy previous military service to us, so now please accept this small token of our esteem.'

A page took the object from King Henry and offered the cushion to Thomas. Lying upon it was a magnificent diamond and ruby ring. Despite his many mixed feelings, when Thomas put the ring onto the middle finger of his right hand, he was overwhelmed at the magnificent quality of the gift - and the sheer *chutzpah* of the giver.

Henry went on, 'We now wish to honour thy companions and to render them Knights and Dame as they deserve. We can give benefit of lands to Steven, and perhaps our treasurer can arrange that shortly, but sadly, we cannot benefit thy Hidalian friends in that way, so they will perhaps be happy to accept our thanks and to become our Knights as a matter of honour.'

The male 'Hidalians' bowed while Kelly used her ballet curtsey to good effect once more. Several pages came forward with low stools and hassocks for the team to kneel on and King Henry stood up and accepted a sword from a page. David felt the familiar dubbing as the sword touched one shoulder and then the other.

After the dubbing, Henry said, 'Arise, Sir David.'

Then King Henry dubbed each of the others in turn, giving a special smile to Kelly.

David found it an extraordinary experience to be dubbed a second time for services to the same realm, but he was surprisingly glad to become Sir David once again. It felt as though he was starting the process of reclaiming his own skin. Kelly thought becoming a dame was a little strange, but she was absolutely delighted with the honour.

'And now,' said Henry, 'It pleaseth me for you to remain at court with us for the evening, to join us for dinner and for our evening ball and entertainment.'

As they left the 'presence', Jack whispered in Kelly's ear. 'Did you know that Fat Henry has a habit of picking out girls he likes from among those he sees dancing at his court balls? If he takes a fancy to you Kel, you might have to do your duty on behalf of the TUDOR team. How do you fancy that?'

Kelly gasped and looked at Jack in horror...

* * *

Several courtiers took the arms of the New Londoners, as they were keen to talk to such an interesting group and to learn about their exploits. A couple of old friends commandeered Thomas, so he happily caught up with all the national and international gossip of his time, while Sir

David sat with an intelligent married couple and quizzed them about his ancestor, Thomas Cromwell.

Servants quickly ran in and set long trestle tables with banqueting cloths and food. The New Londoners were amazed at the type and amount of food served at the banquet, and they were glad they'd brought their own daggers so they could cut it up. There were platters of fish, including fresh salmon, along with roast meats, various kinds of game and a pig with an orange in its mouth on a centre table. There was a selection of 'herbs' that were available at that time of the year, and fresh fruit, along with dried fruit and nuts waiting in bowls on side tables to serve after the many main courses.

Baz found himself talking to a redhead. He could see that she was lovely to look at in her green and white brocade dress and he enjoyed flirting with her, but he didn't consider her a patch on his Margie. Anyway, Baz wasn't the type to stray. Kelly was in full flirt mode with a raffish naval officer, who with his dark curly hair and neatly trimmed beard, looked like something out of *'Pirates of the Caribbean'*. Two young and very pretty girls commandeered Jack, and they were happily letting him take peeks down their low cut bodices while they surreptitiously patted his thighs under the table!

After the meal, Baz and David went off to play cards while the others watched the dancing, and it didn't take long for Kelly and Jack to join in, picking up the moves from a selection of willing partners as they went along. Steven and Thomas drifted off to join Baz and David in the card room, leaving Jack and Kelly to enjoy the dance, while Kelly kept an eye open in case the King started to take too much interest in her...

Chapter Eleven

JACK GETS HURT

I was born with an enormous need for affection, and a terrible need to give it

AUDREY HEPBURN

Jack loved the dancing, but the past week's celibacy was telling on him, so he decided to break his duck later that night. He was also glad that he'd stuffed a quantity of condoms into his doublet pocket on the off chance. Sir David liked being at the heart of power and influence, even though this wasn't *his* era and it was only for one day - but still, it was enlivening to be back in the saddle, so to speak. David could see the way the wind was blowing for Jack, so he gave him strict instructions to get himself back to their digs by morning, reminding him that Sophie was due to fetch them when the church bells struck midday.

Jack was soon chatting to a creamy redhead, who despite her youth, was married. As was common in court circles, hers was a marriage that had been arranged for dynastic reasons rather than for love. A beautiful dark haired girl with a curvy figure also made her interest clear, and he was sure that he could definitely do something for her as well. Like her companion, she was in a loveless (and fun-less) marriage with an elderly man. In common with many of the women in Henry's court, the brunette came from a mixed

French and English background, and she'd spent several years in France, so her French was better than her English, and she was absolutely charmed to discover that Jack was equally at home in both languages. The redhead's name was Jane, and the brunette was Françoise. Like most of her generation and class, Jane also understood French and could keep up with the bilingual conversation, so it made a pleasant change for Jack to use his dad's language once again.

Once the three youngsters reached the redhead's quarters and Jack got close to the girls, he found their ingrained grime a bit hard to take, so he asked if their servants could bring up a bath, bars of soap and plenty of warm water, all of which resulted in a shared splash around and a good deal of amusement in front of the roaring bedroom fire before retiring to the redhead's bed for a wonderful night's romp. Jack was mighty glad that he'd brought plenty of condoms along, because while the girls were young and potentially disease free, they were married - and their husbands could have passed something on to them. He avoided drinking too much wine because he knew that he would need his wits about him if he were to find his way back to Austin Friars on his own. The girls were fascinated with the condoms and grateful that they could make love with no fear of falling pregnant. After they'd finished, Jack gave them the remaining packets to keep.

* * *

The following morning, Jack woke up early, dressed quickly and blew a kiss to the two sleeping beauties before slipping quietly out of the castle. It was still very dark as he made his way to the Thames in search of a boat back to London Bridge. He was completely knackered and a little sad to say goodbye to his beautiful and fun-loving companions.

Jack soon found a boat with a sleepy Waterman sitting in it, so he gave the man a gentle shake and offered him a bonus if he'd forego his rest and row Jack upriver. There was a cold mist rising from the water and every bone in Jack's body felt damp. The mist and the hour of the day made the river eerily quiet, but despite the fact that he couldn't shake a strange feeling of trouble in the air, the trip went without incident. Glad to be on the final leg of his journey, Jack paid the boatman double the normal fare and turned northwards towards Austin Friars. The spooky feeling that had been dogging Jack ever since he'd left the Tower now proved well founded, because he'd no sooner turned into the main road than four footpads ran out of a nearby house.

One of the robbers shouted, 'Here's a fat bird waiting to be plucked!'

A light from a nearby window glanced off a blade. Rather than backing away from the knife, Jack rushed towards it, sweeping the edge of his left hand sharply down onto the robber's knife arm and the blade clattered to the ground. Stiffening the fingers of his right hand, Jack rammed them into the man's throat, the footpad dropped, clutching his throat and making a nasty gurgling noise. Now the heaviest of the four thugs came at Jack, making him stumble and fall awkwardly with his sword trapped beneath him. The foot-pads reasoned that apart from a short dagger, which was pretty useless against their long knives, Jack was now unarmed. Fired up with anger at what he'd done to their companion, the three men came at him, snarling viciously, and Jack's nostrils were filled with the rank stench of their filthy clothes. The heaviest thief sliced his long blade downwards hard and fast. Jack tried to turn away from the approaching danger, but the thick layer of filth on the ground slowed his roll, and he felt a heavy blow to his right side.

Hearing one of the robbers yelling to the others to finish him off, Jack shoved his hand into his doublet in an effort to grab his pistol, but the gun was stuck fast. It had become caught on a piece of thread and he couldn't shoot through the doublet because the blast was as likely to wound him as to hurt one of the muggers. One ruffian ran up and kicked Jack in the ribs; while the blow hurt like mad on top of the wound he'd already suffered, it shifted the padded doublet just enough for Jack to give his gun a sharp tug and break the thread trapping it.

The footpad clearly didn't recognise the pistol for what it was, but he figured that the thing Jack was holding so tightly must be something of value. He tried to grab the pistol, but before he could get his hand on it, Jack pulled the trigger and floored the thug. Not realising exactly what had happened to his companion, the third knife-wielding mugger now tried his luck, raising his knife-arm for a killer strike, but Jack rolled onto his back and shot the man in the head.

The fourth mugger could have grabbed one of the other men's knives and attempted to finish Jack off, but the excitement that had gripped him at the prospect of an easy mugging was now ebbing. Nothing he'd ever come across went bang and killed people, so it was obvious that something unnatural must be going on. The mugger quickly crossed himself and ran off.

Jack figured that, if the pain in his side was a knife wound, lying in wet dirt and animal dung wouldn't do him much good, so he got to his knees and then somewhat uncertainly, staggered to his feet. There was a moon peeping between the roof outlines of the buildings and there was a little light leaking from the nearby houses. Jack knew that the road ahead would get narrower and darker as he went along, so he reached into his pocket for his torch. After walking a fair distance, he found himself feeling increasingly weak and giddy, so he stopped for a while to catch his breath. He slipped his left hand under his doublet, and when he brought his hand back out again and checked it in the light of his torch, he could see it was covered in blood.

Jack was starting to feel very cold and strangely tired.

'Must be losing blood,' he muttered grimly.

Determined to make it back to Austin Friars, he set off once again, inching along the road and occasionally stopping to lean against a wall and catch his breath and reaching Austin Friars with no further setback. He used his key to get into Thomas's house, slipping out through the back door and across the garden to Steven's house, where he found his way to Kelly's room and gently shook her awake. For a moment, Kelly was disoriented, but when she saw Jack's face in the torchlight, she knew something was wrong.

'I've been hurt, Kel,' he whispered, 'can you help me?'

Whispering so as to avoid waking Elaine, Kelly said, 'Go to the kitchen and light some oil lamps while I dig out my Medipak.'

When Kelly reached the kitchen, even in the dim light of the oil lamps, she could see that Jack was looking grey.

'Let's take your top off and see what's going on.'

She gently undid the cloak and took off his doublet.

'What happened, love?' she asked.

'I was on my way back from the bridge when four men jumped me. They must have thought I had big money or jewels on me. One stabbed me and the others were about to finish me off, but I managed to disable one of the muggers and I shot two more. After the last one ran off, I stumbled back here.'

'Christ, Jack…' said Kelly.

Kelly carefully removed Jack's doublet and undershirt and inspected the wound by the light of the kitchen oil lamps and Jack's torch. The volume of blood pooling at Jack's waist horrified her, and she saw that it was coming from a flap of skin that had been pared from his ribs.

'Christ Jacko, I've only ever done basic first aid and you've lost a lot of blood. What you really need is a drip, but I wouldn't know what to do with it if we had one. I'll do what I can, though, so hold still now.'

Kelly talked to Jack in as casual a voice as she could, in order to keep him calm and to keep his heart rate steady while she worked on him.

'You must have turned away as the knife came at you, because it's clearly glanced off a rib. There's a flap hanging on here and the flow of blood has cleaned out the wound, which is probably a good thing. Wearing a real silk shirt under the doublet has helped, because a good silk garment has a tight weave and that will have cleaned the knife as it went in. It may also have helped to deflect the blow a little.'

Still determined to keep Jack alert and steady and keep the blood flow to a minimum, Kelly made her voice smooth and chatty.

'I've read that Japanese warriors wore real silk underwear for just this reason. They had a point, didn't they?'

Jack said, 'My uncle was in the navy in the Falklands war, and he told me that before they went into action, the men changed into clean underwear to keep germs out in case they were wounded.'

Kelly was glad that Jack's mind was still working, so she smiled at him while she poured cool boiled water from the kettle into a bowl and washed her hands. Drying her hands on some tissues, she turned to her patient.

'Hang on now Jacko, this is going to hurt.'

She grasped the flap of skin and pulled it back into place over the wound, fixing a thin strip of Micropore across one top corner to hold it in place while she fitted the skin even more closely over the wound. She added several more strips of Micropore all around the square of flesh until it was sitting firmly back in place. She took more of the cool boiled water and washed the blood from Jack's right side, undoing his breeches and pulling them down to get at it all. Then, carefully blotting the area, Kelly put the shiny side of a Melolin pad on the wound, telling Jack to keep his finger on it while she stuck it down with several strips of plaster. She used more pads to cover up every bit of the wound, finally pulling his hose back into place and tying them up gently.

'I think you've got away with it Jack, but take some of these co-codamol tablets for the pain, and here's a course of penicillin to make a start on. The antibiotic will also be useful in the event of you catching a dose of galloping knob-rot off those two birds you went off with.'

'Galloping knob-rot, Kel!' Despite his fright and the pain that was starting to kick in, Jack managed a smile.

'I wore Johnnies, Kel, and I kept my mouth away from their lower orders. I even washed my hands after the performance, just in case.'

'I'm glad to hear it.'

'Anyway, what about you? I saw you chatting up that rascal. The one that looked like Walter Raleigh getting ready to go a-privateering on the Spanish Main.'

Kelly laughed. 'You're probably right, Jacko. He said he was an officer in the navy, and even in New London, that means a girl in every port and doubloons in every pocket. Unlike you though, I hadn't had the sense to bring condoms with me, and by the time I thought of finding you and mumping a couple off you, you'd gone.'

103

'You are a crackpot, Kel. Weren't you ever a girl guide? I was a boy scout and I've never forgotten to say 'dib-dib-dib, dob-dob-dob' and to be prepared for anything - *especially* for a change of luck in the plump little chicken department!'

'Oh well, Jacko. There's not too much wrong with you if you can still think of nookie. Go to bed now and we'll see how that wound goes later today.' She draped the cloak over his shoulders and folded the rest of his clothes carefully over the arm on his uninjured side. Then she let him out the back of Steven's house and saw him into Thomas's next door. 'Good night, Jack.'

He blew her a kiss and was soon back in Thomas's house, where he crawled gratefully into bed. It was only now that he realised the strength of the brother and sister bond that he and Kelly shared.

Chapter Twelve

GOING HOME

*The ache for home lives in all of us, the safe place where
we can go as we are and not be questioned*

MAYA ANGELOU

The last morning gave the team a strange sense of
Schadenfreude, because while they looked forward to
getting back to re-joining their loved ones, they were also
sad to leave their new friends. Thomas had already said his
farewells to his court friends, telling them the team would
now leave for Flanders, travelling on to Hidalia within a
day or so.

Jack knew he'd treasure the memory of the two Tudor
girls in the four poster for a long time, but he also knew
these things never turned into worthwhile long term
arrangements and that the best of the experience was
already behind him. His side was very sore, but the penicillin was dealing with any potential infection and the
painkillers were helping. He mentally thanked Kelly for
being there for him.

Back in Thomas's office at Austin Friars, the TUDORs
were shocked and upset when they heard about Jack's
adventures, but they congratulated Kelly on dealing with
the situation so efficiently. They piled up the left over
bottles of water, soft drinks and toiletries in a corner for

Janie and her family to keep, while Baz took Janie through the medicines slowly and carefully, telling what each one was for and how to use it. She was extremely grateful for the antibiotics because they would become lifesavers when the winter chest infections and the summer's fevers and plagues came around.

Thomas encouraged Janie and her family to come to his office to witness the arrival of the Project and to meet Sophie, standing everyone by the window to allow space for the Project to arrive safely. Just as the church bells started to ring, the air in the office stirred and the Project materialised. The next minute, Sophie jumped out of the car and into Thomas's arms.

Sophie had loaded the Project with yet more goodies for Janie and her family, and the team soon had the swag unloaded, with the help of Godfrey and Alfred. They gave Wilf, Janie and their family boxes of chocolates, biscuits, donuts, cakes, bananas and a pineapple, along with brandy, tea and instant coffee. Sophie had packed under-wear and toiletries by the ton and she smiled at the sight of Wilf, Alfred, Godfrey and Elaine's eyes bulging as they checked out the bounty.

Baz and Kelly wondered what Sophie was up to when she handed over a jar containing a dozen or more whole nutmegs, but they were even more astounded when they saw the response this gift evoked. Janie gazed at the nutmegs in awestruck wonder, and Sophie later explained that she had given Janie the financial equivalent of a whole row of Austin Friars houses.

The team stayed for a final meal, thoroughly enjoying a cold collation of ham, pickles and cups of Janie and Frieda's precious tea.

It was disorienting for Sophie, who'd only waved them off a half hour previously, to see the change in them all. They were slightly tanned from spending so much time in the fresh air and their hair had grown a little. The men all had the early stages of beards. David and Baz looked slightly scruffy, while Thomas and Jack looked sexier and even more dashing than ever!

'Good God, Jacko, if you keep your hair and beard like that, every girl in London will soon be climbing all over you!'

Jack brightened at that idea. 'Perhaps I will - for a while, anyway.'

Sophie thanked Janie and Frieda for looking after the team so well, and soon Janie, Frieda, Kelly and Elaine were crying their eyes out, while even Alfred, Wilf and Godfrey were struggling to hold back their tears. Jack sneaked a cheeky kiss with young Elaine, and then followed Sophie into the Project with Baz and Kelly, leaving Steven, Thomas and David as rear-guard until Sophie could come back for them and the swords and pistols.

Soon, they were all inside the workshop at the bottom of Sophie and Thomas's garden. Baz climbed out and found Margie waiting for him, whereupon he grabbed his wife and hugged her so tightly that she thought she'd crack a rib. When the Project got back from the final trip, the men climbed out, picked up their swords, scabbard and belts, and tucked their pistols into their doublets. Soon, they were all making their way across the garden towards the back of the house.

The TUDOR team found it disorienting to see blossoms, flowers and trees in their spring glory, having just left behind the bare branches and misty cold of late autumn, but they didn't miss the pervasive smell of dung, discarded meat, sewage and dirt. They could hardly wait to get out of their Tudor clothes and have a good shower, especially as it was so much warmer in the May of New London than it had been in the November of Tudorland. Everyone was happy to be back, and it was a relief to have nothing more than Jack's wound to worry about.

* * *

Halfway across the garden, the group became aware of a disturbance to their left, and to their astonishment, they saw Sophie's drunken and drugged up ex-husband, Gavin, clambering over the wall. The great lump scrambled to his feet, yelling incomprehensibly., and they were all about to start laughing at the incongruous sight when they noticed he was toting a pistol.

'I told you I'd kill you!' screamed Gavin, waving the gun around. 'You and your bloody friends are all going to die. *Now!*'

Gavin let off a shot that whistled past Sophie's ear. It occurred to Sophie that he'd either taken shooting lessons since they split up, or it was a lucky shot. A second shot rang out and the temporary paralysis that had gripped the group swiftly passed.

'Get him!' yelled Thomas, pulling out his sword and running towards Gavin, while Sir David went for his sabre and followed closely behind. Steven brought up the rear, grabbing his sword as he went, while Baz reached for his gun.

Gavin fired again, missing the men whom he'd been aiming for, but hitting Margie and spinning her around. This was too much for Baz and he literally saw red.

Gavin screamed, 'I'm going to kill you all!'

Baz yelled, 'Not if I get you first, you won't!'

Sir David was now between the fat slob and Baz, so he inadvertently messed up Baz's chance of getting off a clear shot, but he brought his sabre down forcefully. Gavin turned away just as the sabre came at him, so it sliced down the length of his upper arm, filleting the flesh from the bone. Gavin screamed and dropped his gun. Kelly picked it up. Out of the corner of her eye, Kelly could see Baz raising his pistol to shoot the unarmed idiot, so she ran back towards Baz, literally throwing herself at him and knocking him off his feet.

'Baz, no!' she yelled, 'he isn't worth it!'

The TUDOR team piled onto Gavin and held him down while Thomas yelled at Sophie to ring for an ambulance. Sophie ran into the house and phoned, then she took a length of washing line from the utility room to use as a restraint, although truth to tell, Gavin was no longer in any shape to give trouble. The team rushed into the house so that they could get back into their own clothes before the ambulance and police arrived.

Sophie was comforting Margie and praying with all her might that the bullet hadn't done too much damage. She was absolutely horrified that it was her crazy ex who'd hurt her friend.

Thomas walked briskly across the garden and gathered Margie into his arms, taking care not to crush her wounded arm.

'We'll get him, you know. If the law doesn't take care of this, we will. You know that, Margie love, don't you?'

Margie nodded weakly.

Meanwhile, Sir David thought quickly and said, 'Let's tell the cops this was an informal meeting of the TUDOR group. I'd been practising my fencing earlier in the day and had picked up the sword on autopilot.'

Steven said, 'I'll tell them you were practising with me.'

Baz said, 'If Gavin goes on about men and women in old-fashioned clothes, I'll tell them it's not surprising he's seeing things, being the drunkard and druggie that he is.'

The others agreed to stick to the story.

Baz changed quickly and went to the hospital with Margie and Gavin. It said a lot for his self-restraint that Baz didn't punch Gavin in the face for what he'd done to Margie.

Meanwhile, the others disappeared into Sophie's bathrooms. Apart from the wound itself, Jack was so bruised and sore that he could barely use his right arm, so when Thomas had finished his shower, he helped Jack, gently washing his young friend and helping him change into clean clothes.

'This is normal for me, you know,' Thomas said in a conversational tone.

Jack's face was a real picture. 'What, washing men, you mean?'

'In Tudorland it's common for a young man who is hoping to become a knight to 'squire' his elders and betters by acting as a valet and helping them wash and dress. In a battle situation, it's vital to have someone who understands the knight's armour and who knows each knight's particular problems, such as where his amour chafes and so on.'

'I guess you're right. I'd never thought about it before.'

'There's a great fear of 'gayness' in our New London world, but it just didn't enter the heads of medieval people to think that way. The few gays who were around were tolerated if they were artists or musicians, but they weren't encouraged to become soldiers, and any who made a nuisance of themselves were quietly executed. So men just helped each other in the same way that footballers and other sportsmen do today.'

'Yes, I can see that. A bit hard on the poor old gays though, don't you think?'

'It was a hard time; individual human rights didn't exist.'

Thomas looked at the area around Jack's bandage and pulled a face. Jack's side was black and blue, and clearly very sore.

'Those footpads did a number on you and no mistake, but the area around the bandage doesn't look inflamed so it probably isn't infected. Kelly did very well with the first aid, but you'll go to the surgery tomorrow and get it dressed, won't you?'

'Yeah, of course, Tom. Truth to tell, I'm more worried and upset about Margie than I am about myself. I could cheerfully kill that Gavin bastard.'

'So could we all, Jack. So could we all,' sighed Thomas. 'This time I hope they bang him up and throw away the key.'

Jack gave a silent nod.

'One thing, I've absolutely decided on is that I can't take a chance on Gavin having another go at Sophie, so when he gets out, I intend to find him, shove him into a Project and throw him out into the Ice Age. Then he can take his lousy moods out on a hairy mammoth.'

Despite his discomfort, Jack grinned at the image.

Soon they were sitting around the kitchen table while Jack, Kelly, Thomas, Steven and Sir David told Sophie about their adventures. When Sophie heard about the attack on Jack she was horrified, and only slightly less upset when she heard about the attack that Sir David and Thomas had fought off.

'Don't you want to go to the hospital now, Jack?' she asked in a worried tone.

'Nah, my lovely. Thanks to Kelly, my side seems to be doing pretty well, but they have a clinic at my doctor's surgery, so I'll pop in first thing. I'll need the dressing changed, because I can't reach it myself.'

'Make sure you do that.'

Steven said, 'Thankfully, we didn't need the grenades and plastic explosives. I'm glad things didn't get that bad.'

Nobody disagreed with that.

When the team told Sophie about being dubbed knights and dame, she was truly amazed - even more so when Thomas showed her the magnificent ring that the King had given him.

Turning to Sir David, Sophie asked, 'Is it at all likely that the tunnel still exists after all these years? After all there's been so much building in London, and there was the bombing during the war and whatnot.'

'The original tunnel can't exist in the form that it was in 1541 because the area is now completely built up, but the weakness in the crypt walls may still be there and it's possible that a short tunnel or cave of some kind may exist as a void behind it. If so, it's still the logical place for explosives to be stored.'

Sophie nodded.

'Anyway, Sophie,' said Jack, 'it's the first real lead we've had and it's definitely worth following up. The old watergate is inland now due to the deliberate narrowing of the Thames, but even that might still be worth inspecting, and I don't think the land around the Abbey itself has been disturbed all that much over the centuries, so we might get lucky.'

'Lads and lasses,' said Sir David, 'I would love to suggest that we all have a week off, but we've still got the Abbey situation on our hands, and if the intel from Alec Blitz is right, we need to do something about the other threats as well. He thinks the London Eye is a target and he reckons the Shard or perhaps the Gherkin might be on the list, so tired or not, I need the TUDOR team to convene in my office tomorrow morning. We won't put in a full day, but we do need to thrash out some details pretty quickly.'

Sir David turned to Sophie. 'Sophie dear, I noticed that your wonderful Project is looking a little tattered, and that some of the batteries are rattling around. With your agreement, I would like to take the Project into TUDOR and ask you and Raj to work on it. Frankly, I would like the whole thing to be cloned, but that means taking you onto the staff to work with Raj, so I will need to know how you and Tom would feel about that.

I wouldn't be surprised if you felt more like destroying the Project than improving it after this episode, but it would be a shame, because I can see many good reasons why Her Majesty's government might use such an incredible machine in the future. If you agree, I would also like to tell the Home Secretary and the Prime Minister about the Project.'

'It sounds like a good idea, Sir David, but Tommy and I need to talk it over first. I'll ring you with an answer.'

'Of course.'

Sir David now turned to Thomas. 'Tom, I know you like working at the CAB, but you're wasted there and I would love you to join TUDOR on a full time basis. If you want to stay at the CAB for the moment, perhaps you can agree to be available to us in an emergency.'

Thomas's head snapped back. 'That's taken me by surprise, Sir David, but as Sophie says, I will need to give it some thought and talk things over with her. I will give you my answer tomorrow, if that's all right.'

Now David approached Steven. 'I understand that you aren't working at all yet, is that so?'

Steven nodded.

'How would you like to join TUDOR, Steven? We could use someone who keeps his head in an emergency, and you showed us you could certainly do that. I can also see that you're more of an admin man than an action man, despite the fact that I think you did amazingly well in

Tudorland. I would be very happy to see you handling some of our more important admin tasks, such as statistics, collating and linking with the police forces here and overseas. We also need someone to do the accounts and budgeting, as the job's getting to be too much for Jill now that we're growing. You'd be great at that and Raj can help you, but you'd need to work for us on a part time basis and spend the other part in college learning the computer and taxation sides of things. There'd be a lot to learn and it wouldn't be easy.'

Steven nodded and said, ' We all prefer to talk things over with our families before making major decisions, so may I also phone you with my answer?'

'Of course. I will await all your calls with interest,' replied Sir David - finally slipping fully back into his role as boss of TUDOR.

* * *

Once the others had gone, Thomas wandered into the garden and walked around, smelling the blossoms and touching the trees. He even went into the greenhouse and said hello to Sophie's young salad and vegetable plants. It was as if he needed to get in touch with reality. The last week had given him a lot to take in, and he knew he'd need time to get over it all.

Sophie left him to his own devices while she took the Tudor clothes and folded them into a couple of bin bags to take to the cleaners. She decided to tell Angels that the outfits had been used for an amateur dramatic play, and to pay them for Jack's ruined doublet.

* * *

Later that day, Sophie phoned Margie to see how she was doing, and her friend answered with her characteristic cheerfulness.

'Hi Soph, Baz is absolutely knackered and he's gone upstairs for a kip. I doubt I'll see him again until supper time.'

'Margie, darling, I'm so sorry you got shot. I'd have done anything for that not to happen. I really wish I'd never set eyes on that bloody man.'

'Don't be daft, Soph. None of this is your fault. And anyway if you hadn't married Gavin you'd never have ended up living in Silas's old flat, playing silly buggers with the Project and marrying Tommy Thumbscrews, would you?'

'I guess that's true. How's the arm, anyway?'

'They've given me a sling. Baz thought it must have clipped the bone and he's right. The doctor said it would hurt like stink for a while, but hey - I'm still doing the housework, aren't I? Where there's life, there's washing, eh girl?'

Sophie couldn't help laughing. 'Is there any news about Val yet?'

'Val's seen the surgeon and she's back at the Nuffield tomorrow for more tests. The unspoken fear is cancer, but the weird thing is that I don't think it *is* cancer. I wouldn't be surprised if it was fibroids.'

'Oh God, I hope you're right. Well, tell her I'm praying for her - if she's happy with a Jewish prayer, that is.'

'She's happy with *anybody's* prayers, Soph. Truth is, Val just wants to know one way or another and it will take a few days yet. Thank God we're private. If we had to rely on the NHS, it could be months of messing around, and that would make it too late if it was cancer.'

'Well, keep me posted about Val, and if you want me to bring a cooked meal over tomorrow or to take the kids off your hands for a while, you've only to ask.'

'Thanks, Sophie, I will definitely ask for help when Baz goes back to work. I'll need to dump the kids on you when Val goes into hospital, anyway.'

Sophie's thoughts lingered on her poor friend, who really had a lot on her plate at the moment.

* * *

Thomas was very quiet during their evening meal and after they'd eaten, he watched motor racing on the television while Sophie took her sewing kit from the shelf in the utility room and caught up with some mending. She'd also had a long and emotionally draining day, because to her, it was still the same day in which she and Margie had filled the Project with gear and sent their loved-ones to Tudorland. She was also extremely upset at what Gavin had done.

Neither she nor Thomas felt like an acrobatic love-making session, so they settled for a good old cuddle, kissed each other goodnight and fell into a deep and very welcome sleep.

* * *

In the meantime, Lucy Sanders was due to meet her friend Riva for a bite and a gossip catch-up that evening, but first, she wanted to spend her rare free afternoon catching up with the five hundred-year old gossip from the Tudor court. She wanted to see how King Henry was coping with his unrequited love for Anne Boleyn, along with his *requited* love for his mistress Elizabeth Blount, and to get a sneak preview of the way Catherine of Aragon and her daughter Mary were coping with the situation...

Chapter Thirteen

BACK TO THE CRYPT

The greatest healing therapy is friendship and love
HUBERT H HUMPHREY – EX VICE-PRESIDENT OF THE USA

The following morning, Sophie and Thomas slept late. When they did get up, Sophie made them a good old-fashioned English breakfast while Thomas went out to buy a newspaper. Later that day, they talked over Sir David's proposals.

'You know, Sophie, now that we're settled in the house, it occurred to me that you might want to go back out to work at least on a part time basis. I know we don't need the money, but you'll feel as though your brain is rotting if you stay home much longer. I'd be perfectly happy for you to work at TUDOR, but the Project is yours, so any decisions and any further implications about it must also be yours.'

'Tommy darling, on the one hand I couldn't care less if I took a hammer to the Project and shoved it into the recycling depot, but on the other hand, it would be lovely to visit Janie and Frieda and their family from time to time, and I can see that the Project would be useful to TUDOR. I agree that the physics required for a job at TUDOR would definitely prevent my brain from rotting, and I'd be glad to do it and to work on other more advanced time and space telemetry if needs be. It will take two people working together to back up everything, and to keep copies of the software and data on a number of computers to prevent any part of the massive program from getting lost or mangled. Once it's safely backed up, we can work out what makes it tick and probably clone the lot.'

Thomas gave a slight nod.

'I can see that you'd be much happier at TUDOR than at the Citizen's Advice Bureau. It's more you, isn't it? The CAB has done you a really good turn, but it's too tame. Truth to tell, I've been waiting for you to show signs of boredom and restlessness, and maybe even resentment at the loss of your old life.'

'It was a clever idea of yours to suggest that I volunteer at CAB at the time, and I was glad to take the paid job when they offered it to me. It's taught me an immeasurable amount about New London, and it's allowed me to see the problems of ordinary people at close range, but you're right, it isn't enough.'

Thomas leaned over and gave Sophie a loving peck on the cheek.

'This is a golden opportunity for me to climb back into a familiar saddle and I really need to thank Baz for it, because the opportunity would never have come my way otherwise. It will enable me to stretch myself and to use the knowledge that I built up during my years of service to King Henry. I would be proud to work for Sir David and for TUDOR.'

'At your level, I suppose most of the work will be strategic rather than a matter of chasing around in the field, so it shouldn't be too dangerous, so I guess I'll be able to sleep at night - most of the time!'

'Men and women who live with spooks must necessarily be kept in the dark, but with us both working for

TUDOR, we'll both know what's going on, and that will remove a great deal of the pressure.'

'Yeah, that's a fact.'

'I'll hand in my notice tomorrow and recommend Teresa for job. She's doing more of the managerial work now anyway and her confidence has grown, so I don't see a problem.'

'Do you think Steven will take the job that David's offering?' asked Sophie.

'I'm sure he will. He wants to earn his own money and to stand on his own two feet.' Thomas took Sophie's hand. 'We can still help Kate and the children with additional funds here and there, but Steve will feel more like his old self when he starts to earn a real wage. He also needs mental stimulation, because he also has a fine brain, and he needs to use it.'

'So it seems as though things are falling into place, Tom.'

'It does indeed.'

* * *

Jack was getting his wound checked and dressed, but the others were in the TUDOR office bright and early. Sir David looked around the table and opened the meeting.

'The first thing we need to do is to get round to the Abbey PDQ and re-check that bloody tunnel.'

Sir David turned to Baz. 'I want you and Kelly to go over there today. I'll get Jill to phone the Abbey and tell them you're coming and I want her to get the Abbey people to set up powerful lights so you can see what you're doing down there.

'When Jack gets in, I need him to get around to his informants, along with anyone else who might have heard something. It seems that Alec Blitz was absolutely right, because we know that something more *is* intended, but we don't know what or where. We need to know if something else is designed to go off at the same time as the Abbey explosion, or whether we're looking at a series of separate events in London or elsewhere, and when they're due to be set off.'

After the meeting, Kelly and Baz stood by the large 'image table' in the open plan office area. This was a table with a top consisting of a massive digital screen, specially made for a group of people to view documents and designs at the same time. It also allowed people to swipe images from their tablets onto the table or vice versa. Kelly set the table's computer to show the photos that she and Jack had taken on their phones while they were in Tudorland.

'This area showed disturbance, so I guess that's where we'll look.'

Kelly held her iPad next to the table and put her finger on one of the images. She swiped it off the table and the image was immediately copied to her iPad. The others followed suit, collecting the images for comparison with the crypt walls when they got to the Abbey.

* * *

Baz and Kelly took the tube to the Abbey, and unsurprisingly, when back in the familiar building, they had strong feelings of déjà vu. They could also see how much had been added to the Abbey since their last visit, and how much older and grubbier it had become.

A serious looking senior church official was waiting for them and several workmen accompanied him, carrying lamps and torches. The first thing Baz and Kelly noticed was the lack of menace in the air, and the eagerness with which the Abbey's officials greeted them.

'I'm Reverend James. I understand you've had intelligence to the effect that there's a cave or tunnel or something leading off the crypt. Is that right?'

Baz said, 'Seems so. And we even have some idea of where the tunnel or cave is supposed to be.'

Reverend James led the way. 'When we find the spot, the men can run cables down and rig up lights, but the crypt is a big place and there's no point doing that until we know what sector we need to examine.'

Kelly led the way with Reverend James, Baz and the foreman of the workforce following behind her. The crypt hadn't changed all that much, so Kelly paced out her steps, moving from one part of the building to the next, until she felt certain that she was in the right area. Then she turned sharp right and walked over to the wall.

'That's the outside wall,' said Reverend James.

'It should be,' said Kelly.

'Let's have some light here,' said Baz.

Even with nothing but their torches, they could see an area of disturbance running for about five feet along the relevant area of wall. When checked against the photos on Kelly's Tablet, the disturbance looked much the same as it had when they'd last seen it.

The foreman's radio wouldn't work in the crypt, so he went back for help and within fifteen minutes there were men moving swiftly towards them with lights on stands, metres of cable and an assortment of tools. Once the lights were working, two men jimmied the wall and pulled several stones away, and soon they were all looking through the hole into a deep cavern. It was a weird and disorienting feeling for the TUDORs. They replaced the stones and removed the lights, cables and all evidence of their visit, and once they were back upstairs, they regrouped in Reverend James's office.

'We'll post men around the Abbey, both close by the crypt entrance and in short sessions in the crypt itself. It won't be nice down there in the dark, but the operatives will have infrared glasses.'

Baz phoned Sir David, telling him what they'd found, and Sir David ordered Baz and Kelly back to the office. Teams of agents from TUDOR's small force, along with other counter-terrorism forces were set in place. Everyone was warned not to talk about the operation until all the terrorists had been apprehended; they hoped it wouldn't take too long.

Soon, seven men were in captivity, three of whom had come from a small country called Parmia, which is on a border of one of the old Soviet satellites, while the other four were from the Argentine. The ringleader had left the country, which was ironic, because this was exactly what had happened during their Tudorland adventure, but they still needed to discover what other developments the gang had in mind.

A couple of days later, it became clear that TUDOR had reached an impasse, because nobody was talking. Any counter-intelligence interrogator knows that most spies and terrorists will break in time, especially if talking gives others who are involved time to get away unscathed, but a breakthrough of this kind could take months to achieve, and the christening was only a few short weeks away.

Chapter Fourteen

QUESTIONING SUSPECTS

Speak quietly, but carry a big stick

HARRY S. TRUMAN

Thomas's superiors at the CAB were very sorry to lose him, and while they didn't know exactly *why* he had been recruited by a government agency, they knew it was important, so they left it at that. Thomas was going over the last few loose ends with Teresa when his mobile rang. Calls on Thomas's mobile were never related to CAB work, so he checked the screen; he was surprised to see Baz's name come up.

'Hi Baz, wait a minute can you?'

Thomas quickly told Teresa to come back to him later if she had any queries, and when she'd left the room, he closed the door and turned his attention to Baz. 'Hello Baz. Family all right?'

'Yeah, they're fine thanks. Val's on the mend. Thank God it was only fibroids, but they gave the old girl a complete hysterectomy, so now it's just a matter of recovery. Val doesn't want to stay in bed though, so she tries to get up and help Margie, and the kids don't want to stay out of Val's room, so Margie's having to put her foot down to all of them. Poor Margie, I'm really sorry for her, and the only time I can help is at the weekend. Anyway, Tommo, thank

God this isn't yet more family trouble, its business. Do you think you can slip out for a pie and pint at lunchtime? I can easily come down your way if you like.'

'Sure Baz. Meet me at one o'clock in the "*Dukes Head*" in Charles Street. Do you know it?' As soon as he asked the question Thomas knew it was a stupid one, because like all London cops, Baz seemed to know every pub in the city.

'Yeah, I know it. See you there then.'

Just before one, Thomas grabbed his jacket and made for the pub. He picked a corner table with a good view of the room, and within a couple of minutes, Baz walked in. Thomas stood up to greet Baz and a man who he'd brought with him. Thomas noticed that Baz's companion was a tall and handsome guy, with dark hair and a dark brown moustache, deep-set dark brown eyes and a jolly white-toothed smile, set into a suntanned skin, all of which gave him a dashing and somewhat piratical appearance.

Baz introduced his companion as Alec Blitz, and Thomas shook the man's hand, while greeting Baz.

Thomas said, 'They do a good burger and chips here. Apparently it's all homemade, so if you're buying, Baz, I'll have that, and a pint of Fosters.'

Baz and Alec settled for the same, and Alec went with Baz to help carry the drinks.

When they'd tasted their drinks, Baz spoke quietly. 'Alec is from Mossad, Tommo. Heard of Mossad, have you?'

Thomas noticed that Baz pronounced the name Moss*ad*, with the emphasis on the last syllable, which is the Hebrew style.

'Certainly have, Baz. Sophie says their agents shoot first and ask questions afterwards.'

Alec laughed cheerfully at that one.

'Alec, Sophie is Tommo's wife and she's Jewish, so she knows her gefilte fish, so to speak. And she also works for TUDOR.'

Alec said, 'I saw her once in a meeting with Sir David. Short, dark hair and very pretty.'

'That's her,' agreed Baz. 'She's a clever girl and she works in our techie department.' Baz was careful to avoid talking about Projects or time machines.

'So what can I do for you?' asked Thomas.

'We're stumped for an answer,' said Baz, 'and as time is of the essence, it occurred to me that a change of face in the interview room might do the trick.'

Thomas couldn't see where this was going.

Alec's warm voice was lightly accented, so Thomas reasoned that Alec's first language must be Modern Hebrew.

'As you know, the point of a terrorist group is to use cells so one lot doesn't know what the other lot are up to, but in the case of the gang that you have under lock and key, Hezbollah have assured us that the group *do* know what the other cell is planning.'

Thomas nodded.

'I got wind of this via my informant at Hezbollah, who told me that their compatriots are miffed at the gang's London operation. Al Quaida hate the fact that the apparently pagan Parmians are working with Argies, who are presumably Roman Catholics, because that offends their purist sensitivities, and much the same goes for Hezbollah, so they want the whole lot stuffed, so to speak.'

'Fuck's sake!' exclaimed Thomas. 'Sounds like a modern version of the Reformation.' Then he asked Baz where the suspects were at the moment.

'Belmarsh,' replied Baz. Thomas noticed his friend seemed to be uncharacteristically embarrassed, but then Baz revealed what was on his mind.

'You see, Tommo, we'd like you to do the interrogation for us on this one.'

Thomas put his fork down and stared at Baz. '*Me?*' he exclaimed. 'You can't be short of good people.'

Baz shifted in his seat. 'Well, TUDOR doesn't have many skilled interviewers on board yet, so the gang know us all, and a fresh face would help, so to speak.'

'Holy-moly Baz, I'm out of *practice*! I've done my share of counter-intelligence interrogation in the army, but not for some time. I'd be rusty - but I'd love the chance...'

'Sure you would, Tommo. You never really forget. It's like shagging: however long you leave it, it soon comes back!'

Alec was laughing gaily by this time and said, 'That's another fine mess you've got him into!'

'Not as much as the mess you're in, Alec,' said Baz.

'What mess is that?'

'That burger's not kosher, so if you die within the next twenty-four hours, you'll go straight to hell,' said Baz.

'Then I'll be there with you lot, won't I!' countered Alec.

* * *

The next day, Thomas dressed even more carefully than usual, because his Tudorland experience had shown him that prisoners always felt scruffy and at a disadvantage when faced with someone who was perfectly turned out. The team worked their way through the complex security system, and soon enough Thomas was ensconced in an interview room with Jack at his side. The prisoners had a solicitor present to ensure the interview stayed within the limits of the law. TUDOR had even provided Parmian and Spanish interpreters in case of need.

Thomas questioned each of the men quietly and persistently, using his penetrating gaze to good measure. He soon saw that what Baz had told him was quite right. Most of the men would be impossible to break in the time they had available to them, but he kept on at them anyway, drip-feeding such evidence as the TUDOR team had against them until he felt himself working towards a weak link. When Thomas and Baz got together later to compare notes, Thomas suggested they push the youngest Argentinean hard, because he could sense that the teenager was nearing the end of his tether. The young man had gone down with a heavy cold and whatever truculence he was trying to hang onto was fast disappearing.

'One of the older Argies is the lad's brother and I think he bullied the lad into joining the gang.' Thomas looked at Baz and Jack. 'I'm pretty sure I can break the kid fairly swiftly.'

Baz, Jack and Kelly kept going at the older gang members, but just as he'd predicted, the breakthrough came from Thomas's teenager. The lad didn't have much English, so Thomas smoothly switched to Spanish, with the interpreter translating for the sake of the solicitor and the tape. After a couple more hours of quiet, but relentless probing the lad suddenly folded, agreeing that he'd been pushed into the job by his bullying older brother. He also said that he was glad it had ended without anyone getting hurt.

When the team arrived back at Millbank and reported their findings, Baz explained that once the youngster had started to talk, several other gang members gave up the ghost. It appeared they'd planted small missiles in boats on the Thames, from where they intended to attack the London Eye, in the hopes of catching a few foreign dignitaries taking a ride in one of the pods. Then they were due to hit the Shard and the Gherkin. The following day, Thomas and the TUDOR team questioned the men again to be sure they had uncovered the full extent of the plot.

They were enjoying a welcome cup of tea after their exertions, when Jack told Baz of an unexpectedly amusing incident.

'The lad said the gang had aimed to drop a missile on the Tower of London, and I thought for a minute that Tom was going to offer to lend them a hand!'

* * *

That evening, Margie told Baz that Jack had popped in to see how Val was getting on, and that she'd sent him through to where the older woman was watching the TV. A few moments later, Margie had thought she could hear Val yelling, but when she ran in to check, she saw her mum bent double with laughter, and Jack looking the picture of innocence. When Val could manage to speak, she'd explained that Jack had told her a funny story.

'What was the story?' asked Baz.

'Well, Margie love, come through to the den and I'll get him to tell it to you himself, because I could never do it the way he did.'

When Baz looked at him enquiringly, Jack held his hands up in surrender and told his tale.

'You see I have a Welsh friend called Jon who has several old aunties. One day, Jon was walking down the high street with his Aunty Flo, when they met up with his Aunty Glenys, and naturally, Aunty Flo asked Aunty Glenys how she was.'

At this point, Jack's voice morphed into a credible Welsh accent.

'Aunty Glenys said, "I'm not too good, Flo love."'

'Aunty Flo asked, "Oh, why's that then, Glenys?"'

'Aunty Glenys replied, "Well, the doctor's told me I've got to 'ave an 'ysterical rectomy, and truth to tell, I'd rather 'ave it behind me than 'anging over me 'ead."'

At this point, Val started to laugh all over again and Margie used her good arm to swipe Jack round the head, saying that if Val's stitches burst, she would happily do a twenty stretch for murdering him. Val however, reckoned Jack had done more to make her better than all the medicines in the world.

* * *

Teresa became the official manager of the CAB branch, and remained good friends with Thomas and Sophie thereafter. Thomas felt comfortable now that he was earning a really decent salary on his own account rather than relying on Sophie to augment his CAB pay, while Sophie told him that she didn't give a toss who earned what or who paid for what, but if earning a good salary made him happy, it made her happy. Indeed, now that she was also earning a salary from her job at TUDOR while also obtaining an income from her investments, their combined tax bill was so horrendous that she reckoned they were financing TUDOR for the government all by themselves.

Steven had already joined the TUDOR team on the admin side and he was taking various technical and finance courses as he went along. As Jack commented dryly, they were all bloody TUDORs now, and if Fat Henry ever reincarnated in London, he'd feel very comfortable.

* * *

Slipping her DVD into the player, Lucy wasn't sure whether to commiserate with King Henry for wanting Anne and a legitimate son or two, or to feel aggrieved on Catherine's behalf. She loved the costumes, though, and wondered what it might be like to have a handsome and brave, doublet-wearing man of her own.

'Ah, well,' she told herself, 'we can all dream, can't we?'

Chapter Fifteen

A PASTICHE OF PERVERSION

It's almost a definition of a gentleman to say that he is one who never inflicts pain.

KNOWLEDGE AND RELIGIOUS DUTY, CARDINAL NEWMAN

Thomas and Sophie were in bed one Sunday morning, when Sophie came out with a real non sequitur.

'I've just read a strange book,' she said.

'What book is that?'

'It's the one everyone was talking about a few years ago. I'd call it kinky-girly-porn.'

Thomas propped his head on his hand and looked at Sophie, 'You'd call it *what*?'

'It's about a girl who'd reached the age of twenty-one and hadn't yet got around to sex, then she meets this alpha male who she really fancies and she goes for it big time. So far, I've got no argument with that. I once had a perfectly normal friend who stayed a virgin until her early twenties because she didn't meet anyone who rang bells for her, but the man in *this* book is clearly perverted and the heroine gets caught up in being hit, tied up and so on.'

'That *is* a taking things a bit far.'

'I don't get it, Tommy. Why on earth would anyone want to hit someone for pleasure and why would anyone find being smacked around erotic. It'd be the finish of a relationship for me, I can tell you.'

'I know it would. You've not said much about it, but I know that your mother took her rages out on you by knocking you around.'

'Do you know, Tommy, my mother would be perfectly all right for weeks on end; then for no good reason, she'd start to weep loudly in a horribly embarrassing way, her temper would rise and she'd start slapping me around. The worst place to hit a child is around the head because it rocks the brain against the skull and disorientates the child. It forces air into the eardrums and that temporarily deafens the kid. The poor child can see her mother's twisted, hate-filled mouth opening and shutting as the woman shrieks and rains curses down on her, but she can't hear properly and she can't make sense of the world. She feels helpless and humiliated. So how something like that could possibly equate to pleasure is beyond me.'

Sophie turned to Thomas and looked into his concerned face. 'I'm not daft, Tommy. I'm perfectly well aware that I'm still fairly ignorant about sex and I know I'm sexually sub-missive. I think that's bred into many women, especially those from an ethnic background. I guess I'll always need a man to turn me on, and none of the men I knew took the trouble - until now.'

Thomas smiled at her. 'There's no need to wallow in perversion, and those who do eventually lose interest in normal love and normal relationships. We all have a dark side, but purely in the interests of knowledge and experi-ence, I'll show you precisely where yours resides, Sophie.'

Thomas pulled her on top of him, reached to his left and pulled a pillow down long-ways, then he slid his hands down Sophie's arms, swiftly gathering her thumbs together and clasping them in his left hand. He rolled her onto her

132

back so that the pillow supported her shoulders and upper spine. Her captured hands were below the pillow line and thus not under pressure, and while her shoulders complained a little and her thumbs complained even more, she wasn't in serious pain.

'I can easily turn you on now,' he said. 'Try to keep part of your brain functioning and watch what happens.'

He set his face and fixed his blazing blue eyes on her, making his gaze icy and pitiless. Then he brought the fore and middle fingers of his free right hand to her mouth and crisply ordered her to lick them, after which he ordered her to do the same with his thumb. Once she'd complied he got to work, and the psychology of bondage kicked in. Sophie bucked as though she'd been electrocuted.

'See?' He smiled at her. 'Wanna come? That won't take long, either.'

Sophie stared up at him in amazement. She was astonished at how quickly she'd responded. Her skin was on fire and her throat constricted. 'Cripes, Tommy,' she croaked. 'What the fuck happened?'

'Standard perversion procedure.'

'It's like those sex-charged episodes of CSI where super-powerful Grissom comes up against Lady Heather,' said Sophie.

'Lady Heather?'

'Lady Heather runs a dominatrix club for sexual nutters, and the highly superior and self-satisfied Grissom finds himself attracted to her.'

'A club for dominants and submissives. That sounds like fun,' chuckled Thomas. 'Remind me to pay the place a visit - but only as a dominant, never as a submissive.'

His face became serious as he ran a few things through his mind. 'At the end of the day, my darling, we can all be led into temptation. What's the Jewish view?'

'Jews have had different views at different periods of history. Throughout the nineteenth and early twentieth century European Jews were very prudish, but once you get past the masculine propaganda and read the Talmud directly, it says that within marriage, everything is permitted and nothing is banned.'

'Sounds very practical.'

'Jewish law and Jewish thinking *are* extremely practical. It isn't metaphysical, like Christianity or Islam.'

'I like the 'everything is permitted and nothing's banned' bit,' grinned Thomas.

'I don't want you getting mad ideas, Tommy. Anyway, my shyness is starting to fade, so I just might fancy trying a bit of charge-taking one of these days.'

Thomas lay back and spread out his free arm. *'Prend-moi. Je suis a toi.'*

Sophie giggled despite the fact that she was still trussed up like a Sabbath chicken, but like Thomas, she was also in the mood to garner information,

She asked, 'Is it true that most women can only come once?'

'That does seem to be the case for many women, but most can do more if they have the right man. Sadly, most men in Tudorland were lazy, and I think they're even worse in New London. However, there are a number of slappers like you who don't know when to stop.'

'Men despise over-enthusiastic women, don't they?'

'I love my over-enthusiastic woman.'

Thomas released his grip on her thumbs and made love in a normal fashion, but when she came down to earth once more, Sophie had a moment of insight.

'Tommy, you've tied up women before, haven't you?'

'Sophie my little lamb, I have never had sex with a man, never had sex with a woman with another man present or had anything to do with pee or poo, but outside those parameters, there's *nothing* I haven't tried.'

'And I *married* it,' muttered Sophie.

* * *

Later, Thomas went in search of wine and glasses, and while Sophie accepted a glass of wine, she said, 'Now I understand why thumbscrews were such a successful instrument of torture.'

'Indeed. Bones hate to be compressed and joints are even more sensitive to pressure.' He took her glass from her and set it down on the side table, grabbed her thumbs again and squeezed them hard for a second or two.

'Ouch!'

He released her. 'Precisely,' he said, handing her glass of wine back to her.

'I can see why prisoners talked in your day. I know I'd sing like a canary in that situation.'

'People talk a lot of rubbish under duress. It's much better to question suspects carefully, cross check the facts, and only if absolutely necessary, frighten them with the *idea* of torture. Even then, if the prisoner's cause is just, they may never break, and that still applies today. Just as some of the men and women of the resistance in the Second World War never gave in to the Gestapo, so I am noticing some of the Christian girls in Nigeria who are being forced into Islam are refusing outright and even accepting martyrdom rather than complying with the demands of some power-crazed tyrant.'

Thomas put his empty glass down on the bedside table and took Sophie's and put that down as well, then he reached for her hands and trapped her thumbs again, but this time in front of her body, fitting himself behind her so they were like spoons in a drawer.

'Er, Mr Thumbscrews, would you mind letting me go?'

'No. I think I'll hang on to your gorgeous thumbs,' he said, leaning over, nibbling her ear and gripping her thumbs until the pressure became noticeably painful.

'I *do* mind, you cheeky devil.'

'Hard luck,' he murmured, as he started to explore.

* * *

'You know,' said Sophie, when they were cuddling up after their crazy lovemaking session. 'Come to think of it, in the book that I read, at no time did the guy use pleasure and pain *at the same time*. He either dished out one or the other, but not both at once, as you just did.'

'I see,' said Thomas evenly. 'Well, as your friend Margie would say, whether we're climbing the ladder of success, playing sport or brushing up on our perversion skills, we Leos like to do everything just that little bit *better*!'

Sophie couldn't help laughing at the sheer arrogance of her husband.

* * *

A couple of days later, they were having dinner when Thomas told Sophie that he'd downloaded the book she'd been going on about and read it during his lunch breaks at work.

'What did you think of it?' asked Sophie.

'I found it so funny that I couldn't help laughing out loud in places and I got some very strange looks. The sex was amusing, but I guess the real talking point is the bondage and smacking stuff, because normal sexual behaviour is hardly taboo these days, so it must be the perversion that makes people hot under the collar.

'I know I can do the submissive bit *by choice*, for instance by laying back with my hands under my head and letting a woman make love to me, but if someone tried to restrain or hurt me, I might actually kill them before they had time to carry it off. However, what if I had a pretty girl manacled to an 'X' cross in a red room of pain, what would I do? Would it turn me on?' Thomas looked up at Sophie with laughter creasing the edges of his incredibly blue eyes. 'I honestly think old habits would take over and she'd soon be spilling every secret she'd ever had - *and* selling her granny down the river at the same time!'

'Yes, I expect that's exactly what would happen,' laughed Sophie.

Chapter Sixteen

WORKING AT TUDOR

Choose a job you love, and you will never have to work a day in your life

CONFUCIUS

Sir David had told Thomas there was no need to come in early on his first day, so he arrived at the office at about quarter to nine, which taught him that the journey was highly unpleasant during the rush hour. He resolved to start his working day at least an hour earlier in future, as he had always done at the CAB.

When the young receptionist spotted Thomas coming through the door, she squealed and rushed over, leaving her switchboard unattended. Two more juniors ran out of the open-plan office and crowded round, followed by Raj who clapped Thomas on the back. Jill Standish walked elegantly out of her office on her super-high heels and stood smiling at their new staff member, while Jack and Baz wandered out to see what the noise was all about. Steven trailed out, looking handsome in his dark brown suit, with the addition of a pair of strange looking headphones slung round his neck. Kelly charged out of the open-plan with no elegance whatsoever, jumped into Thomas's arms and gave him a smacking great kiss on the cheek.

The gorgeous Jack Duquesne strolled languidly out and stared at the scene with disgust.

'Jeez, this guy's an even bigger babe magnet than I am,' he complained.

Needless to say, this was the moment Sir David chose to arrive. He stopped in his tracks at the sight of the pandemonium and then roared. 'Right, you lot! Get back to work, *now!*'

Sir David motioned at Thomas to come into his office, closed the door put his case and paper down while giving Thomas a warm handshake.

'Well, that lot are all happy to have you on board, and so am I. Sophie's happy now that she's moved the Project to the Mews, and she's working for us on a part-time basis, which suits Raj perfectly. I don't doubt for one moment that he'll find other things for her to do once they've cracked the Project situation. He says she's very good at physics, maths, computing and all kinds of techie stuff.'

'She is, but she lacks confidence.'

'That'll come, and Raj is just the right person to help her. He's patient and gentle, but also very professional, and she'll learn a lot from him. Raj says with Sophie helping him, they should be able to build Projects that are much more sophisticated than the original. I don't understand any of it myself, so I'm happy to leave it to eggheads. As TUDOR grows, we're going to need *more* techie help, so Raj is happy to have Steven in the office. He's picking things up amazingly quickly, considering he didn't grow up in an industrialized world, but he's going to be the most use to me by dealing with the budgets and prising money out of the treasury. Do you know that the guys have picked up on his old job in Tudorland and they now call him "Exchequer"?'

'No, I hadn't heard that one,' smiled Thomas.

'Jill will show you your office shortly. It's not large, but it'll serve and it's right by Baz's room. You'll be working with him much of the time to start with, and that reprobate frog, Jack, isn't far away. I'm sure he'll help all he can, as will the others.'

Emma came in with a tray of coffee and left it on a side table, with sugar and sweeteners. Sir David put two pills into his coffee. 'Must watch the weight these days.'

After taking a good sip of coffee, Sir David went on. 'Your first step is to acquaint yourself with our current investigations, read files and catch up on things. Talk to the guys in Raj's department and to Steven and let them show you the links to the police, Interpol, CIA and other data-bases. Also fingerprints, DNA and all the other data-search methods. Go down to Forensics and see all the gutty forensic stuff. Take your time about everything, because I want you thoroughly briefed before you to rush into anything. When you've got an idea of what's what, let me know and I'll confer with Baz and the others to see what we can pass over to you. To be honest, Tom, I see you as a potential manager rather than as a field operative, and while I know you can do the field stuff, you are thirty-eight now and that's not the right age to start training as an athlete or a crack shot. You will do some fieldwork where appropriate and you will definitely be required for interrogation. What I'm saying is that I see you as my deputy.'

Thomas gave a small nod, but there was something he needed to square away before he made his final commitment. Sir David saw Thomas staring at the table so he told him to spit out whatever was on his mind.

'Surely Baz should be your deputy. He knows modern police work and he's been working for TUDOR for several months. I don't want to do anything to make him resent me.'

'Baz and I have already discussed this and he knows the score. Baz is a copper's copper and that's what he wants to be. He's the same age as you, but he's highly trained for fieldwork, so he can direct, instruct and train new agents as they come on stream. He talks their language and they respect him as one of their own, and much the same will apply if he's called upon to work alongside the armed services. I know you've done your share of fieldwork and you will do more when appropriate, but that's not where you're headed, and Baz knows that.

'Baz has seen that I really need a second in command here, and he said categorically that he'd rather see *you* in that spot than have some unknown quantity brought in over his head from outside.' Sir David stopped to allow Thomas to absorb what he'd said, then he started to speak again. 'For the moment, I'm putting you in at the rank of Inspector, but you'll move up through the ranks swiftly once things get going. The Home Secretary, Frances Shulman, is happy, so that's the main obstacle out of the way.'

Thomas still looked thoughtful. 'It's a relief to hear you tell me that Baz is happy with the situation, but on the other hand, won't *you* feel threatened by my presence? After all, I had a similar position to you when I was in Tudorland.'

'Tom, your position was way *above* mine in Tudorland, but this is a different world and it'll take a while before you get to grips with it. I know TUDOR will grow, not because I am trying to build a little empire, but because the threats to our country are growing. Even forgetting the Project, we have a measure of flexibility that other services don't have. There will be times when the job will be too much for one person and we'll need to split it between us. There will be times when I'm needed elsewhere, or when I'll be taken up with politicking at Number Ten. I would also like to be able to take an occasional holiday and even take to my bed if I get the flu, for God's sake, so I need a thoroughly trustworthy deputy.

'If you think about it, Tom, we all worked under you in Tudorland and none of us was uncomfortable with that situation. You have the personality and the gravitas for leadership. As you said yourself, you refused to stab Thomas Cromwell in the back even when his life was ending and yours was due to be sacrificed as a result, so judging by your loyalty to my ancestor, the chances are you will just as loyal to me and to TUDOR. Believe me, I'll be glad of the help and I won't feel at all threatened - and if you do something particularly well, I can always take the credit for it, can't I?'

'You've really thought this through, haven't you?' smiled Thomas.

'I have, Thomas, and so has Baz. So don't worry.

'Jill has found a good PA for you, and unusually, your helper is a young man. He's a top-flight amateur golfer, but he says that he needs an interesting job as a balance to the physical and competitive stuff that he does as a sportsman. He's helping Jack and Kelly at the moment, but as of today, he's all yours.'

Thomas said, 'I always had male clerks in Tudorland, so the situation will be normal for me.'

'Nothing new under the sun then?'

'Nothing.'

'Well, all I can say for now is "welcome on board", Tom.'

'I'm very glad to be here, Sir David, and so is Sophie.'

* * *

Sir David buzzed Jill and asked her to show Thomas his to office, whereupon he discovered that Jack and Baz had screwed a beautifully engraved brass plate to the wall of his office that carried the legend, *"Sir Thomas 'Thumbscrews' Hatherleigh"*!

The office wasn't over large, but it was adequate for his needs, and best of all, it had a great view of the Thames and of the buildings on the opposite bank. The furniture was pale beech veneer and the carpet tiles two shades of dark blue. There was a PC, printer and a laptop waiting for him, but he could see he'd need to buy himself a diary and other accoutrements to replace those he'd left at the CAB.

Ten minutes later, a light knock announced the arrival of a russet haired young man who held out a hand and introduced himself as Ryan Andrews.

Ryan showed Thomas his own workstation in the open-plan area, and he took Thomas through the somewhat confusing telephone system.

'It's going to take me a while to get to grips with all this, Ryan, so you might need to take me through some things more than once,' said Thomas. 'How long have you been working at Millbank?'

'Ten months, Mr Hatherleigh,' answered Ryan.

'I understand that this suits your lifestyle.'

Ryan nodded. 'Do you play golf, Mr Hatherleigh?'

'Never tried it.'

Ryan was surprised. 'You're joking! It's a good game, you should give it a go.'

'I probably will. I've seen it on the television and it looks like the kind of game I'd enjoy. I've played quite a lot of tennis and I really ought to get back to that soon. Life gets busy though, doesn't it?'

'It sure does. By the way, we use first names here, even to the bosses - apart from Sir David, that is - so is it all right if I call you Tom?'

'If that's the norm, that's fine by me.'

'Good. Now let me take you through some of the drill before I wheel you down to security for fingerprinting, your photo pass and whatnot.'

'Fingerprinting?'

'And DNA. Got to know whose blood's on the floor, haven't we.'

Thomas found the casual atmosphere a little strange, but he decided that it was a case of "when in Rome". In his previous life, his clerks had bowed to him when entering or leaving his presence, as he had done with his previous superior, but this was a different world, and none the worse for that.

* * *

It took a while for Thomas to get a handle on the work at TUDOR. On top of the tricky nature of the job itself, he was still getting to grips with modern language and spelling. Sophie sent him to an evening class for English, she also bought several children's spelling books, and they spent many evenings testing and correcting his spelling. He had to learn to cope with computers and software, but he wasn't afraid to ask for help when he needed it, while Sophie was always happy to take him through things on his home computer. Still, there were still times when the poor man felt as though his head was bursting. An occasional chat with Steven helped, because he was going through the same struggle and the two guys were able to encourage each other.

Sophie bought Thomas a briefcase that would take a laptop and a tablet as well as everything else he needed, along with a beautiful wooden desk set and a framed photo of the two of them for his office wall.

Thomas bought Sophie a new Honda Jazz in a girly shade of metallic lilac. He'd wanted to buy her a seriously expensive car, but he knew she'd fret if it got bumped, and anyway, she was delighted with her new Jazz. They passed her old one to Kate, as she was still getting to grips with driving herself to the shops and taking Robbie to school in the London traffic.

Sophie worked three days a week with Raj in a warehouse at the back of the Mews, which wasn't far from the TUDOR offices. While Thomas went to work every day looking gorgeously handsome in his perfect clothes, Sophie often worked in old jeans and sloppy tee shirts that were stained with whatever materials she was working on. She even had her own boiler suit. One day, Thomas wandered into the Mews on business and as he couldn't see Sophie, Jessica pointed him in the direction of a pair of brown boiler-suited legs tipped with safety boots, that were sticking out from under an aged Volkswagen Transporter. Thomas called Sophie and she scooted out on her wheeled trolley and smiled up at him. Sophie had dirt on her nose and oil on her forehead, but Thomas thought she'd never looked lovelier, so he squatted down, tugged the zip on the boiler suit and reached into her lacy bra.

'For the love of Mike, Tommy, not here!' hissed Sophie. 'Go and ask Raj or Jess for whatever it is you want and then bugger off, I've got work to do.'

Thomas pretended to look crestfallen. 'I'll catch you later,' he said.

'I'm doing really physical work today, so I'll be knackered by the time I get home, Tommy, so forget it.'

'That's your problem, not mine,' he chuckled, strolling off in search of Raj and whistling cheerfully as he went.

Jessica had caught the exchange and was giggling at Sophie's predicament. When Sophie emerged for a coffee break, Jessica commented, 'That husband of yours is a real handful, isn't he?'

'You can say that again,' sighed Sophie.

'I wouldn't mind one like that, though,'

'Well, with a bit of luck, you'll be able to test out a new Project one of these days and trawl through the whole of history in search of one just like him.'

'Lovely,' mused the romantic nineteen year old, 'something like a young Indiana Jones would do nicely for me.'

* * *

When Thomas arrived back at Tamerlane Square, Sophie was soaking her aching limbs in a hot bubble bath. After changing into tee shirt and jeans, Thomas carried two glasses of cool white wine into the bathroom. 'I'm taking you over to Riccardo and Marco for dinner tonight, Sophie darling. You're too tired to cook, so dinner at their trattoria is a better idea.'

'Thanks, love.'

'How's it going?'

'Raj and I are finding snags all over the place. Silas's notes are helpful, but it's still tricky, so as we solve one problem, we run into the next. We'll work it out eventually, but it's tiring at the moment.'

Thomas ruffled Sophie's hair. 'Now that life's settling into a pattern, how about a holiday? I'm not doing anything vital at TUDOR yet, so they can spare me for a bit, and Raj could get on with something else if you weren't around, couldn't he?'

'Any idea where you'd like to go, Tom?'

'I just want to relax and forget everything for a while. It's been a heavy few years for us, hasn't it?'

'Florida would be nice, Tommy. It's a holiday area and you can do lots of touristy things, or nothing at all, just as you fancy.'

'Sounds good to me.'

Chapter Seventeen

A WELCOME BREAK

Live and work, but do not forget to play, to have fun in life and really enjoy it.

EILEEN CADDY - AUTHOR

Sir David granted Sophie and Thomas three weeks' leave from TUDOR, and soon enough they were on their way. Those who have to travel frequently soon learn to detest airports and airplanes, but this was Thomas's first experience and he loved it, while the flight was made all the easier because they travelled business class. Sophie chose the Raleigh Hotel on Miami Beach, partly because it was in a busy area with shops, restaurants and the beach nearby, but also because the Tudor name amused her, despite the fact that Sir Walter's time had been several decades after Thomas's.

The hotel was old, but it had been nicely refurbished, so they spent their first day recovering from the journey, dozing on the beach under colourful umbrellas and reading whodunits. Sophie chose to read a really old book by an author called John D. MacDonald, because his stories were set in the Miami area.

They wandered into the town, gazed at the cafes and shops while enjoying the Latin American music that was seeping out of the many restaurants. They chose a

Spanish restaurant for a meal of calamari, fries, salad, olives, bread and Californian wine. Sophie ended the meal with fruit salad and Thomas worked his way through a huge confection called "death by chocolate".

'You'll get fat if you eat too much of that, Tommy,' teased Sophie.

Thomas's bland look indicated that he wasn't about to rise to the bait. He commented dryly, 'I understand that exercise helps prevent weight gain.'

'So they say. Why, what have you got in mind?'

'Oh, this and that,' he drawled.

'Hey, can't I have a holiday for once? *I* need a rest too, don't I?'

'What you *need* is to love, honour and *obey*.'

'We don't do the '*obey*' bit these days, Tommy.'

'This marriage runs on Tudor rules, so obedience isn't negotiable.'

Sophie knew when he was teasing, but he did it so well that he sometimes caught her out nicely, but she also realised that there could be worse fates than being loved so much. She pretended to be put out by pouting and sighing, while Thomas's intense lapis-lazuli gaze bore into her big brown eyes.

They ended their first evening with a leisurely walk, but soon they were in their room and making love. Sophie always felt a thrill when she was in her husband's arms, while for his part, Thomas needed the warmth and reassurance of her love as much as she needed his, and he took great pleasure in the passion he engendered in his wife.

Over the next few days, they took a tourist trip to the Everglades, visited Sea World and went to the cinema to see a film about spies that made them laugh. They rented a car and made for the Keys, where they enjoyed the tourist traps of Key West, before turning back and renting a little apartment on Tavernier Key where they sat on the tiny beach and read books on their tablets.

Thomas put the swimming sessions that Sophie had given him in London to good use in the warm water. He also treated himself to a cheap rod and line, and relearned a skill that he'd last used as a child, when he'd fished with his father. He was utterly elated when he caught a couple of yellowtail, which Sophie cleaned and barbecued for their supper. It was a wonderful holiday and a real break.

* * *

Lucy, meanwhile, had worked her way through her finals and was beginning to consider what her future career might be.

Part Two

Chapter Eighteen

QUATTRO STAGIONI

The secret of getting ahead is getting started.

MARK TWAIN

'Thank God it's nearly Friday,' said Riva.

'Is that what you're calling Thursday these days?' laughed Lucy.

Riva and Lucy were in the *Quattro Stagioni*, which was Riccardo and Marco's new restaurant. The trattoria in the Borough was doing so well that they'd decided to expand and open the kind of affordable café that everybody liked. According to Riva, the salads at the Staggy were delicious and perfect for her latest diet.

'How's the boyfriend?' asked Lucy, knowing that Riva had at long last found someone who wanted to make a commitment.

'Great,' said Riva between mouthfuls. 'We're off to Majorca for a week at the end of the month and I can't wait. It'll be good to get away from all the aggro at work and laze about on a beach for a bit.'

'And shag yourselves stupid, no doubt,' laughed Lucy.

'Not a bit of it,' said Riva looking shocked. 'We intend to spend the week reading uplifting literature, eating boiled fish, drinking tap water and keeping up our good work for the *Junior Anti-Sex League*.'

Lucy nearly choked on her pizza before telling Riva that she looked far too happy for someone who belonged to the *Junior Anti-Sex League*. In turn, Riva asked Lucy about her new job.

'As far as I can see it's secret, mysterious and stuffed with gun-toting James Bond types,' said Riva. 'What's it called? Something historical, isn't it? And how on earth did you find the job, Loo? And while we're on the subject, what do you do there?'

'Well, at the moment my work is mainly number crunching for what they call "Exchequer", which is the budget and statistics department, but they tell me it will get more interesting in time. Anyway, Reev, I didn't set out to work in security, I just needed something that could make use of the stuff I'd done at Uni.'

Riva helped herself to a slice of Lucy's pizza while nodding for her to go on.

'As to finding the job – well, it was by accident, really.'

Riva's mouth was still full, so she could only give Lucy an enquiring look.

'You remember the couple in the flat below mine, Reev? Well, their flat has a garden and they sometimes have friends round for a barbeque. Knowing I'm on my own, they take pity on me and invite me. They're a nice couple, so I made up a bowl of salad and took it along as my contribution to the meal. Anyway, while I was there, I got into conversation with an older guy who turned out to be a copper, and I ended up telling him that I'd just got my results and that I was now looking for a decent job. He asked me what subjects I had taken and when I told him, he suggested that I contact Raj Patel at TUDOR. He said they employed youngsters with computing, maths and physics qualifications like mine, and he thought it would be worth a try.'

Riva gave Lucy an encouraging look.

'You know how we're supposed to research jobs before applying, don't you?'

Riva nodded.

'Well, I couldn't find much out about TUDOR on the 'Net or anywhere else, but I figured I had nothing to lose by applying, so I wrote to Mr Patel, and a few days later he called me in for an interview. He seemed happy with me, so as soon as the agency had finished the background checks on my family... well, that was it.'

'Background checks?' Riva's eyebrows went up.

'Yeah Reev - they checked everyone in my family and even looked into Chris, despite the fact that he's no longer living in the UK.'

'And me?'

'Oh yes, Reev. They know all about those two guys you were banging – and the fact that one was a Russian spy.'

'Russian spy!' hissed Riva. '*What* bloody Russian spy? And when was I ever shagging two guys at the same time? Don't tell me you've dropped me in the merde with your bloody spook organisation! Am I going to get a visit from the rubber heelers some time soon?'

'Oh for sure, Reev.' Lucy was struggling to keep her face straight. 'They won't need to investigate you, because they already have you down as a real honey trap. The head spy told me that when they next need to compromise some old married official somewhere in the Russian Federation...'

Realising her friend was winding her up, Riva pulled a face and stuck her tongue out. When the waiter had cleared the table and taken their coffee order, Riva asked Lucy if there were any eligible men at TUDOR.

'Most of the guys have partners and the rest are real Casanova types – and anyway, Reev, I don't want to date anyone from the office. I'm beginning to consider clubbing, pubbing or the 'Net or something, though.'

Riva pulled a face. 'Why not leave it for a while and see what turns up?'

After the meal, the girls hugged each other and made their way back to their flats. It had been a good night, but Lucy wasn't sleepy, so she decided to watch a couple more episodes of her Tudor DVD. She set up the player, smiling slightly at the coincidence of the name of the show and of her place of work.

Lucy soon found herself absorbed in the fascinating soap opera of the Tudor court, but there was an event at the end of one of the episodes that didn't look right to her. Like many people, Lucy had read a couple of books on the Tudor era, and what she had seen wasn't adding up. While pondering the anomaly, she remembered that one of the men at the office was said to have studied the Tudors for his degree and was something of an expert on the era, so she made up her mind to ask him about it at some convenient moment.

Chapter Nineteen

BATTERIES

Hard work spotlights the character of people: some turn up their sleeves, some turn up their noses, and some don't turn up at all

SAM EWING

The workbench was piled high with shiny black boxes, each of which had wires leading to monitors that flickered, while computers showed graphs and figures. Sophie was leaning over the bench, watching the flow of data and jotting down notes. She was dressed for action in a faded black tee shirt that was slightly ripped at the back where she'd caught herself on a stray piece of metal, while the front of the garment was adorned with red glass stones arrayed in the Rolling Stones "licky-lips" logo. The outfit was finished off with a worn pair of tight black jeans, and light brown engineer's safety boots. Her shiny dark brown hair was mussed up, with one side tucked behind her ear and the other falling forward as she worked. She had a smudge on her left arm and another on her right cheek.

Jack Duquesne strolled into the workshop, but Sophie was so absorbed in what she was doing that it took her a while to register Jack's hand giving her bum a friendly squeeze.

'Hi, Jacko,' said Sophie, 'I'll be a few minutes. There's a clean stool just there if you want to wait. Today's paper is on the bench.'

'Actually, Soph, I'm looking for Jess.'

'She's out getting a jar of coffee and something for lunch. She'll be back soon.'

Sophie went back to her task, but she soon felt another hand giving her tempting backside a pat and once again, she recognised the touch.

'Hi Tommy. Won't be a moment, I've just got to jot down these figures.'

Jack looked at Thomas, glanced at Sophie's backside and grinned.

'How did you know the first hand was mine and the second Tom's, Sophie?'

'You two buggers grope me so often that I know who it is the minute you start.'

Thomas laughed. 'You know Jack, if anyone but you laid a finger on my wife, I'd floor him, but we all know that if there's a female backside sticking out anywhere in the world, you're going to give it a rub. You remind me of a Tudorland pilgrim rubbing the big toe on a saint's statue for luck.'

Sophie turned round, and when Jack saw the saucy logo on the front of her scruffy tee shirt, he gawped.

'Kerrrrist, Sophie! That's more than I can bear! How does Thomas stand it?'

Thomas grinned at his cheeky oppo.

'Seriously Tom, if you ever decide to pack it in and return to Tudorland for good, please tell me straight away, because I need to be at the head of the queue for a Sophie takeover before some other bastard gets in there.'

'No chance, Jack,' laughed Thomas, 'she's far too sexy for you.'

Jack's eyebrows went up and his mouth fell open.

'Will you two please *stop it*! You're making me feel like a prize cow in a cattle market!' complained Sophie.

At that moment, Jessica came in lugging several Marks & Spencer shopping bags.

'I thought I could smell testosterone,' said Jessica. 'I swear it's seeping out from under the front door.'

Jack pretended to be affronted, but followed Jessica to her office to get what he needed.

Jessica handed Jack his file and asked Sophie and the lads if they wanted coffee. Jack had to get back to Millbank, but Thomas and Sophie nodded.

'I've got biscuits and some sugar free oatcakes if you fancy them, and there's chicken and salad for later, Sophie.'

'That sounds lovely, Jess,' said Sophie.

Thomas pulled up the stool that Jack had vacated and smiled at Sophie. The men and women in the Tudor offices never knew whom they might meet during the course of a day, including Members of Parliament, foreign dignitaries or even Royalty, so they were always well dressed. Adding an overdose of male vanity to the mix, it became easy to see why they decked themselves out well. Thomas was the sharpest dresser of all, and his very dark brown, slightly unruly hair, patrician looks and intense blue eyes, atop a tall, toned body made him one very good-looking guy - a fact of which he was perfectly well aware. Today's choice of John Smith charcoal with a pale blue shirt and deeper blue tie worked well on him.

Sophie put down her notepad and focused on her husband.

'You lot at the office always make me feel such a scruff when I'm working here. Young Jessica is always smartly dressed, but Raj and I spend so much of our time lying under cars, tool-making and welding that we don't stand a chance.'

'Jack had a point though, Sophie love. You look amazingly sexy, especially with that Stones logo and all the grease and muck on you. I'm looking forward to giving you a thorough wash down when we get home.'

Sophie rolled her eyes.

Thomas loved teasing his wife, but today he'd come across to the Mews for a purpose, which was to acquaint himself with what Sophie and Raj were working on.

'I've got a bit of spare time, darling, so I thought I'd catch up with what you and Raj are up to.'

'Raj has gone up to Milton Keynes to see about these batteries. They're called Solabrites and they're so new that nobody really knows what they're capable of, but we think they'll do well.'

'Are they more powerful than normal ones?' asked Thomas.

Sophie nodded. 'Each Solabrite battery is a hundred times more powerful than a normal one, both in terms of what it can do and the length of time it keeps on before needing to be recharged. We'll need a lot of power to move larger vehicles through time and space, and then to work everything that requires power to make it run.'

Sophie downed her coffee and signalled Thomas to follow her. She led him through to an area at the back of the original Mews offices, which had been extended into a large warehouse and workshop. Sophie pointed to various vans, caravans and smaller vehicles.

'We're calling these three static caravans *lodges,* and they will be used for accommodation. Others will carry supplies of drinking water, food, batteries, weapons and whatever else might be needed. Small vehicles, even including the old Peugeot, can ferry people and goods back and forth as required.'

Sophie showed Thomas the inside of one of the caravans and then walked him to a large van parked at the side of the warehouse. Thomas climbed inside, but found it to be empty.

'That will become our *Command Centre* and it'll contain whatever's needed to run an operation. We can still use computers to good effect in the field, although we're unlikely to have access to the Internet.' Sophie pointed to the top of the vehicle. 'We're fitting solar panels on every vehicle to give us direct power and also to recharge the Solabrites, and we'll have solar powered lamps and other solar gizmos of all kinds. We're looking into various kinds of field telephone system, but we'll use cheapo Walkie-Talkies while we're in the vicinity of the Command Centre. Believe it or not, Maplin sells sets that can be used over a distance of ten kilometres.'

'Thomas ventured into one of the accommodation vans. Are you planning any dry runs with this lot?'

'Definitely, but we've got a problem. You see, we were thinking of asking the army to help on Salisbury Plain or something, but we're concerned about security. We don't need some squaddie getting pissed and yakking about time machines and whatnot, do we?'

Thomas bit his bottom lip and stared at the ceiling for a moment, finally coming to a conclusion.

'I think I can solve that one for you.'

'How's that, Tommy?'

'Do you remember Kate telling you that we had one remaining relative in Tudorland?'

'Yes I do,' said Sophie thinking. 'Come to think of it, he had an Italian name.'

'His name is Charles Hatherleigh, but someone called him Carlo when he was little and it stuck. He lives in Devon and he farms there. He's a good bloke and I'm sure he'll be happy to help.'

'Going back to Tudorland would certainly keep our activities away from the press. I'll suggest it to Raj when he comes back.'

Sophie pushed a stray lock of shiny dark brown hair out of her face and tucked it behind an ear.

'What's this Carlo bloke like?'

'He's ten or eleven years younger than me, so he's in his late twenties. He runs the Hatherleigh farm and estate, and before I left I heard he was also working part time for the local Sheriff. If that's still the case, he must have fairly extensive experience of police work by now.'

'Is he married?'

'Carlo? Nah,' laughed Thomas. 'Too many pretty girls out there, though he may have settled down a bit since I last saw him. He has a policy of never touching the female servants or getting involved with women in his area, because he says that kind of thing leads to trouble, but when he visits other parts of the country or comes to court, nothing with tits is safe - or wants to be, as far as I can see.'

'Christ, not another Casanova! That's all we need,' laughed Sophie. 'Does he look like you?'

Smiling, Thomas said, 'Very much so, but with pale grey eyes rather than my blue ones.' Ruffling Sophie's hair, Thomas said, 'I'll talk to Sir David and if he agrees, I'll take a trip to Hatherleigh Hall, see if Carlo's around and ask him if he'll help.'

'Take Baz with you in case of trouble.'

Thomas was agreeing to that when Jessica popped her head out of her office to tell him he was wanted back at Millbank.

* * *

The following morning, Sir David was away, so Thomas called the meeting.

'It feels as though we've been here forever, but it's a little over two years since TUDOR was formed. We started life in the Mews premises before moving to our current Millbank offices, but we are growing and recruiting more agents and more techies as well,' said Thomas.

Kelly asked, 'Where are we going to put everyone?'

'Good question, Kelly. As it happens, the two floors immediately below us have become free, so the boardroom and the executives will stay here, while everyone else will move down. We'll have a proper ops room and places where we can look at surveillance DVDs or whatever, and somewhere for training purposes.'

Thomas now turned to the subject of fitness.

'We're sending everyone on fitness courses with help from our friends in the Royal Navy over the next few months, so the agents among you will be taking part in their normal basic training scheme, with added elements that are like the US Navy Seal programme. They are drawing up less adventurous courses for the older TUDORs and for our women. So Sophie, Jessica, Julie and Emma will also be required to do a three day course of PE and a bit of running about and climbing around.'

Kelly interjected. 'Sophie? She's not strong, Tom - what with her diabetes and so on.'

'The Navy people will encourage her to test her sugar, and she'll take her jellybeans along in case she feels her sugar level falling too quickly. She's used to controlling her condition, and as she says, if a type-one diabetic can do sports and so forth, an unstable type-two like herself can also do it.' Thomas smiled at Kelly. 'To be honest, I will worry myself sick and I'll probably phone her every few hours, but if I know Sophie, she'll have the whale of a time.

'Anyway, in addition to this, every member of TUDOR will take part in sport or work out in the gym or both. Julie will keep a weekly log and you will report your exercise times to her.'

This brought groans all round.

Kelly's face was a picture of innocence. 'Does that also include you and Sir David? I mean, you're all getting on in years and…

'Sir David fences and rides and we play tennis once or twice a month. He has even been known to beat me some-times - when I let him. Sophie and I swim, and Steven and his family often join us. I visit the basement gym here with Baz and Jack, while Ryan is teaching Raj and Steven to play golf. Sophie is a keen gardener, but her job is pretty physical anyway, while Jill and her husband enjoy their ballroom and Latin American dancing, so the answer is that the 'crumblies' will log in our exercise hours just as you youngsters do.'

Thomas talked about the reports that had been logged into TUDOR over the past year.

'Julie has produced figures showing the number of reports that we've received and what they amounted to. Many are idiots talking rubbish on Facebook, but we've logged anything of real interest into our system. There have been several potential problems, but we've managed to stop any actual incidents in good time, while we've dealt with those that have actually taken place, before too much damage could be done. Apart from the many physical threats, there's no shortage of cyber activity, and while MI5 and GCHQ deals with most of that, we do our bit.'

Thomas needed to wake the team up from their "quarterly report torpor", so he decided to tell them something interesting.

'A few weeks ago, Sir David and I and were on our way back from a meeting with Mrs Shulman, which as you know, always leaves us in a state of shock, so as it was lunch time, we decided to reward ourselves with a decent meal and a restorative glass of wine at the "*Cafe Regina*".'

This was greeted by murmurs of "jammy sods", and "what about the workers".

Thomas ignored the jibes. 'We hadn't been there long when Sir David spotted a woman sitting behind me, as there was something about her that caught his attention. He pretended to take a photo of me on his mobile while he was actually snapping her. When we got back to Millbank, we gave the mobile to Julie in the techie department and asked her to check the woman out, but nothing showed up. The woman didn't appear to exist. She didn't have a passport or any kind of ID. It was all very strange.'

Thomas took a sip of coffee and went on with the intriguing tale. 'As it happens, I had to go by Regina's a week or so later, and I spotted the woman in there again, so I rang Sir David and suggested that he come over ASAP. Sir David soon joined me, and when the woman finished her lunch, we decided to follow her.'

'Oh Christ,' laughed Baz. 'James Bond and Simon Templar hanging onto their Zimmer frames. I wouldn't let you two follow a blind woman with a bag over her head - she'd be sure to spot you!'

Thomas snorted and pulled a face. Sophie and Kelly were trying so hard not to laugh that they couldn't drink their coffee.

'Zimmer frames indeed, Baz. You're the same age as me.'

'Yeah, but less ground down by dissipation, drink and sex.'

'Bloody cheek,' complained Thomas before going on with his story. 'Well, we strolled along, chatting and looking casual, but to our surprise, the woman turned around and addressed us by our full names and ranks. The cheeky bitch even asked us if we'd enjoyed our walk!'

Kelly regretted the fact that she was trying to eat a biscuit at this point, because she laughed so hard that it went down the wrong way. Thomas ignored the spluttering and carried on talking.

'It appears that her name is Irina Grodzinska - which is apparently pronounced *Grojinska* - and she's the deputy head of spookery at the Polish Embassy.'

'Polish *spookery*!' exclaimed Raj. 'I didn't know they had such a thing.'

Baz jumped in. 'Who do they spy on? Russians? Germans? Do they think they're likely to be invaded again?'

'I don't know what they do but I've invited her here tomorrow for a courtesy visit, so if you're not doing anything useful when she arrives, you can ask her yourself.'

* * *

When Irina Grodzinska arrived at the office the following day, it became clear that what had originally been envisaged as a mere courtesy visit was now something much more. Sir David took the attractive lady into his office and buzzed Thomas over to join them.

'Would you like coffee, Ms Grodzinska?' he asked.

'I'd love some, Sir David, but please call me Irina.'

When Thomas came in, she gave him a winning smile while he leaned over to give her hand a shake before settling into one of Sir David's armchairs.

To their surprise, Irina asked if they knew anything about a country called Parmia.

'Indeed, we do, but what's your interest?'

Well nothing as far as Poland is concerned, but our people have heard a whisper over the Russian airwaves that the Parmians are out to cause trouble. The Russians don't like the Parmians at all, but when we spoke to our Russian contact, his feeling was that the Parmians are cooking up something else - and that it may be aimed at London.'

Sir David picked up his Mont Blanc and started to fiddle with it.

Thomas asked, 'Do you have any idea what they have in mind?'

'Unfortunately, no. The Russians tell us the Parmians are putting together a training camp close to their border, but it's still in the early stages. My contact in the Kremlin is a General Valeri Balabolin, and he's happy for us to keep you in the loop, but he feels that in the current climate, it would be "politically incorrect" for him to talk to you directly, or for him to have direct dealings with the British government, so he asked us to act as intermediaries. This Parmian problem may be something the Russians can deal with themselves, but if they can't, it may drop into your lap. In short, you need to know what's going on.'

'Do you think we need to pay the Parmians a surprise visit?' said Thomas.

'That would be ideal. The Russians don't yet know where the encampment is, but their satellites will pick something up sooner or later and we'll pass on news as soon as we get it. What I don't see is how can you reach the Parmian Kush quickly or without anyone spotting you? An airlift perhaps? Paratroops? It's like being half way up Everest and just as rocky. You could attack the camp with drones, but then you wouldn't find out what they're up to, and Balabolin or the Brits might have to do it all again later by frontal attack, and that wouldn't be much fun.'

'You're right,' said Sir David, 'it's a poser... but I expect we'll come up with something.' Sir David had another question for his pretty visitor. 'How come we couldn't find you on our computer system, Irina? Even deputy heads have profiles, but yours is hidden.'

'I'm new to the post and my department has been keeping my details under wraps. I guess it'll be different now that I'm out of the closet, so to speak.'

* * *

After they'd seen Irina out, Sir David gave Thomas the benefit of his opinion.

'Fucking Parmians!' he spat. The Mont Blank was doing cartwheels. 'Pardon my French, Tom, but Irina wouldn't have been given leave by the Poles or the Russkies to tell us all this stuff unless there was a real possibility of it landing right here and right into our laps. Also, we know exactly who the Foreign Secretary will call on to transport the SAS up a twenty-eight thousand foot mountain in a fucking blizzard, don't we?'

Thomas said 'well, we'd better have a chat to Raj and Sophie and see if they've got any bright ideas.'

* * *

Later that day, the team had reassembled.

'Our "village" now comprises three lodges, two smaller caravans for supplies and the Command Centre,' said Raj. 'We're fitting smaller vehicles with electric engines that run off Solabrites so that we can drive them around. We decided on electric partly because the batteries are so good and partly because we can take the vehicles to places where there is no petrol available.

'Most importantly, we won't have to shift and lift each lodge and vehicle separately, because all the vehicles will be linked to a central computer in the Command Centre and the whole lot will move through time and space in one fell swoop. Once on site, we can detach the smaller vehicles from the network and use them as shuttles between the site and the Mews. The shuttles all have a separate quick-use tablet system that flips down from the glove compartment. The tablet starts up as soon as someone opens the compartment and then it's just a case of touching the section marked Mews, or selecting whatever destinations we might need.'

'What are the lodges like?' asked Jack.

'The lodges are like those static caravans that you see at holiday camps, but we've adapted them to suit our needs, so each lodge will have four large single beds. Each lodge has a galley, and a loo and shower, but there will also be two dedicated "ablution" caravans with loos and showers for trips that are likely to last more than a couple of days. One will be for men and the other for women. Nothing is luxurious, but everyone should be comfortable.'

That's a relief, thought Kelly.

'The Command Centre will be fully equipped with everything we can think of, and we'll soon have a decent field phone system.'

Sir David looked round his team and said quietly, 'There is a lot for Sophie and Raj to think about, so I want you all to visit the Mews over the next week. Have a good look around and make any suggestions you think worthwhile.'

The fact that Sir David was fiddling with his Mont Blanc made the team aware that this meeting constituted more than a casual update, and his next words confirmed their suspicions.

'We've heard a whisper that our old friends the Parmians are planning something, but so far we don't know precisely what it might be or even if we will need to be involved. I know that you lot are gung-ho enough for anything, but if this comes off, it'll be a job for the SAS, and our role will be to transport them. We don't yet know whether we'll need to stay in Parmia throughout the operation or drop the men off, come back here and return to the site to fetch them later.'

'Christ!' said Baz. 'The Parmian Kush isn't going to be much fun. How are we going to land on a mountaintop? And what if the weather's lousy?'

Sir David looked as sober as he felt.

'Well, there's no news yet and it will be some time before there is. It's most likely that the armed forces or MI6 will take care of the problem, and it's unlikely that we will be needed at all, but we might just… so we must be ready. We've always envisaged that most of our jobs will take place in the present time, so time travel isn't likely to be an issue for the most part, but instant "space travel" will be, so we need to do a dry run to see how the village operates. In the short term, Thomas is trying to set something up that will take us back to Tudorland for a while.'

Sir David signalled Raj to take over.

'Sophie and I need to try out the Solabrites and the complete village system. Our original idea was to ask the army to accommodate us, but we're worried about security, so Tom suggested that we avoid leaks by paying a visit to his cousin Charles. The year will be 1541, and as we can hardly phone Charles and ask if it's convenient for us to land our village on his lawn, Tom and Baz are looking out the doublets and swords they bought themselves after the Abbey operation, and paying the cousin a visit later today.'

'Wow! A trip back to Tudorland sounds exciting!' exclaimed Jack, 'Especially as there won't be any baddies coming after us this time.'

'Well, we hope not,' said Thomas. 'By the way, Charles is a "Sir" in his own right, as he inherited the family title from his father. My title was conferred on me by Henry later. And by the way, Charles is known as *Carlo*. Someone called him that when he was a toddler and the name stuck - to the point where even King Henry calls him Carlo.'

Jack suddenly thought of something. 'Hey, that means Tom, Baz, Kelly and I will regain the honours King Henry gave us last time we were in Tudorland, and I will be able to take my proper place in society as *Sir* Jack Duquesne!'

'Yeah,' said Baz, 'I'll be *Sir* Baz Baverstock, Sir David remains Sir David, Tommo will regain his original Sir Thomas Hatherleigh title and Kelly Vance will be a lady for a change.'

Kelly pulled a face.

Chapter Twenty

LUCY LEARNS THE TRUTH

Perplexity is the beginning of knowledge
KHALIL GIBRAN

Lucy Sanders was working on an Internet conundrum in her shoebox office when she spotted Jack through the open door and waved him over. 'Can I have a word with you, Jack, or perhaps later when you can spare a minute.'

'Sure. Is it a work problem?'

'No, work's fine. It's just something I wanted to ask, but I don't want to hold you up.'

'I'll look in when I stop for a coffee if that suits.'

Lucy smiled her thanks.

* * *

Later that morning, Jack wandered into Lucy's room, carrying a two steaming mugs of coffee. He handed one to Lucy, perched himself on her visitor's chair and blew on his coffee while waiting for her to speak.

Smiling over her paper-strewn desk, Lucy asked, 'Am I right in thinking you studied the Tudors at college?'

Jack nodded and gingerly sipped the hot drink while wondering what was on Lucy's mind.

'I went out with my friend the other day, and when I got home I didn't feel like going to straight to bed, so I put the telly on, and watched a DVD about the Tudors. The episode that I saw centred on the fall of Cardinal Wolsey, and at the end of the programme, it showed him cutting his throat and falling down dead. Well, I'm the first to admit that history wasn't my subject at college, but I've read a couple of books on the Tudor period and I don't remember reading anything like that, so I was wondering if the TV people put that in for dramatic effect, or if there was any truth in it.'

Jack was surprised at Lucy's question, but more than happy to answer her.

'Dramatic effect rather than what one might call verisimilitude, eh?'

Lucy smiled at his use of words while Jack asked if she would be interested in hearing about the history of the time. When she nodded enthusiastically, he proceeded to tell her the story – in his own, idiosyncratic way.

'You're quite right Lucy, it didn't happen that way. Wolsey was ousted from his job as Henry's First Minister because he couldn't persuade the Pope to declare Henry's marriage to Catherine of Aragon invalid. Popes tended to support the powerful Spanish court, and of course, Catherine was Spanish, but it's also possible that Henry had a few beefs with Rome independently of his desire for an annulment. Anyway, try as he might, poor old Wolsey couldn't get the Pope to back down on the annulment question. Meanwhile, Anne Boleyn was keeping King Henry at arm's length, which was probably getting on his nerves. Needless to say, Fat Henry never went short of pussy, but he was having to keep off from this *particular* piece of pussy, and Henry didn't like being told what he could or could not do.'

173

By now, Lucy was intrigued and also highly amused by the ancient story.

'My personal view is that when it all came to a head, Henry put a plan into action that may have been growing in his mind for some time, which was to detach the English church from Rome and make himself its head. Such an idea might have seemed preposterous at almost any time during the preceding millennium, but over the preceding couple of hundred years, several things had happened to change the public perception of the religious establishment. Firstly, the Black Death in the mid-1300s showed that, contrary to what people had been led to believe, the Church and those who worked in it hadn't the power to stop it, while on a personal level, prayer and donations didn't help, either.

'Then there was that weird business whereby one pope sat in Rome while a rival set up a separate papacy in Avignon. If that wasn't enough, a third contender turned up and said that the guy in Avignon should climb off the throne and let him get on, all of which helped make the papacy a laughing stock. Even after the Avignon nonsense was shut down, there were just too many snouts in the trough. Consider modern politicians who were caught fiddling their expenses or the corrupt buggers who took cash for questions in Parliament. Now multiply all that by a million percent and you'll see how far the Catholic Church had fallen.

Individual monasteries looked after people very well, often taking on the role of social workers, the health service and charities, but didn't compensate for the corruption that was going on in the higher echelons all across Europe.

'All this coincided with, and encouraged, the many new ideas that were coming out of Europe, starting with Erasmus in Holland, Luther in Germany and Zwilling in Switzerland, among others. The northern Germanic peoples had never been never overly committed to the Roman Church, so they found it easy to turn away, and even France seemed to be leaving the fold for a while. For the first time since the birth of Islam in the sixth century, if someone wanted to start a new religion based on his own ideas, the door was open.

'All this put poor old Wolsey in a quandary, because he may have harboured genuine religious beliefs that he just couldn't rescind. He was sixty by this time, so he decided to pack it in, taking himself and his common law wife to York and going into retirement.

'Unfortunately, the people in the north of England weren't taking kindly to the dissolution of the monasteries, and there was a hint of rebellion in the air, so Henry thought - with some justification - that the rebels might use Wolsey as a rallying point for an insurrection. Henry sent someone to fetch the old boy and bring him to London for a trial, partly to punish him and partly as a means of extracting him from Yorkshire. When you think about it, a journey of that length, at speed, and with no protection from bad weather, must have been hard on a man of Wolsey's age. Now add the fact that the poor man was well aware that he was being asked to go to London for the express purpose of being slagged off and then bumped off - well, he must have been under a massive strain, mustn't he?

Lucy was entranced by Jack's explanation. Somehow, it made her dusty old history books come alive, with all the fear and the urgency of the era coming sharply into focus. Meanwhile, after drinking most of his coffee, Jack went on with the story.

'Wolsey's party got as far as Leicester, where Wolsey was reported to have eaten lunch with friends, after which he collapsed in pain and died. There was some talk of poisoning, and an even more persuasive suggestion that the old boy had poisoned himself, but that seems to me to be far-fetched. I remember an old police inspector once telling me that people who commit suicide do so in private, so the idea of Wolsey eating a nice lunch with his pals and poisoning himself in front of everyone makes no sense at all.'

Lucy gazed raptly at Jack and he smiled gently back at her.

'Nah, Lucy my duck. It was a straightforward coronary. The portraits of the time depict an overweight man who'd obviously spent years eating rich food and probably taking little or no exercise. Apparently, he also had some kind of stomach upset, but a death from that source would have been clearcut, so what with one thing and another, a heart attack was well on the cards.'

Something else occurred to Lucy. 'If the Cardinal was a lifelong Roman Catholic who couldn't give up his religion to suit King Henry, how could he consider committing a major sin like suicide?'

Jack suddenly realised that he was being faced with a choice. He could leave the conversation where it was, or speak out and change Lucy's life forever. In true Sagittarian style, Jack decided to take the gamble.

* * *

'Suicide *was* considered a grievous sin, and it still is to Roman Catholics, but what isn't commonly known is that a thorough investigation *was* carried out shortly after Wolsey's death, and the evidence clearly pointed to natural causes.'

'Investigation? I never read anything about that? There wasn't any mention of an investigation in my history books.'

'It was kept under wraps,' said Jack quietly. He put down his coffee mug, scowled a little and chewed his lower lip while he thought over his next words. Then he took the final decision.

'Look Lucy, there's someone here who knows a lot more about Wolsey than I do, and that's Tom. I'll see if he's around and see if he can spare time for a chat later.'

'That's very kind of you Jack, but it isn't necessary. Tom's one of the big bosses and he wouldn't want to faff around with a junior member of staff, would he… and to talk about Cardinal Wolsey… I mean, it doesn't make any sense.'

'It might, actually. Look, I'll buzz you down about it later if there's any chance.'

To Lucy's utter amazement, Jack rang back an hour later.

'Hiya, ducks. Tom'll meet us in the canteen for lunch, so be there around one o'clock, okay?'

Lucy put the phone down and gazed at it in blank astonishment. The big boss was going to join her for lunch and to chat about Cardinal Wolsey of all things. Why would Thomas know more about the Cardinal than Jack? After all, Jack had a degree in the subject, didn't he? She shook her head in wonderment and then turned back to her paperwork.

At ten to one, Lucy grabbed her bag, took the lift down to the fifth floor and made her way to the big canteen that served the various government offices in the building. She was just setting her jacket potato and salad on the table when Thomas and Jack joined her, each carrying a tray of chilli beef with rice.

'The chilli smells good today, doesn't it, Tom? Hope it *is* beef and not some old horse that's been through the knacker's yard!' said Jack.

'I hope you're right,' replied Thomas laughing.

Turning to Lucy, Thomas said that Jack had told him about her Wolsey query.

Lucy was extremely embarrassed to be bothering someone as important as Thomas about a silly television programme. Truth to tell, she'd been a little nervous about approaching Jack. She knew Jack wasn't stuffy and that he was kind hearted, but now she found herself apologising lamely to Thomas for bothering him.

'Don't worry, Lucy, that's fine. I'm happy to help and I do have something to tell you about the Wolsey affair. You see, there certainly *was* an investigation into his death and it was a very thorough one. I should know because I was *there*. Indeed, it was my team who carried it out on behalf of Sir Thomas Cromwell,' said Thomas.

'He gets everywhere, doesn't he?' laughed Jack.

Lucy didn't know what to make of this. It made no sense whatsoever, so she stared blankly at Thomas, wondering if this was some kind of wind-up.

Jack ate his chilli and chuckled quietly to himself.

Lucy looked from Thomas to Jack and back again; trying to make sense of a world that seemed to have gone raving mad.

'I think you'd better let the cat out of the bag, Tom. After all, we're going to need Lucy with us on the dry run, aren't we?'

Lucy couldn't understand one word of this. Well, she could understand the *individual* words, but not when they were arranged in the order that Jack was using. What dry run? And what the blazes were her bosses talking about? How could Thomas have been involved in an investigation that took place four hundred and eighty years ago? Was he an amateur archaeologist, perhaps? That might be an explanation, because the alternative was that two of her bosses had gone completely potty. Or, perhaps it was she who was going nuts? She shook her head and tried to eat her prawns, but then she became so absorbed in what Thomas told her about Sophie's uncle, the Project, their trip to Westminster Abbey in 1540 and all the rest it that she couldn't bother to eat.

When Lucy realised who Thomas really was, her jaw dropped so far that she was afraid it would land on the table. Her throat felt very dry, so she sipped some of her juice and tried to focus on what he was telling her. She felt as though the earth had suddenly tilted several degrees to form a completely new angle.

'You'd either have to be kept completely out of the loop as far as the Projects are concerned, or you would learn about them sooner rather than later. You see, if the trip I'm going to make with Baz tomorrow works out, you'll be travelling to 1541 with Sophie, Kelly and the rest of us. It's not compulsory, so you don't have to come with us if you don't want to.'

'Want to!' cried Lucy, 'Of course I *want* to. I'd be mad to miss out on an experience like that!'

Lucy gathered what was left of her wits, while the scientific side of her nature started to kick in. 'How do we travel? What do we go in? How's it done? How many of us are there? Where do we go from? Is that what Sophie and Raj do at the Mews? Do we ride down a wormhole? Where do I get a Tudor dress? What powers the Projects?' Her mind was spinning from the dozens of questions buzzing around inside her head.

Jack was laughing merrily at the poor girl's confusion. 'Look, Lucy love, let's give Jessica a ring and see if she can show you around the Mews this afternoon and you can pester her with your questions.'

'Just one question that I'd like to ask you, Mr Hatherleigh, if I may?'

'It's Tom, Lucy,' said Thomas, indicating that she should continue.

'How did you investigate Wolsey's death? I mean there weren't any forensics in those days? I mean, how did you satisfy yourself that the Cardinal died of natural causes?'

'Oooh Jack, she's good isn't she?' smiled Thomas, 'we'll have to teach her how to interrogate, won't we?'

Jack chuckled into his chilli. 'She's doing a very good job of interrogating you, Tom. It's a treat to see you on the receiving end for a change!'

Thomas grinned and went on.

'Well, Lucy, I didn't boil anyone in oil - or even in chicken soup. It was pretty much like a modern investigation, because we interviewed everyone who was there and cross-referenced their replies, all of which led us to the conclusion that Wolsey's death was natural. Also, we also did what forensic work we could within the limitations of the time, but I have to say that I knew in my bones even before I'd left London that Wolsey had suffered some kind of seizure, so I wasn't surprised by what I found.'

'How did you test for poison in those days?'

'Doggies and moggies.'

'Whatties and whooies?' asked Lucy.

Jack was laughing openly by this time, but Thomas's face was perfectly straight as he ploughed on.

'I got a couple of my men to round up as many stray dogs and cats as they could find, telling them to focus on smaller animals rather than large ones, while I despatched a trooper to buy a quantity of chopped meat and offal from the local butcher. We didn't feed the animals or give them water for a day or two, so they became very thirsty and hungry. Meanwhile, we removed every piece of crockery and utensil that we could find and took the lot outside, and when we were ready, we put out bowls of water and dishes of meat into all the pots. Then we let the animals out a few at a time and watched closely to see if any of them took sick. If anything had carried even a trace of poison, some of the animals would have died.'

Lucy pulled a face. 'Christ, Tom, that's horrendous. You'd be had up for that these days, but I can see why you did it that way. I mean you'd hardly have had a CSI lab on hand there, would you?'

'We had some clever apothecaries in London who could do a certain amount of testing, but that would have taken time, and my boss always wanted answers yesterday. After all, he was being pressured by Henry, and we needed to know whether we were up against a conspiracy, or if it *was* just natural causes. To be honest, I was glad I looked into it myself and I was very relieved at the result, because Sir Thomas Cromwell and I already had more aggravation on our plates than we needed.'

Jack and Thomas finished their lunch, leaving a stunned Lucy sitting at the table and staring into space. She parked the tray of congealed food and treated herself to a couple of bars of chocolate from the machine to take back to her office. She hadn't been back long when a call came through from Jessica, suggesting she come over to the Mews around three o'clock for a look-see.

* * *

Jessica showed Lucy everything and answered all her questions, even explaining that they didn't travel down wormholes, but changed matter into anti-matter and back again. When Sophie had finished what she was doing, she joined Jessica and Lucy, smiling gently at this girl whose enquiring mind was so much like hers at the same age. To Lucy's astonishment, Sophie suggested that Lucy might like a quick whiz back in time there and then. She explained that they were in the habit of testing the system by returning to the day after V.E. Day, because nobody ever noticed them when they walked among the crowds thronging the main road.

181

Sophie ushered Lucy and Jessica into the old Peugeot while fishing out the velvet jewellery roll containing the safety rings. She demonstrated how the stone on the ring flipped back to reveal a little button inside, explaining that Lucy should press it if there was a problem, as it would whisk her back to the Project. Sophie keyed the coordinates into the computer and in no time at all, she transported the three of them back to May 1945.

The three women walked out into the Mews and round to the main road, where they mingled with the cheering crowds, and soon they were clapping, cheering and singing "God Save the King" along with all the other 1945 revellers. When they got back, Lucy admitted that it had been the most interesting day of her life, and that she couldn't wait to pay a longer visit to the past, the future or any-where else for that matter in one of TUDOR's magical time machines!

Chapter Twenty One

THE DRY RUN

*You know more of a road by having travelled it than by all
the conjectures and descriptions in the world*

WILLIAM HAZLITT

Baz and Thomas were fishing their Tudorland gear out
of the Mews lockers.

'I still find this stuff bloody awkward to get into
Tommo,' grumbled Baz, holding up the doublet.

'I'll squire you, Baz.'

'You'll *what* me?'

'Squire you. It means to help you dress. Young gentle-
men act as esquires to their elders. It's especially important
for them to know how to dress a knight in armour, because
it can chafe or slip its moorings if it isn't put on properly.
You may remember that I washed and dressed Jack after he
got hurt and he also found it strange until I explained about
the job of a Tudorland squire.'

'Bloody Nora, Tommo, I've never thought about it, but
it makes sense. We do the same thing when we help each
other get into Kevlar. And if that isn't armour, I don't know
what is?'

'Of course it is.'

Thomas soon had Baz tucked into a Tudor shirt, hose,
doublet, riding breeches and knee boots. When his sword,

dagger and hat were in place, Baz no longer resembled a modern copper. The change of clothes brought out the strength of his courageous personality and gave him a real air of command.

Thomas dressed himself in a dark blue velvet doublet with white embroidery on the front panels, and once he was fully kitted out, he gave Baz a respectful Tudor bow, murmuring, 'Sir Baz', and Baz returned the compliment.

Sophie and Raj loaded toiletries, bottled water, tea, coffee, dried milk and groceries, along with scarves, socks and gloves for Carlo's housekeeper Bessie, and once in the car, Thomas started the process of travelling back to 16th century Dartmoor. Raj leaned in through the open door and watched the laptop screen intently; when he was satisfied that the computer was correctly set, he closed the door and stepped away. Raj, Sophie and Jessica watched while the Toyota shimmered and disappeared.

* * *

The Toyota landed with a slight bump in a woodland glade. Thomas climbed out and looked around until he found what he was looking for, which was a substantial house that was just visible through the trees to the south. All the Project vehicles had been painted with a dull camouflage pattern so they weren't easy to see at a distance, but now Baz pulled out a wad of camouflage netting from the back seat and tossed it over the car. As they turned towards the house, Baz kept his hand on the Glock 23 in the rig under his cape.

When they reached the house, Thomas used the heavy doorknocker and a few minutes later, a hard-faced woman in maid's clothing opened the door and Thomas asked for Sir Charles Hatherleigh. The surly maid said he wasn't in, so Thomas told her to fetch Mistress Bessie and to say that Sir Thomas Hatherleigh wanted to speak with her right away. A few moments later, a tubby middle-aged woman bustled down the hall, and when she saw Thomas, she gave a respectful curtsy before rushing up to give him a hug.

'It's wonderful to see you, Master Thomas - and looking so well! Are you back from Hidalia now? Are you and your friend staying with us? How long are you here for?'

The questions poured out while Thomas held Bessie's hands and laughed gently at her.

'We'll tell you everything later, Bessie darling, but I need to talk to Carlo. Is he around?'

'He has an office over by the stables and he's in there with Jackson, the farm manager. Why don't you walk across? Carlo would love to see you.'

'We'll do that,' answered Thomas.

As they walked across to the stables, Baz asked, 'How come Carlo is also a Sir? I know King Henry knighted you for service in the Holy Land, but what did Carlo do?'

'Carlo is ten years younger than me, but his father was my dad's older brother, so when my grandfather died, Carlo's father inherited the lands and the title of Baron Hatherleigh. When he died, Carlo took the title and farm lands. He offered to share the Hatherleigh lands with me and for us to work them together, but I'd been brought up in London and my life was there, so I declined his kind offer and left him to it.'

'Is he all right? Carlo, I mean.'

'He's fine. You'll get on well with him.' Thomas motioned with his head and said, 'That's him over there.'

From the back, Baz could see a tall well-dressed man talking to a chap in work clothes. The workman signalled to Carlo to turn around, and when he saw Thomas, he rushed over.

'Tom! What are you doing here?' he yelled, dragging Thomas into a massive bear hug, 'It's soooo good to see you! Who's your friend?' As with Bessie, Carlo's questions tumbled out.

'I've got a lot to tell you, Carlo, so I suggest we go somewhere private,' said Thomas quietly, while quickly introducing Baz.

Carlo bowed politely to Baz, who bowed smoothly back in true Tudor style.

Once back at the house, Carlo ushered them into a comfortable sitting room, calling the maid and ordering wine and cake. A few moments later, Bessie brought in a tray and set it on a side table.

Baz studied Carlo and noted the strong family resemblance. Carlo was a younger version of Tom with the same great looks and athletic body, but with eyes of a silvery shade in place of Thomas's intense blue.

Over the next couple of hours, the men worked their way through a flagon of wine and a fair sized fruitcake, while Thomas told Carlo of his adventures. To Baz's astonishment, Carlo had received news of the Abbey operation and he was delighted to meet one of the so-called Hidalians who had taken part in it, but when Thomas told him the *real* story, from the moment Sophie had decided to rescue him, Carlo nearly choked on his wine. Thomas went on to tell Carlo about Baz and Margie, the Projects, the CAB and TUDOR - all of which left Carlo utterly dumbfounded.

Baz was now so used to the Tudor way of speaking that he no longer found the "thou, thee, giveth and taketh away" stuff difficult. It occurred to him that if he'd been able to spend time in Tudorland as a schoolboy, GCSE Shakespeare plays would have been a doddle. He noticed Carlo had a slight West Country drawl, but like all the

Tudor people with whom Baz had come into contact, his accent had an American tinge, and Baz suddenly realised that it wasn't the Americans whose accent had drifted away from Standard English, but the English themselves who had changed.

When Baz drifted back to the present, he heard Carlo asking Thomas if he could visit New London after the dry run, and Thomas saying that he'd be delighted to show him round. The conversation now turned to the details of the Tudorland trip. It became clear that Carlo had done a stint in the army and that an instinct for military logistics started to kick in.

'How many of these vehicles will you bring? How big are they? How much land will you need?' asked Carlo. 'What about supplies, weaponry, clean water?'

Baz answered Carlo's questions, in addition to what he and Thomas wanted to achieve during the field trip. Baz was impressed with Carlo. This handsome young man shared the Hatherleigh intelligence and Thomas's instinct for running a successful operation.

Carlo gave Baz's answers some thought and then suggested the best place for them to set the village down.

'Aim for a field that's to the east of the woods that you're in now, Baz. There's a slight dip and the area is surrounded by woodland, so you will be shielded from sight. It's also a little nearer to the house, which makes it more convenient. I will tell Bessie the truth about you and your team and also Jackson, my farm manager, but nobody else needs to know anything other than the fact that you are from Hidalia.'

'By the way, when do you hope to arrive?' asked Carlo.

'Tomorrow if you like, or the next day. It's up to you,' replied Thomas.

'Make it the day after tomorrow, Tom. It'll give me time to sort a few things out at this end.' Carlo was silent for a few moments while he was thinking things through. He sipped his wine and ticked off what he needed to do.

'Bessie has a widowed friend who comes in whenever she needs extra help. Alice is trustworthy, as are her daughters and the women who come in to clean and light the fires and do other rough work, but I'm not happy about the maid who let you in. She joined us when the previous girl left and there's something about her that doesn't feel right. There's a big house about ten miles to the south of here that I've heard is taking on staff, so I'll give the woman a note of recommendation and get Jackson to run her over there in the pony trap first thing.'

* * *

A little later, Carlo walked Thomas and Baz to the area he'd suggested to them.

'Is this area safe?' asked Baz. 'I mean, will we need to post sentries through the night?'

'The area is very safe as a rule. We can get occasional pirate raids from the sea, but they have to travel a fair distance before reaching us, so they're usually stopped well before they reach our lands, but even so, we have to keep our eyes open. If anything happens, the Sheriff's troopers will soon let me know. As far as my work with the Sheriff is concerned, if something big happened to blow up, I'd have to drop everything and deal with it. I also get involved if there is something to investigate or if there is any interrogating to be done.'

'That figures,' murmured Baz.

Back at the woods, all three of them climbed into the Project while Thomas used the "adjust" feature to move it to the spot that Carlo had recommended, before setting the coordinates in readiness for the dry run. Carlo clung to the back of the seat in front of him for dear life, but he soon found there was hardly any sensation of movement and the landing was soft. When they climbed out, Baz and Thomas could see that they were indeed in a slight depression and surrounded by woods. After they'd taken a good look around the area, the three men unloaded the car and carted their booty to the house.

'Bessie and Alice will really like the shampoo, Carlo, and so will you,' said Thomas.

'What's shampoo?'

'It's stuff you use with water when you wash your hair. It will make you very clean and you'll smell like a bouquet of flowers.'

'I'll use it next time I pay a visit to one of my lady friends,' laughed Carlo.

When his visitors had gone, Carlo went in search of Bessie. He took her into the sitting room and told her all about Thomas, Baz and the dry run. She was as dumbstruck by the news as Carlo had been, but she looked forward to what the next few days would bring.

* * *

Sophie was on edge. She was always twitchy when any of the TUDORs were away, especially if it was Thomas and Baz, so she was heartily relieved to see her "boys" back in one piece, but when she saw Baz and Thomas giggling and falling out of the Toyota, she instantly morphed into a put-upon housewife.

'We've all been worried sick here, but it's clear that you've both had the whale of a time!'

Jessica was giggling and even Raj was trying to conceal a laugh.

'Get changed and report to Sir David Cromwell PDQ. And while you're about it, you can tell *him* why you're both pissed as newts. I'd love to hear what he'll have to say about that!'

* * *

As it happened, Sir David didn't do much more than give a "hurrump" when the men arrived and apologised for being "tired and emotional", because if getting plastered was what it had taken to find what they needed, he wasn't particularly bothered.

'Is the dry run on, Tom?'

'Yes, it'll be fine. I've left Carlo to make preparations at his end and we'll land there the day after tomorrow "his" time. Incidentally, the weather was generally better in Tudorland in the 1540s than it is here right now, and Carlo reckons there'll be a week or two of hot weather to come.'

'That will be a bonus. It'll be easier on you than messing around in rain and mud. When do you want to leave and who do you want to take with you?'

'Sophie says the Projects are ready to go, so it's only a matter of loading up and everyone getting their gear together. We won't need to bother with Tudor costumes for this trip as we're unlikely to leave the camp.'

'Well, that'll please the Exchequer, won't it?' said Sir David. 'He always moans when you have to order up clothes and stuff. Was he always this stingy when you were both back in Tudorland, Tom?'

'Steven has always been extremely generous to Katherine and the rest of the family, but very parsimonious when it came to the country's treasury. I reckon he saved King Henry a fortune, all of which gave the fat sod even more money to waste on jousting, eating, going on the piss, showing off to foreign dignitaries, buying presents for his girlfriends and giving his hanger-on friends a good time. I'm sure there were times when Steven and your ancestor, Thomas Cromwell, could cheerfully have committed regicide.'

Sir David chuckled, but despite hiccoughing a little, Thomas wanted to talk about the forthcoming trip.

'Raj and Sophie want to take Lucy along to help with the techie stuff, and I'll take Baz, Jack and Kelly. Anyone who wants to pop out and visit the site while we're there can do so. I know you and Steven will want to come out for a visit, and I think Jessica ought to be given the chance. The guys will have to work out a rota to ensure there are enough senior staff here to cover, and if something does arise, we'll simply abort the operation and come straight back.'

Sir David said, 'By the way, Kelly's become our designated chooser of operational names, and she decided to take a name from *The Midsummer Night's Dream,* so this one's to be called *Operation Oberon.*'

Chapter Twenty Two

OPERATION OBERON

*It is questionable if all the mechanical inventions yet
made have lightened the day's toil of any human being*
JOHN STUART MILL

Raj checked the team's safety rings and suggested that
Sophie and Lucy stay with him in the Command
Centre to keep an eye on the main computer, while Jack
and Kelly sit in the VW with Thomas and Baz. He told
them to keep their windows open so he could shout
instructions at them.

'Sorry to use such a low-tech method of communication, but it's all we've got for the moment. Once Sophie and
I have given the computer a final check, we'll on our way.'

Everybody was tense. The old hands weren't sure that
an entire "village" would "fly", let alone land safely, while
those who hadn't time-travelled before were nervous about
everything. When Raj was happy with the coordinates, he
took a deep breath, stuck his head out of the window and
yelled: 'Close your windows and hang on. Lift-off will be
in one minute.'

Jessica was waving like mad from behind her office
window as Raj hit "enter". The vehicles started to shudder
and the air in the Mews shimmered. From the vehicles, the
team saw vague outlines of people and things arriving and

leaving the warehouse, and shadowy people walking around, but then everything went black.

A moment later, the vehicles were flooded with light and the team were safely in the glade. Thomas, Baz, Jack, Sophie and Kelly jumped out confidently, while the others crept out cautiously and looked around. Amazingly, the space adjustment feature of the Project system had spread the vehicles out at safe distances from each other, but the order they'd landed in was disorganised. The Toyota, Transporter and a Smart car were inconveniently in the middle of the laager, so Thomas suggested they drive them out of the way once they were disconnected from the central computer system. Soon, Baz and Kelly had the vehicles neatly parked under nearby trees.

Two hours later, the village resembled a holiday encampment, and the hot weather enhanced the illusion. The team had left the Mews in a London spring, but now it was so hot that they changed into shorts and vest tops; the aroma of sunscreen soon filled the air.

Mike and Kelly went in search of cold drinks, and once everyone was refreshed, they split up to deal with a variety of tasks. Raj and Lucy ran tests on the computer systems while Thomas screwed together flat-pack desks and chairs for the Command Centre. It was already obvious that the village was nowhere near coping with a "hot" field operation, and they could see just how necessary this dry run was already proving to be.

Among the many snags, it had become clear that some of the solar panels hadn't been properly screwed down, so Jack was sitting on the top of one of the lodges, holding one of the heavy panels in place while Sophie was softly tapping at a bracket with a rubber mallet. It was while she was on her hands and knees with her dark brown shorts waving in the air that a mounted man rode slowly into the glade. Baz strode over to greet him.

'By Thor's hammer!' exclaimed Carlo, getting off his horse and gazing in rapture at Sophie's rear, 'I've never seen anything like that in all my born days!'

'Good, isn't it?' laughed Baz.

'Is the rest of it as alluring as the part that's waving around up there with its legs on view?'

'Oh yes, it's all very alluring.'

'I'll have to get to know her then, won't I?' said Carlo.

Baz started to chuckle. 'I wouldn't recommend it.'

'Why on earth not?'

Baz was laughing out loud now.

'That's Sophie, you idiot. She's Tommo's wife, and I doubt he'd be keen to share her.'

'Trust Tom to take the pick of the bunch,' said Carlo sourly. 'If you've brought any others with you, I bet they look like the back end of my best cow.'

'You'll be glad to know that we have two others here for you to choose from, and several more arriving for short visits while we're here, and I'm glad to report that none of them look remotely like the back end of your best cow.'

Carlo brightened considerably, while Baz walked him round the Command Centre where they found Thomas staring at the various parts of what was supposed to become a flat-pack desk. He was muttering to himself.

'It might be easier if they'd left the bloody instructions in Hidalian because then I could translate them into something sensible. What does "affix the tail leg board to the side leg fixture on the left and right side" mean, for God's sake?'

'Tommo, your cousin's here,' called Baz.

Thomas was only too glad to give the desk building a rest and greet Carlo.

'He's fallen in love with Sophie's backside, Tommo,' said Baz, pointing out the aforementioned bum.

'Christ on a donkey, Baz! She could fall off that bloody lodge, and Jack's stuck there holding onto that damned panel.'

'I'll get up there and give her a break.'

'I wish you would.'

Looking around at all the activity, Carlo asked if he could lend a hand, so Thomas took his cousin to the lads' lodge, suggesting that he get out of his Tudor gear and use their shower. While Carlo was enjoying his first ever shower and shampoo, Thomas broke out a new pack of underpants and looked out a spare tee shirt and shorts. Once Carlo was ready, Thomas smeared suntan on him and put him to work helping to decipher the desk-making instructions. Somehow, by dint of studying the illustration and a fair bit of guesswork, they managed it, and soon Baz called the Oberon team together to grab a sandwich. While they were eating crisps and sandwiches, Thomas introduced Carlo to the team, and they all remarked on how alike the cousins were, while Baz decided to make mischief.

'Carlo fancies you like mad, Sophie,' he said. 'It was the sight of your bum waving at him from the top of the van that did it, Soph, but I told him Tommo wouldn't take kindly to the competition.'

Sophie looked closely at Carlo and said, 'I admit I hadn't thought of it up to now, but Tommy will be thirty-nine on his next birthday and a toy boy might make a nice change...'

Thomas snorted, 'Toy boy indeed! I'll take you into the woods in a minute and make you forget all about bloody toy boys!'

The TUDORs giggled at the minor domestic con-tretemps and Carlo joined in the laughter, deciding that the events that had brought the New Londoners to his door looked like being fun. For one thing, it was a relief to feel really clean and to discard his heavy Tudor clothing in such hot weather. Jack asked Carlo if his horse would like a drink and when Carlo nodded, Jack fetched a washing up bowl from the stores, decanted some of their drinking water into it and took it to the grateful animal.

* * *

Jack was staring thoughtfully at several crates containing weapons when Thomas found him.

'Are we likely to use these, Tom?'

'In theory not on this trip, but theory and reality are two different things.' Thomas also gazed at the weaponry. 'Jack, do you think you could show me how to use these guns? I've had some pistol training and I'm confident with the Glock 23 now, but I've never shot any of these other things.'

'No problem,' said Jack. It looks as though we have a dozen rifles and a dozen assault weapons. I'll need some help with cleaning and preparing them, though, because it looks as though they're brand new and covered in grease.'

'Sure, we'll all help.'

Later that day, the three techies, Raj, Sophie and Lucy were up to their necks in computer printouts, maps, maths and other such matters, while Thomas, Kelly, Baz and Carlo were taking rifles apart and reassembling them. "Sergeant" Jack walked up and down the line adjusting things until he was happy with his "troopers". They spent some time letting off a few shots and getting used to the weapons. As sergeants go, Jack didn't make much noise, but neither did he let the team get away with anything. When they took a break, Jack asked Carlo if what they'd been doing bore any resemblance to the training given in a medieval army.

'It's remarkably similar. Other than the fact that you're much nicer to your troopers than our sergeants were.'

Jack grinned at the image, but his interest was piqued, because while he'd studied the Tudors at college, he'd never studied their weapons or their war tactics.

'How many ranks do you have in your army?'

'Well there are knights, sergeants and troopers, but there are also many separate specialities, such as pike men, halberdiers, and longbow men and so on. Bowmen are trained from childhood and they can't let up, as they need to keep up their strength and skills, but where other skills are concerned, our sergeants train batches of men in much the same way you were doing. As a knight, I could already use a sword, but I wanted to know what my men were going through, so I often joined their training sessions. The longer weapons are hard to cope with and very tiring to use, so I always had a lot of admiration for those who wielded pikes, poleaxes and so on.'

'That makes sense,' said Jack, stretching himself out languidly like an oversized cat. 'Did you enjoy your time in the army?'

'I did. As a mounted knight, my life was easier than that of a foot soldier, but chain mail and armour are tiring to wear. The one thing I really hated though was the siege of Lillientours. Luckily for us, it was over fairly quickly, because if a siege goes on long enough, the besiegers run out of food and get ill. They often go down with deadly forms of diarrhoea, and if they're really unlucky, plagues can set in.'

'Crikey!' said Jack, pulling a face. 'You know, studying history from books doesn't really bring it to life in all its uncomfortable reality.'

Carlo stretched out on the grass, burping a little as the unusual experience of drinking lemonade brought up a few bubbles, while Jack was still bent on taking the golden opportunity of learning about medieval warfare at first hand.

'What about guns? From what I know of your era, guns were starting to take over from the longbow. I read that it took years to train a powerful and accurate bowman, but only a couple of weeks to train a man with a musket.'

'Musket?' asked Carlo.

'An early type of long barrelled gun that's the forerunner of our modern rifles.'

'They may be coming in soon, but I ended my term of service a few years ago. I know of the harquebus and of heavy siege guns that knock down the walls of a city, and there were some handguns around, but I never trusted them. More likely to damage the shooter than the enemy, I always thought.'

'What propels the bullets in your hand guns?' You know, like the bullets in these rifles.'

'There's no bullet in that sense. The gun shoots out a slug of metal or a small stone, and we propel it by pouring a little gunpowder into a trap and setting it alight with a small bunch of burning straw that we call a match.'

'Oh crikey, matchlock guns!' cried Jack 'I've heard of them, and flintlock guns, too!'

'Ummm,' said Carlo, 'The flintlocks are new and they aren't yet in service, as far as I know. I've seen one though, and it's very good. It's certainly an advance on the matchlock mechanism.'

'I'm going to train the lads on the American assault rifle soon, so if you like flintlocks, you'll just *love* that, Carlo. It shoots out streams of bullets and you don't need even one tiny flint to get it going!'

* * *

Towards the end of the afternoon, the Oberon troopers were flat on their bellies with their eyes stuck firmly to their rifle sights, and thinking longingly of cool showers and even cooler beer, when the air behind one of the lodges shimmered and several nearby trees lost a few of their leaves. A moment later, a VW Transporter materialised and Sir David stepped out, followed by Steven, Julie, Kate, Jessica and Margie who almost fell over each other in their rush to reach their friends and loved ones and give them a hug… but it was the other two passengers who were the greatest surprise.

Even in black cargo shorts and a magenta polo shirt, Emson Barotse managed to look like a Vogue model, while Frances Shulman looked surprisingly good in pale green slacks and an even paler shirt. She'd clearly been to the hairdresser, where some genius had tamed her dreadful perm and applied a dark blonde tint to cool down her usual carroty look. The woman almost looked human - as long as one ignored the prominent teeth, beaky nose and those sharp, miss-nothing eyes.

* * *

Later that day, the cleaned up team put together a barbecue while Baz handed out cans of beer. Solar lights and an MP3 playing quietly made the evening very pleasant indeed, while coils of mosquito repellent kept the bugs off. Sophie and Margie were soon catching up on family news, while Kate, Steven and Sir David sat with Emson and Kelly. A remarkably relaxed Home Secretary talked to Carlo for a while, but she was now chatting happily with Baz, Jessica and Jack, while Raj, Julie and Thomas discussed the problems the techie team were coming up against.

Both Jack and Baz were certain that Carlo and Kelly would get it on. After all, they were a similar age and

Kelly was a confident woman who took the occasional lover when someone captured her fancy, but while they liked each other well enough and shared a joke or two, it was obvious that something unexpected was developing between Carlo and Lucy. Carlo wasn't stupid. It was obvious that gentle girl lacked confidence and she seemed naive, and while he knew that it would be no problem for him to talk her into his bed, something stopped him. The fact of the matter was that he liked and admired her, and that was unusual for him.

Now that she'd spent a little time washing and drying her hair and had released it from its usual pins, Lucy's brown hair fell softly to her shoulders, with the fire highlighting its reddish glints. Her clear hazel eyes shone up at Carlo as she concentrated hard on his archaic English. For his part, Carlo's intuition told him that Lucy was highly intelligent and absolutely lovely, but that there was something emotionally fragile about her, and it was triggering his protective instincts. He took her hand and started to use a skill he'd picked up while campaigning in France.

Carlo pointed to her palm in the area near the thumb, but beneath the index finger, showing her the separated lines where the lifeline and head line start their journey. The lines were not only separated, but there were several crossing lines between them.

'Wow, you're a very independent lady, and the circumstances of your life have increased that tendency. You are desperate to stand on your own feet and you hate the idea of asking others for anything. It's as though you discovered early in life that asking wouldn't work, so you either learned to do without or find ways of getting what you needed yourself. The link between the lines suggests that you have studied hard and long, so that you could make your own way in life.'

Lucy's breath caught. In one single moment, Carlo had touched the very things that had made her life so painful, and the reasons for her fierce desire to stand on her own feet.

'The broad Mount of Luna and the skin-ridge loop coming into it shows a love of plants, trees and the countryside. These things are important to you.'

Lucy was gobsmacked at this insight.

And so, the pleasant evening came to an end, the "visitors" returned to New London, the team turned in for the night, and Carlo rode slowly and thoughtfully back to the farmhouse.

Chapter Twenty Three

WEAPONS OF WAR

You can't say civilization don't advance... in every war they kill you in a new way.

WILL ROGERS

Things progressed much the same way the following day. Thomas worked alongside the "techie team" as they worked out the problems related to communication and orientation, while the "fight club" continued their weapons training in the woods. They were taking a rest when Baz asked Carlo about medieval weapons, and especially about bows and arrows.

'Can you use a bow and arrow, Carlo?'

'Of course.'

'I remember schoolteachers telling us the English longbow took years to master. Is archery that difficult?'

'Not at all, Baz,' said Carlo getting up, 'come with me to the barn and I'll get some gear and show you all how to do it.'

'We haven't got doublets with us,' said Jack.

'It won't be a problem. The farm workers are out working and Jackson knows the score, so it doesn't matter if he sees us. I had to tell him something, and as with Bessie, I decided the truth was the best explanation. He won't talk out of turn.'

An hour later, they'd erected some target butts, and Carlo was getting Baz ready for his first shooting lesson.

'The reason for the years of training was the power of the bow and of the bow string, because the tighter the string, the further the arrow can go, but with the advent of gunpowder, bows and arrows are no longer the main means of artillery. The future that you have already shown me must have started right about now, I guess.'

Baz agreed with Carlo's conclusions, and Carlo went on with his explanation.

'However, unless you are shooting at an army or trying to pick off enemy knights in full armour, there's no need to use such a heavy bow or string. You'll soon see that this isn't a difficult technique to master.'

'What about me?' asked Kelly, 'Will I be able to shoot?'

'Women do very well at archery, Kelly. You'll be fine.'

Carlo attached a leather protector to the inside of Baz's left arm and gave him what looked like the finger part of a leather glove to put on his right hand, tying the leather string round his right wrist to anchor it in place. Then he tied a quiver to the right side of Baz's belt.

'I thought archers carried their quivers on their backs,' said Baz.

'They might when mounted, but this is the best way when on foot. It's easy to get the arrows out and it stops them getting knocked about. The better condition your arrow is in, the better it flies.'

'I guess that makes sense.'

Once Baz was ready, Carlo prepared Kelly and Jack in the same way, telling them to stand well back and keep still. Now he went back to Baz and gave him a bow to hold. Baz found the bow light and smooth to hold. It was gently curved and it didn't have the Cupid's bow re-curve shape at the ends.

Jack asked, 'What kind of bow is this, Carlo?'

'An English longbow.'

Jack gaped. 'You don't say! The famous English *longbow*? Of Agincourt fame and all that?'

'Well yes,' said Carlo turning to speak to Jack. 'They certainly used these at Agincourt. Theirs were heavier than these are, although these bows will kill a man well enough, even at a distance.'

Jack couldn't believe he was about to learn how to shoot with an English longbow. Everything he'd loved about history came together for him in a sudden rush, and he felt tears gathering in his eyes.

Carlo corrected Baz's stance so that he was facing side-ways on to the target, with his feet at shoulder width.

'Hold the bow without completely straightening your arm, Baz. Keep your left shoulder down and your left hip forward. Now pull the string back without an arrow in it just to get a feel for the position.'

Baz did as Carlo asked.

'Do you see how high your right elbow needs to be and how straight your back is?'

'Yeah, I guess the whole upper body needs to be in line with the arrow.'

'Exactly. Your body is the power behind the arrow.'

Carlo showed Baz how to fit the arrow onto the "nocking point" on the string, which was an area marked off in the centre by two pieces of thread that had been wound around the string and stuck into place with fish glue. Baz "nocked" his arrow carefully - and it promptly fell to the ground.

'This is more awkward than it looks,' said Baz, inspecting the notch at the back of the arrow. 'I notice there's no broad head, just a smooth metal cap. Would it be right to say these arrows are specially designed for training purposes?'

'Yes, these have a smooth head, which makes them easy to draw out of the target after use. By the way, getting the arrow to stay in place on the string takes a bit of practice, and even expert archers sometimes mess up the nock and drop an arrow. It doesn't matter. Try it again slowly and you'll get it this time.'

A moment later, Baz was holding the string firmly back with three fingers of his right hand and with the nail on his middle finger pressing the side of his upper lip. Carlo told him to aim somewhere between the centre of the target and the lower edge - but fairly close to the bottom of the target. It seemed to Baz that this would be too low to hit anything useful, but he was happy to do as Carlo said. On Carlo's command, Baz opened his fingers, and the arrow flew. To Baz's surprise, it landed a little to the right of the bull's eye.

'Try another arrow and aim at the same point as before, Baz,' instructed Carlo.

The second arrow landed beside the first one, just to the right of the bull.

'Stop a minute and lower the bow while I retrieve the arrows, and we'll have another go.'

When Carlo had removed the arrows, he told Baz to adjust his aim slightly to the left, but still keep it low. This time the arrow landed squarely in the centre of the bull. Baz stared at it in open-mouthed amazement while his brain tried to catch up with what his eyes were telling him.

'I can't believe this. I've just shot a bull's-eye at around thirty feet with a bloody longbow. That's incredible!'

Carlo laughed at Baz's amusement and then suggested he try another half-dozen arrows, fitting them to the bow and aiming slowly and carefully. Some arrows flew a little wide of the bull while others landed firmly on it, but all landed squarely on the target. Then it was Jack's turn, and he did equally well, while to her amazement, and although pulling a lighter weight bow than the lads had used, Kelly did even better.

Carlo wasn't surprised and he told the men that it was often the way. Something about the way women's eyes functioned or the way their bodies were made, worked in their favour and they were often excellent archers.

Jack commented that he'd never read of female archers in his history books, but Carlo said they must have erased them from history, because they certainly existed before and during his time. He told Jack that women had fought hard when defending their families and their farms during the Wars of the Roses, and many of them saved their home-steads from destruction by that means.

The team spent the rest of the afternoon competing with each other, using flights of six arrows in each session. To her amazement, Kelly was the winner, with Jack and Baz a few points behind her. Carlo said they were all very good indeed, mainly because they had listened to his instructions and focused carefully on what they were doing.

'So you'd take us on as troopers?' asked Jack.

'I'd have no problem with that,' said Carlo, 'but you'd have to learn how to do it with a smaller re-curve bow and from the back of a galloping horse.'

'As the bishop said to the actress!' laughed Jack.

* * *

By Wednesday evening, the team had solved most of the technical problems and made lists of the jobs they'd need to complete when they got back to the Mews. The batteries and solar panels had all worked perfectly, and the Walkie-

Talkies and the longer distance radiophones that linked to an aerial arrangement on top of the Command Centre were also working well. Lucy and Raj were the chefs that evening, so they made eggs, oven chips, bacon and baked beans for everyone, followed by fresh fruit salad. The weather had turned a little chilly, so the team gathered in the girls lodge for their last meal, which included a chocolate cake and several bottles of fresh white wine that Baz fished out of the supplies van. After dinner, Carlo and Lucy went for a walk.

'I'm coming back with you to New London for a week or two, Lucy, and I'll be staying with Tom and Sophie. Would you show me around when you can take time off?'

Lucy felt her heart contract, and when Carlo took her hand, she felt her insides starting to spin. Her mouth felt so dry that she could hardly speak, but she managed to tell Carlo that she'd love to show him around her city. They walked to Carlo's house, where he called for Bessie and asked her to come to the lodge to share some cake and a cup or two of wine with the team.

The whole trip would have been like a dream holiday, but for two problems. The first was the fact that Thomas, Baz and Raj were only too aware that the Russians hadn't yet solved the Parmian problem; which meant that the team might have to use the encampment for real before long, and in a much less kindly environment than sixteenth century Devon.

The second problem came later that night.

* * *

The storm woke Raj, and it wasn't the thunder or rain that bothered him, but an insistent feeling that something was amiss. He opened the lodge door and stepped outside. The worst of the storm had passed over and the rain had eased off, so he walked out of the Village area and listened hard.

Hearing nothing more, he turned back. He hadn't gone far when a hard blow to his right shoulder knocked him to the ground. Raj twisted his head around to see what was going on, and even in the pale light of the moon as it flitted in and out of the clouds, he could see the fletch of an arrow sticking out of his back. He knew better than to stand up and present himself as a fresh target, so he lay flat in the wet grass and groped around until his handed landed on a stone, which he lobbed left-handedly at the nearest van. Fortunately for him, it was the men's lodge, and the noise woke Baz, who put his head out the door. Raj yelled at him to keep his head down because people were shooting arrows at them. Baz ran for his Glock while yelling at Jack and Thomas to get up.

'Jacko! Tommo! Get up. We're under attack!' screamed Baz.

Baz and Jack tumbled out of bed and shoved their feet into running shoes, while at the same time, snatching up their guns. Jack spotted the extra Glock sitting on the side and tossed it at Thomas who thanked his lucky stars for his recent weapons training while he removed the safety and cocked the gun. The men ran out to where Raj lay and fired into the woods. They were soon joined by Kelly who lay down on the soaking grass and joined in the shooting. They heard shouting and the sound of men running off, then the area fell quiet. Thomas was the first to reach Raj, so he helped him up and walked him back to the lodge. They all turned abruptly to face the sound of approaching hooves, but they were relieved to see that it was Carlo. He'd heard the noise and was riding into the camp, sword in hand.

When Carlo saw what had happened to Raj, he cursed.

'Do you know who they are?' asked Thomas.

'Carlo shook his head. Pirates don't usually get this far south, so no, I don't know who they are.' Carlo turned to Baz. 'Do you know if you hit any of them?'

'There's no way of knowing, but we'll ride out tomorrow and see if there are any bodies lying around.'

'Or signs of blood,' agreed Carlo.

Back in the lodge, Kelly and Jack lay Raj face down on the bench and inspected his back. Kelly found a pair of scissors and carefully cut Raj's tee shirt so that a small circle of cloth remained around the arrow. It had been carried into Raj along with the arrow.

Jack spoke to Raj in a calm and cheerful manner to stop him getting into a state.

'You know, Raj my old beauty,' he said, 'I think you've got away with this one. The tip of the arrowhead is just into your shoulder blade, but it hasn't penetrated far. If the barb had gone in properly, it would be a major problem, because we would need to push it all the way through and out the other side to prevent the broad head from doing even more damage. My guess is that the shooter was a fair way off and the arrow must have passed through a few bushes en route, which slowed its progress. Even your tee shirt has done its bit to slow it down.'

'Do you think you can get it out, Jack?'

'Yeah, it's not that bad.' Jack hoped his diagnosis was right and that the arrow tip hadn't cut anything vital.

Kelly fished out the first aid kit and was poking through it to see what she could find, but she put the box down again when Jack told her to hold Raj down and keep him still. Kelly lay right across Raj's waist and pressed her weight firmly down on him.

'Raj my old duck, this is bound to hurt, so take a deep breath and hold your horses.'

209

Raj did as he was told while Jack got hold of the arrow and waggled it slightly to see how deeply it was embedded. Raj groaned noisily. Jack waggled it again and saw that it was fairly free, but Raj decided not to put a brave face on it, so he moaned, groaned and complained bitterly.

'Play around with it, Jack, why don't you? I mean, it's only my shoulder-blade that you're mucking about with.'

Jack was sorry for Raj. It must be uncomfortable, but he needed to see what he was dealing with.

'It's moving Raj, so I think the best thing is for me to pull it straight out. Hold on now, I'm going to give it a tug.'

Jack grabbed the shaft of the arrow with both hands and with one swift movement, yanked it out of the poor man's back. Blood oozed from the wound, but it was clear that the arrow hadn't cut any vital blood vessels.

Meanwhile Raj had jack-knifed from the shock; his mouth fell open and he flopped back down with a loud groan.

'For fuck's sake, Jack,' he yelled, 'did you have to schlepp it out quite that fast? It bloody hurt. Excuse my language, Kelly love.'

'I forgive you,' said Kelly quietly.

Jack examined the arrow. 'It's all out, thank God. The broad head is complete and thankfully, it doesn't look dirty or rusty. Better still, the bit of tee shirt that it took in with it remained intact and the tee shirt looked clean, so it couldn't be better, really. There's no question that it's pitted your scapula and bashed it about, and I think it's a torn a muscle. You'll mend, but it's going to hurt like stink for a few days. I remember what it felt like when I got hurt on the Abbey jaunt.'

'Yeah, Jack, but you'd just enjoyed a pleasurable evening with two ladies of the court. All I've had in the way of entertainment before I got injured was sharing the lodge with you, Baz and Tom farting and snoring all night long.'

'Good thing too, Raj old bean. Janessa would be most unhappy if you'd spent the night in the sack with two court girls, but I'm sure she won't be put out by you bellyaching about having to sleep with us. And by the way, none of us fart or snore in our sleep, if you don't mind.'

The only perceptible response was a disgusted "humph" coming from the direction of the patient.

Kelly intervened, 'Stay where you are, Raj, I'm going to spray around the spot and it's going to sting. I guess this is like a stab wound, in that as long as the thing is clean inside, you won't even need stitches. It's bleeding a bit, which is all to the good, as that also helps to clean out a wound. It's bound to hurt, but I don't have much choice.'

'Okay, Kelly love, get on with it.'

When she'd finished, Jack helped Raj into a sitting position. His complexion had taken on a greenish tinge and sweat beaded his brow, but Kelly thought this was as much from fright as from any real trauma.

Kelly bent down looked closely at him. 'I think you'll be all right, Raj, the worst is definitely over.' She handed him several tablets. 'Here's two penicillin pills, two co-codamols for the pain, and a vitamin C for healing. It's just as well you don't drink - you're best off without alcohol at the moment, with all that shock going on and whatnot, but I reckon we could all do with a cuppa.' She gestured for Jack to pick up a fleece rug from the end of the bed and tuck it round Raj to keep potential shock away.

A few minutes later, Lucy and Sophie turned up, followed by Thomas, Baz and Carlo.

'Did you see anyone?' asked Jack.

Thomas shook his head. 'We'll take another look in daylight, but it looks as though the noise of the gunfire frightened them off.'

'We'll know more when the gossip machine starts up tomorrow,' said Carlo.

Baz bent down to look at Raj's face. The colour was coming back now that the painkillers were kicking in, and he was gratefully sipping the sweet tea that Lucy had handed him.

'You know Raj,' said Baz conversationally, 'when you play cowboys and Indians in the woods, the Indians are supposed to be *redskins* not *Paks*.'

'Very politically correct, I'm sure, Baz... *redskins* and *Paks* indeed.'

Sophie handed round a large tin of biscuits and was glad to see Raj helping himself to a couple of chocolate digestives.

'Talking of political incorrectness,' said Sophie, 'I remember someone telling me that in the old days, there weren't enough real Native American Indians in Hollywood to play the part of the Indians in the cowboy films, so they used Jewish and Italian extras who they called *"shmo-hawks* and *woppa-hoes"*.'

'I hadn't heard that one,' laughed Raj, 'but I did once hear about an American film called *The Fighting Seebees* or some such thing that was supposed to have Japanese soldiers in it. The film was made while World War Two was still in progress, so there were no Japanese actors available. The casting office rounded up all the oriental looking men they could find and got them to mutter, *"I tie my shoe, you tie your shoe"* because that made them sound Japanese - or so they hoped.'

* * *

They all went back to bed and even Raj managed to get some sleep. By morning, he decided that when he got back to New London, he'd tell everyone that he'd fended off a hoard of armed-to-the-teeth pirates all by himself. He knew the lads would take the almighty mickey out of him, but he was determined to enjoy the fuss while it lasted.

* * *

The next morning Carlo trotted up, leading two more horses on long leather straps. Thomas handed Carlo a pistol and asked him to give Jack a quick riding lesson. Jack being Jack, it didn't take long for him to get the hang of it, and the horse soon learned not to mess him around. The three men rode off to see what they could find.

The others cleared up the camp and packed everything away in preparation for the flight back to New London. Raj wanted to oversee the work in the Command Centre, but Sophie and Lucy made him sit still to prevent the wound from opening up. It was a little awkward working round him in the confined space, but they managed.

A couple of hours later, Jack, Carlo and Thomas came back saying they hadn't found anyone or any clue as to who had attacked them, although they'd picked up several arrows that had fallen short during the attack. They walked the horses back to the stables and went over to the house to say goodbye to Bessie. Back at the village, Thomas handed Carlo a pair of jeans and a sweater as his cousin got ready to see what New London was all about.

This time, Sophie took charge of the flight, so she shoved her head out of the window and yelled to the others in the Transporter that it was one minute to lift-off. Everyone closed their windows and soon the TUDORs were flying back to the Mews.

Chapter Twenty Four

CARLO VISITS NEW LONDON

Just when I think I have learned the way to live,
life changes.

HUGH PRATHER

The team landed at the Mews to find a reception committee of Sir David, Jill and Jessica, who were aghast when they learned about Raj's adventure.

'Raj of all people,' said Sir David scratching his head. 'We've got all these soldiers on board and it's you who gets clobbered. How bad is it?'

Now that he was feeling better, Raj milked it for all he was worth, telling Sir David that Jack and Kelly saved his life - after he'd chased off the pirates single-handed and saved theirs. He said he was proud to be the only member of TUDOR who had ever been shot with an arrow and he was happy to report that it was a very painful and unpleasant experience. He might have got away with his bid for sympathy if it wasn't for the fact that Jack and Baz were standing behind him and rolling their eyes.

'Right,' said Sir David briskly, 'I want Tom and Baz at Millbank right now for debriefing. The rest of you can go home, but I will need Raj and Sophie in first thing so that we can see what we learned from this adventure.'

Turning to Raj he said, 'If your injury gives you any trouble - any trouble at all - go straight round to Harley Street and get it seen to. We have a dedicated doctor and a full clinic for our use now, so we no longer have to worry about hospitals asking awkward questions when any of us come home with gunshot wounds or Robin Hood's arrows sticking out of us.'

Sir David looked around at his crew and thanked them all for their efforts. Jessica called a limo for Sophie and Carlo and told them to go home and not to worry, as she'd shut the "factory" for them.

Just as Thomas, Steven, Kate and Robbie had looked around in wonderment at New London when they first arrived, so was Carlo astounded at the sheer number of people in the city, the motorised transport and the shops. Let alone the variety of dress styles sported by the populace. Once Sophie had belted him into his seat, Carlo grabbed the handle at the top of the door and hung on for dear life, but having already been through this routine with the other Tudorlanders, Sophie left him to discover that road travel in central London was much slower and safer than he feared.

* * *

Lucy Sanders decided to call in on the garden centre on her way home and ask for the next two weekends off. She had never asked for time off before, so she didn't expect there to be a problem.

'I'm glad you've come in Lucy; I have some news for you.'

Lucy picked up a whiff of embarrassment.

'I've decided to retire, and I've sold the land to developers, so the centre will close at the end of the week, and

215

unfortunately, your work here is at an end.' Mr Parker gave Lucy a sad look. 'Have you been paid up or is anything still outstanding?'

'There's nothing owing, Mr P, but thanks for thinking of it.'

'You've been a very good worker, Lucy.' He waved a hand around the office. 'I'll miss you and all of this, of course. By the way, if you need a reference… '

'No, Mr Parker, I have a good job now. To be honest, I was finding it hard to cope with a demanding full time job and coming here at weekends, so while the garden centre has been a big part of my life for the past seven years, I guess it's time for me to move on. As it happens, I came in to ask for the next two weekends off because for me too, life is starting to change.'

'Lucy love, the Wheel of Fortune turns for all of us. Sometimes we ride up on it and at other times, we go down. It's the way of the world.'

* * *

Carlo spent two weeks in New London, mainly working unofficially at TUDOR and going out on a couple of jobs with Jack. He spent time with Kate, Steven, and their children and he asked everyone endless questions. He even bought copies of farming and agricultural magazines to get an idea of what the rural scene was like in the twenty-first century.

Carlo learned to flick Thomas's remote and to find the reality cop shows and motoring shows that fascinated him; he played tennis with Thomas and helped Sophie and her gardener with a few heavy jobs. At the start of his stay, he offered a few pieces of gold to Thomas in exchange for some New London money, but Thomas waved him away and gave him a bundle of cash to run around with.

Sophie decided to take Carlo and Thomas to a new dining place called *"King Henry's Feast",* which specialised in "Tudor evenings" where they could dress in Tudor costume and eat mock-Tudor food. Sophie wondered whether Carlo would prefer a bit of younger company for the evening, so she asked if he'd like to invite Kelly, Jessica or perhaps Lucy. Carlo jumped at the chance of asking Lucy.

Sophie wasn't surprised, as she'd thought this was the way the wind was blowing, so while chopping veggies with her back to Carlo, she kept her voice light and innocent, saying, 'I'll ring her for you now, if you like.'

'I hope she's free on Friday,' said Carlo.

'She'll be free,' answered Sophie.

'How do you know that?'

'Woman's intuition.'

* * *

Not only was the evening at the "*Feast*" a great success, but when the evening came to an end, Lucy and Carlo decided to spend the next day together. At the end of the day, Carlo accompanied Lucy to her flat, and at the front door, he bowed slightly but he didn't kiss her and neither did he ask to come in for a nightcap.

The next day, Sophie threw Carlo and Thomas out of the house and told them to find Steven and take him for a pub lunch, because she was going to be busy in the kitchen. Later that day, the Baverstock crew and the Byers gang would be joining them for high tea. Sophie asked Carlo if he'd like Lucy to join them and once again, he jumped at the idea. Carlo and Lucy spent the next couple of days in each other's company, walking through Regent's Park and wandering the shopping streets and seeing the sights, but

Carlo still didn't offer anything more than friendship. If Lucy had been less naive, she would have questioned his behaviour or perhaps made a move herself, but she just assumed that he saw her as no more than a friend. She couldn't help the intense yearning that had set itself up in her heart though - and an answering heat slowly boiling away in her belly whenever she was near him.

* * *

Lucy's downstairs neighbours were due to have one of their barbeques on the Saturday evening, and as usual on these occasions, they invited Lucy to join them. As it happened her friend, Riva, had phoned for a chat that morning, so Lucy asked her neighbours if she could bring some friends to their party, and she offered to bring some salads and a few bottles of wine along to cater for the extra mouths. They said they'd love to have some younger company and that the contribution would be appreciated.

Later that evening, Carlo and Riva were sitting together under a tree, when he took the opportunity of buttonholing her.

'I like Lucy a lot, but I have to go back to Hidalia soon, so I'm not sure where we're going with this, but there's something about her past that I would love to know. I'm not unreasonably jealous by nature and I'm not the slightest bit bothered about the men she may have known in her past, but I get the feeling that something happened that was strange and hard to understand.' Carlo bit his lower lip and looked across the garden at Lucy, who was chatting away with a couple of her neighbours' friends. 'Do you know anything about it?'

Carlo turned his silvery eyes on Riva and lifted an inquisitive eyebrow.

Riva knew she shouldn't gossip, but she'd already downed a good few gins and Carlo was due to go back to Hidalia the next day, so she figured there was no harm in speaking out.

'I got to know Lucy during our last year at college, so I actually met Chris once or twice. I thought at first he was just a flat mate and I was sure he was gay.' Riva wondered whether Carlo knew the word "gay" and its meaning, so she checked that he did before going on.

'Lucy opened up to me one evening and told me he'd moved in with her when she was still only sixteen.'

Carlo nodded and said nothing. His experience of questioning people who were innocent of any crime had taught him that if he sat still and stayed quiet, they would rabbit on, and in Riva's case, this was exactly what happened.

'Apparently Chris tried to make love on a couple of occasions when he was tipsy, but it didn't really work. Lucy thinks he may have found someone gay to spend time with soon after, but she didn't know for sure and she didn't ask. To be honest, I doubt that Chris had much sex drive, one way or the other.'

Riva hiccupped a little and sipped a little more of her gin and tonic before delivering her final verdict. 'According to Lucy, Chris hadn't a clue as to how to turn her on – not that she had much clue herself.' Riva leaned more closely to Carlo so she could breathe gin-laden whispers into his ear. 'She told me that Chris lacked the requisite equipment for sex – and especially for the gay life – because from what I understand, men are very demanding of other men.'

'You mean he wasn't well built? That he was not shaped as a man should be?'

At this point Riva told Carlo about the turkey giblets and pigeon giblets, and while he'd never heard of a turkey, he got the idea and started to giggle.

'Lucy told you that?' asked Carlo.

'Her very words,' said Riva, slurring a little over her refreshed glass. 'Even our inexperienced and naïve Lucy could sense something was wrong, so she researched the masculine "crown jewels" on the 'Net and discovered that poor old Chris was missing an inch or few, if you see what I mean.' Riva hiccupped into her gin. 'And she said his testimonials were the size of shrivelled grapes.'

Carlo was laughing so hard by now that he had to hold his hand over his mouth to avoid drawing attention to himself.

* * *

At the end of the evening, Carlo stood on the steps leading to Lucy's flat and took her into his arms. He kissed her gently.

'Lucy darling, there isn't much time to talk now, but I want you to come back with me to Tudorland tomorrow and I want you to be my wife.'

Lucy was so taken aback that she stared at Carlo open mouthed. Then she wailed at him.

'I can't do that! I love you totally. More than I have loved *anyone* or *anything* in my entire life! But how can I give up all I have striven for over the past ten years to become dependent upon someone else? And in such a strange environment. And what do I know of the duties of a Tudor wife? Your women are trained from birth to… to… to scrub sheep and shave pigs or whatever. All I know is physics, maths, science, computers and office work. Maybe my years in the garden centre could be useful, but even that knowledge is directed towards city horticulture. I don't know the first thing about rural life in my *own* world, so how the blazes would I be any use to you in yours? It won't work. It would be an absolute disaster for both of us.'

Carlo looked so crestfallen that Lucy's soft heart melted, but she just couldn't see herself giving up all that she had done to ensure her survival in New London, or of living in such a dissimilar environment.

With tears streaming down her face, she tried once again to impose the truth of the situation on Carlo and also on herself.

'I know you love your life in sixteenth century Devon and I respect that, but just as I wouldn't ask you to tear yourself away from your world for my sake, neither can I see myself doing so for yours. Even if I did, I just couldn't see it working - for either of us. It would destroy us.'

Carlo was too upset to talk, so he turned away and found a cab to take him back to Tamerlane Square. The next morning, he asked Sophie to fly him back to Tudorland. He didn't even stop to say goodbye to his friends in the Millbank office.

Chapter Twenty Five

LUCY UNRAVELS

A woman's life can really be a succession of lives, each revolving around some emotionally compelling situation or challenge, and each marked off by some intense experience.

WALLIS SIMPSON

Lucy went to work the next morning and tried to put her mind to her job. She worked harder than ever, but now she was quieter than ever. Her world shrank down to her job and evenings spent studying the subjects she needed for her work at TUDOR. She sat in on interrogations and began to understand the way terrorists thought, along with those who hunted them. She loved her country and her job, but nothing else made an impression. It was as though her world had gone from colour to grey.

She fell into a pattern of heating a tin of soup or baked beans at night, or making do with a piece of cake and a cup of tea. She increasingly relied on the Millbank canteen for nutrition, but she was steadily losing weight. The weeks trudged by, and Lucy's rotten diet, along with the depth of her depression made her tired and dispirited. When the weekends came, she didn't always bother to get dressed, but sat on her sofa with her feet tucked under her, and staring into space. Eventually, she reached a point where getting up and going to work took a major effort.

Lucy tried not to think of Carlo, but every time she switched on the television, there seemed to be something about life in the sixteenth century. She tried innocuous property programmes, but most of them were set in the West Country, and even Caroline Quentin's programmes about Cornwall brought great gulping tears of utter misery.

She gave up watching TV and often ended the day with such a cold lump in her stomach that she couldn't even get warm, and she couldn't face food at all. She got into the habit of curling up in bed and hugging herself to sleep with a hot water bottle. She came to the conclusion that, while *she* still existed, life that had any meaning or value didn't. Not any more. Her heart was breaking, and so was she.

* * *

A large middle-aged women, sporting a pair of jutting over-sized breasts and a quantity of dark wavy hair who worked in some Civil Service department somewhere else in the Millbank building, had decided to designate herself boss of the canteen queue. Like all well-practised bullies, she was accompanied by a skinny faded blond acolyte who hung on her every word. Day after day, the big woman pushed herself and her "familiar" to the head of the queue where she picked out the choicest items for herself and her friend. If the fried fish, roast chicken quarters or whatever the bullying woman fancied that day weren't ready, the queue would have to stand by until the requisite tray had emerged and she and her acolyte had been served.

This bully spotted the now insubstantial looking Lucy as perfect victim material, so day after day, the woman and her friend made a concerted effort to push Lucy to the back of the queue. By the time the poor girl reached the serving area, everything worth eating had gone, so Lucy made do with tired sandwiches, unloved sausages or greasy scraps. One day, the woman actually elbowed Lucy out of the queue altogether, making it clear to Lucy that she wasn't even to *enter* the canteen from now on. Exhausted by the extent of her depression, Lucy shrugged and turned away.

Unfortunately for the two women, Sophie happened to be in the canteen that day with her phone in her hand, so she took a short movie of the exchange. She knew that when she showed this to Thomas and Sir David, the two women would lose their Civil Service careers and their fat pension schemes. It was also entirely possible that Thomas could conjure up a charge of "attempting to prevent a TUDOR operative from performing her duties" or some such thing, to put the frighteners on these two pigs, but in the meantime, Sophie had more pressing matters to consider.

Sophie polished off her own lunch, deposited her tray and left the canteen, taking the lift and walking smartly into Lucy's office. With her face set into unaccustomedly severe lines, she told Lucy to grab her handbag and come with her. Right now!

A puzzled Lucy did as she was told, whereupon Sophie took the startled girl by the upper arm and frog-marched her across the road to the Mews. Jessica gazed in wonderment as Sophie opened the passenger door of a Smart Car and shoved Lucy inside. She walked briskly to her locker and pulled out a travel backpack that contained toiletries and several sets of underwear in a small size, ran back to the car, climbed in, powered up the tablet and punched in a set of coordinates.

* * *

The Project landed at the side of Hatherleigh Hall, where-upon Sophie jumped out, ran round and wrenched open the passenger door, and dragged Lucy out. She marched the startled girl to the front door and banged hard on the knocker. It was opened by one of Bessie's young maids, but without even stopping to acknowledge the servant, Sophie propelled Lucy down the hallway and into the kitchen. Still keeping a tight grip on her charge's arm, she asked Bessie if Carlo was around. Bessie stood transfixed, with her mouth agape and holding a wooden spoon in the air, for all the world like an orchestra conductor waiting for a concerto to begin. The young maid backed into the hall and gaped at the scene. For one thing, she couldn't help staring at the weird clothes that Sophie and Lucy were wearing.

While Bessie was still gathering her wits, the back door opened and Carlo stood on the threshold. He'd obviously been doing something messy on the farm, because his unruly dark brown hair had fallen into his eyes and his old woollen doublet was streaked with dirt, as were his breeches. He used a metal boot-remover to pull his boots off and stepped into the kitchen. Somehow, the scruffy look made him appear more handsome than ever.

He stood in the doorway with his mouth falling open. A golden retriever tried its luck and attempted to enter the for-bidden realm of the kitchen, but Carlo caught its collar and held it back.

'What the…!' exclaimed Carlo.

Sophie's fury at Lucy's untenable situation boiled over and she laid it on the line. Pointing at Lucy, she declared, 'She can't be arsed to eat, and a pair of bullies are making things ten times worse by harrying her out of the Millbank canteen. Her lunch today was a glass of water! You can bet she doesn't bother to feed herself at home, so that canteen was her lifeline, and now it's gone.'

Sophie literally shoved her charge at Carlo, while she glared angrily at her cousin-by-marriage. 'She's bloody *pining*. For *you*, you stupid prat. She won't *live* much longer if something isn't *done* about it!' she yelled. 'For God's sake, do something useful, Carlo! Turn her on and shag her stupid, and keep on doing it until she doesn't know if it's Tuesday or Christmas. Get her pregnant, marry her and make her happy – and keep her here with *you*!'

Turning to Bessie, she said sharply, 'And you can give her a bit of mothering. You can be sure it'll be the first she's ever experienced.' Totally rigid with fury, Sophie turned back to Carlo. 'This kid's like an unwanted pup, so either drown her or love her. Either way, it will be better than the slow death she's putting herself through. I can't stand watching it, so even if you end up drowning the silly bitch, it will be a relief to the rest of us.'

As her rage started to dissipate, Sophie's voice quieted down. 'I will come back here on All Soul's Day. I will be here at noon and you can tell me how it worked out - or not - as the case may be.'

With that, Sophie tossed the backpack at Lucy, turned on her heel and made her way out of the kitchen, stomping down the hallway towards the heavy front door. She wrenched it open, stormed out and banged it shut behind her.

On her return to the Mews, Sophie sat alone in the Project with tears streaming down her face. Jessica ran over and asked her what on earth was the matter. When she'd calmed down, Sophie asked Jessica to make her a cup of tea and then told her the whole story.

'I think Carlo asked Lucy to marry him and she turned him down, Jess, probably for what she considered to be sound and practical reasons, but they were ultimately bloody stupid ones.'

Sophie went on to tell Jessica what had been going on in the canteen and she gave her the phone with the movie on it so she could check it out.

'Bloody Norah,' said Jessica. 'I can see why you're so upset, but there's no doubt you did the right thing. It couldn't go on like that.' Jessica picked up her own mug and leaned a hip against the kitchen counter. 'I've been wondering what could be the matter with Lucy myself. I thought maybe she had cancer or perhaps type-one diabetes or something. She's lost so much weight recently and she's looking grey.'

Sophie looked into her tea, as if trying to find answers in the fragrant liquid. 'I hope I've done the right thing, Jess, I really do. I couldn't go on seeing her like that. Those bullies in the canteen... that was the last straw. She's at the end of the line, Jess. Something had to happen.'

Sophie looked up at the canteen calendar. 'Today's the 23rd of August and I said I'd go back for her on All Soul's Day, which is a couple of months away, so I guess we'll just have to wait and see.'

'What will Tommy say about you hi-jacking a member of his staff - or Raj for that matter?'

Sophie suddenly felt very tired. Gazing into her tea, she shrugged her shoulders.

'Do you know what, Jess? I couldn't give a flying *fuck* what Raj or Tommy think. Something had to be done and I did it.'

'Jeez,' muttered Jessica, shaking her head.

Chapter Twenty Six

CARLO AND LUCY

Never be afraid to trust an unknown future to a known God.

CORRIE TEN BOOM

Carlo was the first to gather his wits, and he started issuing orders.

'Deborah, take Miss Lucy into my sitting room and get her a cup of milk.' Turning to Bessie, he said, 'Get one of the girls to take my boots to Billy for cleaning and leave Lucy to me, I'll deal with her.'

Carlo went off to change, and when he strode into the sitting room, he'd changed into a beautifully embroidered forest green doublet and breeches. Lucy had set the cup on a table beside the settee. When Carlo looked into it, he saw she'd drunk half the milk. He pulled a chair over to the settee and sat down directly in front of the girl, stretching out one long leg while he sat back in the chair and waited. His eyes were the colour of a dark, angry sea.

Lucy looked thoroughly miserable, and the lack of the customary happy smile on Carlo's face added to her melancholia. She cleared her throat and tried to speak.

'I suppose you want me to tell you about everything and whatnot…'

Carlo's only response was to raise an eyebrow. Lucy had sat in on enough TUDOR interviews to recognise an experienced questioner when she saw one. Even the eyebrow trick was familiar, as she'd seen Thomas pulling it when putting the frighteners on some poor sod. Lucy shrugged and looked away. Truth to tell, she didn't know for sure herself how she'd got into this mess, but perhaps articulating things would help sort it out inside her own head as well as getting Carlo off her back. When she started to speak, her voice was rusty, which made her realise just how rarely she'd bothered to use it in recent weeks.

* * *

Lucy told Carlo the story of her life up to taking her degree, realising in her own mind how disconnected she'd become from the world around her.

'Chris had gone, Riva went overseas on family business and even the job at the garden centre was sliding downhill, so those I had known and liked had all moved on. Patrick was in Sheffield and my parents were deeply into their second families – not that they'd ever been interested in me in the first place, so I guess I was completely isolated.

'By the end of September, I got the job at TUDOR, and luckily for me, the Millbank building has a canteen so I could make lunch my main meal as I had done in college. I'm too shy to push myself on to people, so I make friends slowly and I was making a real effort at my job. I spent my evenings reading up on law and government stuff. I guess that even then I wasn't looking after myself properly. I can see that now.'

Lucy felt unbelievably stupid, but she plunged on.

'Then there was *Operation Oberon*. Those few days were the very best time in my life - ever. The girls were friendly,

229

the lads were kind and it was fun. I knew I was putting my education to good use at last and being appreciated for what I could do, while the great weather and the holiday atmosphere were a real tonic. I was so sorry for Raj when he got shot, though.'

She stopped talking for a while as tears started to slide down her face. Carlo didn't move, and neither did his expression change. She struggled on like an exhausted channel swimmer.

'I fell in love, and I didn't know what to do about it. I loved spending time with you in New London, but you didn't seem to have any feelings for me other than friendship. It was a shock when you asked me to marry you and to come back with you to Tudorland and I panicked. I couldn't see myself depending on anyone to that extent, because in my experience, people just aren't dependable. I couldn't see how I would cope in such a different environment if it all went wrong. I thought I would muck it all up. I still do.'

Lucy licked her lips and spoke so quietly that Carlo had to strain to hear.

'I tried to put you out of my mind, but I couldn't. I'd rejected the only person who had ever meant *anything* to me. The fact that it was *me* who pushed *you* away rather than the other way around somehow made it worse. Carlo. I think I broke my own heart. I couldn't believe the depth of pain it brought me.

Lucy stopped for a moment and then looked Carlo squarely in the eyes. 'It was like a bereavement but worse, because there wasn't even a grave to visit. I felt bereft and I couldn't see any way forward... or any point...'

Lucy brushed the tears from her face and took another breath. 'I trudged through each day feeling like some kind of ghost, but while I was invisible to most people, those two women in the canteen saw me just fine, and they decided to make my life impossible. When they shoved me away from the good food, I made do with whatever greasy scraps were left, but the situation came to a head when the bloody cow decided to eject me from the canteen altogether. That's what Sophie saw and it's what made her bring me here.'

Lucy looked up at Carlo, and saw concern in his face.

'I could get through the days at work, but I couldn't cope with the rest of it. A cold lump took up residence in my stomach and it wouldn't shift. Sometimes I just went to bed as soon as I got home because I felt so cold and so miserable. I missed you horribly and I wasn't sure I wanted to wake up in the mornings. I had pushed away my only chance of happiness. I still believe that.'

Lucy looked into Carlo's eyes. They weren't as stormy, and the silvery twinkle was beginning to reassert itself.

'Sophie knew, didn't she?' Lucy gulped and tried to get her breath. 'I guess she was aware of my distress, but she's not pushy and she never said anything to me. Anyway, she's mostly at the Mews while I'm at Millbank, so we don't see that much of each other.'

Carlo nodded as Lucy continued,. 'She witnessed that final scene in the canteen though, and I guess it was the last straw somehow…'

Carlo was looking away from Lucy and considering the situation, while she finished her story.

'I'm sorry I turned down your proposal, Carlo. It was panic. I guess I needed time to get used to the idea. I never expect support from so called loved ones, and I couldn't see how I could support myself in this era if it all went wrong.'

Lucy looked down at her hands, as if seeking some kind of answer there. 'Look Carlo, if you don't want me here, I'll take myself off to the woods. I like trees and I'd enjoy their company… at the end… really.'

Carlo still didn't speak. He silently handed Lucy the cup of milk and watched over her while she drank the rest of it down. Then he surprised her by taking her hand and announcing that they were to take a tour of the home farm.

* * *

He led her out of the house and took her to the stables where he introduced her to a young mare. The nervous girl tentatively stroked the animal's neck while Carlo told her she would ride it the next day.

'I don't know the first thing about riding, Carlo. I've never even *sat* on a horse.' To Lucy, this was a vindication of her assertion that she had no useful skills to offer in this alien environment.

'It's not difficult. I'll teach you the basics and you'll soon be proficient enough to get around.'

Lucy smoothed the horse's neck and risked a pat on its nose. 'She's beautiful, Carlo. What's her name?'

'I don't think she's got one, Lucy. What would you like to call her?'

'Hazel.' Lucy gently patted the horse again. 'She's the colour of a hazelnut so I'd like to call her Hazel.'

'Well, Hazel it is then. She'll soon get to know her name and she'll like you all the more if you feed her and brush her down from time to time.'

'I've heard that horses like carrots. Would Hazel like one if I could get one from somewhere?'

'I'm sure she would.'

* * *

Their next port of call was the kitchen garden, and Carlo saw Lucy light up at the sight of it. They walked through the orderly rows of plants to an area of sheds and storage huts. When they got there, Carlo introduced Lucy to an elderly man who was sorting pots on a bench outside one of the sheds.

'This is Fred,' said Carlo. 'He's in charge of the gardens. He grows most of the fruit and vegetables we use on the farm, and he sells the overage in the market, so that way he makes a little extra income for himself and the home farm workers.'

Lucy inspected a row of young cabbages, and noticing some distant raised beds with green fronds peeping over their wooden sides, she asked, 'Do you grow those carrots in raised beds to keep insect infestation away, Fred?'

'That I do,' said a surprised Fred in his West Country burr. 'I've heard you and your friends are Hidalian. Do you grow carrots in Hidalia, miss?'

'Oh for sure, but perhaps not the same variety as yours.'

They discussed the fields of peas that the farm workers were harvesting, but then they came back to the kitchen garden, and Fred surprised Lucy by asking if she'd heard of a strange plant from the New World that someone told him was called a tomato.

'I can get seeds and I'd love to grow them, but I've heard they're poisonous.'

'Yes and no. If you are eating raw tomatoes, it's important to eat them when they're red or they can cause tummy upsets, but green tomatoes can be cooked and turned into a relish that we call by an Indian name, which is tomato chutney. The problem comes with cooking - regardless of whether the fruit is red or green when it's cooked. You see, cooking pots of the kind used here sometimes contain lead, and that *is* poisonous. Tomatoes have a high acid content, so they strip a little of the lead, and people end up eating it.'

'So you're saying that tomatoes encourage the lead to leach out into the food and become ingested?'

'That's it, precisely. However, if you try a tomato raw, perhaps sliced on a piece of buttered bread with a little salt, I know you'll love it. The taste of a fresh, ripe tomato explodes in the mouth like nothing else.'

Soon the conversation about various plants in Fred's kitchen garden grew even more technical, while Carlo stood quietly by and watched the makings of a relationship develop between the fragile girl and the aged gardener.

* * *

Carlo pointed to hillsides full of sheep and explained that his land covered the western side of Dartmoor down to the Tamar River. It reached the sea in the north in one small area, and it almost reached Tavistock in the south, although he didn't own the village of Hatherleigh itself. Lucy began to realise just how wealthy the Hatherleigh family really was. It was clear that Carlo could have lived in a much larger house with many more servants than he had, but that he lived the way he wanted without concerning himself with his status or worrying about the opinions of others.

'Do you have tenants?' she asked.

'Lots,' answered Carlo, brushing a stray curl out of his eyes. 'Many of them work on my land, but some live here and run businesses that are useful to us, such as smiths, carpenters, cloth weavers and so on. We run supplies up and down the river as well.'

They made their way back to the house via Bessie's chicken coop and Carlo encouraged Lucy to dip a cup into a box of chicken feed and toss it into the coop for the chickens to pick up. So far, things were going really well, but then everything changed...

Carlo showed Lucy how to use what he called the garderobe, which he pronounced *garda-roba*. It was surprisingly clean, and there was a bucket of water ready to pour down the loo, along with a jug of water and a basin for washing. She noticed that someone had laid out her own toiletries on a shelf. When she returned, Carlo told her that he'd taken the idea of the bathing caravans from the TUDOR village and had now attached a bathhouse to the side of the house, explaining that it took advantage of a small spring that passed nearby. A permanent fire burned under a water tank, which meant the inhabitants of the house and the home farm could take showers or baths whenever they felt like it and they could wash their clothes in hot water.

Lucy was astonished. He also explained that, as Lord of the Manor and Master of the Household, he should by rights take his meals in the great room, but he preferred to eat in the kitchen with Bessie. Lucy became apprehensive at the thought of food, wondering if she would be able to push anything down.

When mealtime came around, Bessie dished up roast lamb for herself and Carlo with several different vegetables and a hunk of fresh brown bread and butter. Carlo knew Lucy wouldn't be able to eat much, so Bessie gave her a small plate with a little meat and gravy and a sprinkling of peas and carrots, accompanied by a small slice of bread. Bessie also pushed a small mug of ale in her direction. Lucy felt her stomach lurch, so she fiddled about with the food, finally pushing the plate away.

Six years earlier, Carlo had been a knight in charge of a large troop at the siege of Lillientours in southeastern France. When the siege came to an end and the troopers had had their fill of raping and pillaging, Carlo tried to help the survivors, on the basis that the civilian inhabitants of the town had been pawns in their master's games and weren't responsible for the resulting mess. He saw that however much they wanted to eat, they could only manage a little or it would come back up again. He also witnessed those who had gone too far down the road of starvation die even after food had become available to them.

He judged that it wasn't any mental sickness that had made Lucy stop eating, but a combination of lack of opportunity, shortage of money, lack of companionship and then a thoroughly broken heart, along with the most hurtful thing of all, which was her coruscating self-blame for all that had happened. Now though, it had to be stopped and he decided that he wasn't going to put himself to the pain of witnessing her slow rundown to death, and neither could he allow Bessie to do so.

Carlo pushed the plate back in front of Lucy and taking her hand, he spoke quietly to her.

'If you don't eat this meal, I will have you taken to Lydford jail and I will leave you there. It's a dark, damp, cold place with nothing but cold stone and old straw to lie on. There are fleas, lice and a few hungry rats for company. You'll be serenaded by the moaning of other prisoners, if there are any left alive from the last intake.'

Bessie was staring at Carlo in horror. She knew he meant business and Lucy could see it too. The poor girl looked terrified.

'If you give me any reason for refusing to eat Bessie's good vittals or if you give me any lip whatsoever, my man at the jail will strip the clothes from your back and tie you to a whipping post. A few stripes on your back will encourage the rats to taste your blood and bring your life to an even quicker end. It won't be nice.'

Large wet tears ran down Lucy's face. She was so dismayed that she picked up her knife, sliced off a tiny piece of meat and slowly started to chew.

'There's no rush,' said Carlo softly. 'You'll eat it all, you'll drink your ale and you'll keep it all down, because if you sick it up, the result will be the same, which is that you leave here tonight and spend what little remains of your life in Lydford jail.'

Slowly, but surely, Lucy's small dinner went down, and it stayed down. She slowly sipped the low-alcohol ale and sat still while it settled into place in her shrunken stomach. Carlo and Bessie ate steamed pudding and cream, but not Lucy, because Carlo judged she'd taken all she could manage for the time being.

Then Carlo noticed Lucy shaking uncontrollably. Her face was taking on a bluish tinge and her eyes were staring off into the distance, and when he touched her bare arm, despite the warmth of the room, her skin was freezing. Her condition reminded him of the cases of battle shock he'd witnessed in the army.

Carlo promptly swept Lucy up into his arms and carried her to his room, whereupon he pulled off her clothes apart from her knickers. He dug one of his old shirts out of a cupboard and dragged it over her head. The shirt was like a voluminous nightdress on Lucy. Now Carlo pulled pillows up upright and tugged back bedclothes, before picking the poor girl up and tossing her into the bed, ensuring she stayed upright to keep the food down.

He found one of the firelighter blocks that the TUDOR team had left for him, and set the fire alight, piling logs on top once it got going. He opened a cupboard and fished out two more pillows, which he stacked against the head of the bed. Pulling off his own clothes and climbing in, he dragged Lucy none too gently onto his lap and held her tightly until the shaking subsided and she fell into an exhausted asleep. When he was sure she was sleeping soundly, he propped her safely onto the pillows and left her to rest.

Chapter Twenty Seven

FRED'S PREMONITION

*Do the right thing. It will gratify some people and aston-
ish the rest.*

MARK TWAIN

B essie was frying eggs and Lucy was wielding a toast-
ing fork in front of the fire when Carlo came in
through the back door carrying a pile of clothes, which he
dropped onto a chair.

'Eggs for breakfast, is it?' Carlo smiled at Bessie and
turned to Lucy, pointing to the clothing. A pair of boots
stuck out from under the pile.

'A lad came to us some time ago, asking us to train
him as a groom; we'd just got some clothes made up for
him when he was called up to join the army, and that was
the last we saw of him. I think the breeches, boots and
hose will fit, and if the shirt and jacket are a bit large,
well that doesn't matter too much. I think you'll be more
comfortable around the farm in this gear than a long
dress, so why don't you try it on.'

Lucy took the toast from the fork and laid it on a
wooden board.

'I've told Billy to saddle Hazel for you, because today
will be your first riding lesson.'

* * *

Lucy found rising Hazel surprisingly easy and she soon learned to control the pony the way that Carlo showed her.

'You have to show your pony that you're the boss, because her safety and yours are in your hands. She doesn't have the brains or judgement that you have, so don't hesitate to give her a kick or whack her with the crop if necessary.'

Lucy found this particular piece of advice hard to stomach, but she could see what Carlo was getting at, so she did as he said, and soon Hazel got the idea of going where Lucy wanted her to go and doing what Lucy wanted her to do. They rode around for a couple of hours, with Lucy becoming more proficient and confident as the day wore on. Later on, Lucy and Carlo picnicked on bread and cheese, washed down with New London Coke, eventually making their way back to the farm.

Lucy's back, bottom and legs were very sore, but otherwise she felt better than she had in years. She also felt hungry, so when Bessie served up a salmon pie and vegetables that evening, Lucy asked for an adult portion - which she soon polished off - followed by a bowl of raspberries and redcurrants poached with honey and slathered with thick cream from the ubiquitous cream jug. Lucy washed the lot down with a tankard of ale. After her feast, Lucy made herself a nest of cushions at the end of the settee and dozed off, while Carlo got down to some letter writing.

The next two days saw Lucy riding with Carlo or with the home farm stable lad, Billy, if Carlo was busy, and she also spent a good deal of time in the garden with Fred. On the Thursday afternoon, Carlo came looking for Lucy, but she was busy at the far end of Fred's smallholding. Fred dragged a battered chair out of the shed and set it down next to his own equally battered seat, so he and Carlo could catch the sun while they talked.

'What's Lucy up to?' asked Carlo.

'She's hoeing onions over yonder.' Fred took a draught of his ale, and looked out across the rows of leeks and beans while thinking whether he should speak out or not. Then he made the decision to open his mouth.

'You're going to marry her, aren't you, Master Carlo?'

Carlo nodded.

'She doesn't look much because she's too thin at the moment, but I think that has come from illness or from some inner pain. She will plump up soon, although she will never become an ungainly lump.' Fred spoke in a low and urgent voice. 'Master Carlo, yon girl is courageous, kind hearted, gentle, enduring, highly intelligent, hardworking and extremely fragile. She's also sensual - and that will matter to a man like you.'

'Whatever do you mean?' teased Carlo. He was perfectly well aware that Fred occasionally foretold the future – and always with absolute accuracy.

'She turns her face to the sun, feels the earth with her hands, strokes leaves, sniffs the honeysuckle and admires the bean sticks. She sees, hears, feels and touches life. I doubt she knows much about men or the private side of marriage, but I think she will appreciate it when you teach her.'

'How do you know all this, Fred?'

'I see things, Master Carlo. And I was married myself once. It was good while it lasted.'

'What happened?' asked Carlo, sensing that he already knew the answer.

'She died and I never married again. She was going to have a babby when she died. I lost my whole family to the summer fever, all in one dreadful day. I couldn't bear the thought of loving and losing anyone else after that…'

Carlo became aware that Fred was looking into some distant past, then Fred shook himself slightly and quietly said, 'It was a long time ago.'

Fred searched Carlo's face and spoke quietly, but with a sense of purpose. 'You will marry Lucy and you will be happy and God willing, she will soon have a babby of her own on the way - a boy babby - but there's danger, Master Carlo, much danger.' Fred spoke with increasing urgency. 'We must all be gone from here very soon or none of us will survive - not even you, Lucy or the babby.'

Carlo was shocked and highly disconcerted by Fred's pronouncement.

'What do you mean?' he asked. 'What kind of danger?'

'Something will happen to make us leave. I don't know where the danger is coming from, but you must act fast when it happens or you and Lucy will never get away. 'Fred gazed off into the distance. 'You will have to act very quickly indeed if you are to survive the fire, but I will be gone from here even before that...'

'Fire? Christ.' Carlo compressed his lips while thinking through the implications of Fred's premonition. 'I think I can see where trouble is likely to come from, Fred, but I'm not sure when or how.'

Fred nodded, but said nothing more because Lucy was wandering back down the path, hoe in hand and a look of contentment on her face.

'I don't fancy ale, Fred. Is there any Coke?'

Fred smiled and went to the shed for a Coke. Soon the three friends were enjoying a well-earned rest in the sun.

* * *

Lucy settled into life in the Hatherleigh household. She'd loved her time in the garden centre, and she was delighted to be able to bring the knowledge she'd gained from that job to Fred's kitchen garden. Bessie told Lucy that Carlo could have chosen to live in a far grander style than he did, and she also mentioned that Thomas had also chosen to live in a relatively modest style when he was in Tudorland, despite being one of the wealthiest and most influential people in the land. If Lucy became Carlo's wife, in theory, she could expect to live in grand style - if Carlo wanted such a lifestyle. Assuming she could cope with sitting around with nothing but a bit of embroidery to occupy her mind, and - more importantly - if Carlo made a move in that direction. So far, however, there was no indication that Carlo viewed her as anything more than a really good friend.

What Lucy didn't realise though, was that Carlo was determined to give her time to recover from her various ordeals and time to adapt to life a half-millenium in the past before he made his move. He wanted her more than he'd wanted any woman, and he knew he was in love with her. He knew, too, that she'd do her level best to adapt to what-ever life threw at her, but he didn't want her on those terms. He wanted Lucy to be sure she could live in his world. Meanwhile, Lucy didn't know where she stood, so, as with all the situations she'd encountered in her past, she made no demands and did her best to go with the flow.

* * *

Lucy took her Tudor shirt, hose and underwear to the bath-house, washed her clothes and took a shower. She couldn't wear the riding boots without hose, so she decided to don her New London shirt, skirt and shoes, adding her Tudorland lad's jacket for warmth. When she wandered back into the kitchen, Bessie took one look at Lucy and

243

made a decision. She went to her cottage and found a dress for Lucy to borrow, then she went in search of Carlo. When she returned, Carlo was striding in through the kitchen door and looking more handsome than ever in his dark red woollen doublet and breeches, with his windblown, dark brown hair falling onto his forehead. Lucy felt her heart contract, but Bessie on the other hand turned to Carlo and told him to wake up.

'It's time you did something about Lucy,' she said in no uncertain terms.

'What about Lucy? What do you want me to do?'

'Look at the girl,' said Bessie, rounding on Carlo, 'you never hear a word of complaint from her, but she can't go on like this. Even the cleaning maid is better dressed than her. I'll lend her one of my dresses for respectability, but you need to take her to Mary Paget's right now. Tell Mary that Lucy needs everything. She'll know what to do.'

'I can't just drop everything because…'

Bessie cut off his objections. 'You're not doing anything vital Carlo, so you *can* drop everything. Saddle the horses and take Lucy to the town. *Now!* Get going.'

The dress she had loaned Lucy was a shade of sage green that was far from flattering. It was also far too big and also several inches short, but the long socks that Bessie had found worked well enough, so Lucy shoved on her riding boots and made the best of the situation. When Bessie saw her, she sighed, and when Carlo looked properly at her, he suddenly understood the miserable situation he'd put the poor girl into.

* * *

The owner of the dressmaking establishment was a middle-aged lady called Mary Paget, and when Carlo told her that

Lucy was a refugee from Hidalia who had nothing, Mary said she'd take care of it.

'And make her a decent wedding dress while you're at it. I'm going back to the farm, but I will return in about two hours, then Lucy and I will go to see the vicar to get him to put up the bans.'

Lucy stared at Carlo's departing back with her mouth falling open. She felt as though she had fallen through a hole in the universe, and when Mary Paget noticed the colour draining from Lucy's face, she asked her what on earth could be the matter.

'Well, nothing really, Mrs Paget. It's just come as such a surprise.' Lucy turned to face the dressmaker. 'I know Carlo likes me, but I had no idea he wanted to me to be his wife. He hasn't said anything up to now…'

'I've known Carlo for years,' smiled the dressmaker. 'I also remember his cousin, Sir Thomas Hatherleigh, when he used to visit us with his late wife, Anne, in years gone by, and I can tell you that they are both good at keeping their feelings hidden. Carlo is kind hearted, and if he decided to take someone into his household and help them, he would arrange for their needs to be met, but he wouldn't attend to them in person. The moment I saw the two of you riding up Fore Street together, I knew the score.'

Mrs Paget's chief assistant and her young apprentice were thoroughly enjoying the unfolding soap opera, but now the two of them had a burning question for Lucy. The older girl was married and therefore, like Mary Paget, somewhat worldly; so, it was she who decided to ask the million pound question: 'Has he… you know?'

Lucy knew what she was asking, so she slowly shook her head. 'Nothing so far,' said Lucy. He hasn't laid a finger… he did kiss me once, but it was a gentle kiss – perhaps the kind of thing a good friend might do.'

Lucy looked into the eager eyes of her young questioner, 'I had no idea of his intentions until just now.' Lucy fell silent, and then speaking quietly, admitted she knew very little about the physical side of married life. 'So I guess that's yet another thing to worry about.'

Mary snorted, while her assistant and even the young apprentice laughed out loud. The three dressmakers gathered around Lucy, while the chief assistant's voice became conspiratorial.

'My friend is a lady's maid to a wealthy woman,' confided the chief assistant, 'and one day the wealthy lady went up to Gloucester to visit her widowed sister. While they were staying there, my friend became pally with the widow's own lady's maid, and that's where she heard the story. You see, a few months earlier, Carlo had happened to be in the area, and as is the custom with grand people and grand houses, he called in to pay his compliments. To everyone's surprise, he stayed over for a few days, and my friend told me that after Carlo left, it took a full fortnight for the smile to leave the widow-lady's face!'

Now Lucy resembled a stranded fish, gasping for air with her mouth opening and closing. The two young dressmakers were laughing merrily, and now the chief assistant decided to deliver her coup de grace. 'You'll need to eat plenty of red meat if you're going to be his wife, because if a once in a lifetime visit had that effect, imagine what a permanent arrangement would be like!'

Lucy made for the nearest chair and sat down heavily. She put her hands up to her forehead and murmured to herself, 'I'm not sure that I can cope with all this.'

Mary told Lucy not to worry about scurrilous gossip, but to be glad that she was marrying a lovely man like Carlo. 'They're just jealous,' said Mrs Paget in a reassuring voice. 'They'd love to be married to Carlo and so would I, and there isn't a woman in the whole West Country who won't envy you. Nevertheless, it wouldn't hurt to eat an extra lamb chop once in a while, and drink a little red wine from time to time. After all, when a loving man gets busy, it doesn't take long for his wife to be expecting, if you see what I mean.'

'Now that's something I'd really like,' smiled Lucy.

'And so would Carlo,' agreed Mary.

'And so would we!,' said the chief assistant.

Lucy smiled happily at that idea.

Mary and her team took Lucy to the back of the shop and removed the dreadful dress. A moment later, Lucy stood in her New London knickers and bra.

'You're very thin, Lucy. You've been ill perhaps?'

Lucy nodded.

'That means you will gain weight soon enough, so we must find clothes that we can tuck and pleat for now and release later, and those with laced bodices that can be drawn in or loosened.'

Mary explained that she made clothes to order, but she also took in good quality, nearly-new clothes to sell on. Lucy tried on a dozen outfits, along with cloaks and hats. Mary used her extensive experience to select outfits that suited Lucy well. A couple were fine as they were, but others needed a bit of alteration. Mary asked one of her girls to call round to the shoemaker, and get him to bring his measuring kit, and to bring anything suitable that he had on hand for Lucy to wear in the short term.

Meanwhile, Mary helped Lucy into hose that were like tights and a dress of fine wool sections of cream, stone and coral. The bodice fitted nicely and Mary laced it up for her in the front, ensuring it wasn't too tight.

'Take what you need for now and I'll get the rest sent on by trap first thing tomorrow.'

When the maid had been dispatched to the shoemakers, Mary told Lucy she had something really special to show her.

Mary went to a room at the back of the workshop and soon returned carrying a large wooden box, which she laid down on her workbench. Looking reverently at the box, Mary said, 'This came from a ship that foundered in a bad storm and when the storm passed, our local men salvaged what remained.' Lifting the lid carefully, Mary went on, 'the ship must have come from the Orient, because the goods it was carrying were very exotic. The salvage men knew to bring any cloth they found to me, because I would pay the salvage fee without dispute. Some of the cloth is fine cotton, which is rare enough in itself, but some is silk, and in colours and designs we can't begin to create in England. The only client I have for goods of this quality is Lady Isabel Foxley, but she hasn't been in for a while, so these things have just lain here.'

Mary reached into the box and drew out a length of silk. 'One odd thing Lucy, is that the silk pieces are cut in specific lengths and I can't help wondering what they're meant to be.'

Lucy knew what the silken lengths were the moment she set eyes on them - they were saris.

Mary chose a length in a deep blue-green and another in a pale shade of duck-egg that had a slight swirly pattern of fine lines here and there, in a deeper shade of greens and blues. The feather-light silk shimmered with a silvery glow while it moved against the light. Mary explained that the deeper shade would become an overskirt and a fitted over-jacket that would tie in front with fine ribbons, while the aqua length would make the under bodice and skirt.

'We can make a headdress shaped like a halo with tiny seed pearls defining its edge, and we can make up a draw-string handbag of whatever is left over from the dress.

248

Other than the pearls on the edge of the headdress, I think we should avoid any other ornament, as it will detract from the silk. That material will flash green, blue and silver as you walk.'

Lucy could see how utterly sublime the wedding dress would be, and while Mary showed her other silks in yet more amazing colours, Lucy decided to leave it at that. Her life as a farmer's wife - albeit a wealthy and titled one - meant that she needed to focus on practical garments for the most part.

The shoemaker turned up and discussed colours, materials and styles with Lucy and Mary, while he measured Lucy's feet for the cobbler's last that he would need to make.

All the attention made Lucy feel so very special.

* * *

When Carlo returned, he asked Mary to show him the wedding dress material. He nodded, turned and walked Lucy out of the shop and down the road to the home of the local jeweller. When he told the Jeweller he was interested in blue and green stones, the man opened a safe and took out a box that contained a beautiful white-gold necklace set with sapphires and aquamarine topaz.

'I have a ring that accompanies this necklace, if you would like to see it,' said the jeweller.

Carlo nodded, and the jeweller handed Lucy a white-gold ring, set with more stones from the same batch of sapphire and aqua-topaz. She put the ring on and it fitted perfectly, as did the matching white gold wedding ring.

Before going to the jewellers, Mary Paget had dressed Lucy in an attractive dress in shades of dark cream and coral, and helped her into a pair of soft brown riding boots that the shoemaker had left for her. Mary's assistant fitted a couple more dresses and a pair of pretty shoes into the saddle bags on Carlo's horse, and a small bag of linen hankies into the smaller bags that bounced astride Hazel's haunches. With everything finalised, the couple slowly rode out of the village and back down the sunny lane towards Hatherleigh Hall. However, while they both should have been ecstatically happy, something was wrong. For one thing, Lucy was silent, and she wasn't behaving like a girl who'd just been given a fortune in jewellery and a wardrobe any woman would envy - let alone being informed that she was shortly to be married to the most eligible bachelor in the West Country.

Carlo reined in his horse and dismounted, indicating to Lucy that she should climb down, but when Lucy slithered down, her eyes still faced forward along the lane rather than turning to look at Carlo. Her face was set and her expression serious.

'What's the matter, Lucy?' Carlo asked gently.

To be honest, Carlo already had some idea. It occurred to him that his idea of moving very slowly to allow Lucy to recover her mental and physical strength had backfired, and she couldn't really know the strength of his feelings for her. Today's sudden switch to a fast forward gear had taken the poor girl by surprise. He had charged ahead with what *he* wanted, without giving Lucy time to absorb the new state of affairs, or to express an opinion about what was, in effect, her own future. It had become abundantly clear that Lucy could form happy relationships, because she had done so with both Fred and Bessie. Truth to tell, she was far more at ease with the farm manager, Jackson and with the stable lad, Billy, than she was with Carlo. There was a polite formality in her dealings with Carlo that arose from a kind of void that didn't exist between her and the others.

Carlo had slept with many women, but he'd never actually *courted* one. All he'd ever needed to do was show a measure of interest for females to toss themselves willy-nilly into his bed. Lucy was different. She wasn't part of the army of unhappy and unsatisfied Tudor wives who had been locked into arranged marriages with men who didn't care about them, and neither was she a lonely widow. She wasn't in need of a short-term romp or the pseudo feelings of closeness and affection that come from short-term sex. Lucy was honest, sincere, fragile and gentle, and he'd foolishly gone about things in a totally arse-about-face manner where she was concerned. Was it possible that despite Fred's premonitions of a marriage soon to come, he might lose the woman he loved, due to nothing other than his own arrogance and stupidity?

Meanwhile, Lucy spoke up: 'I want to thank you for the clothes,' she said, 'and for looking after me, and for giving me Hazel, and for everything else that you have done for me.' Still looking down the lane, she stopped for a moment, gathered up her courage and said, 'I love the dresses, and the jewellery is breath taking, but this business about bans and weddings has thrown me, Carlo. It's come as a complete surprise. Frankly, I didn't think you liked me that much... I... er...' Lucy had run out of steam.

'Oh, Lucy,' said Carlo, shaking his head at his own stupidity. 'I'm so sorry. I haven't made my feelings clear to you, but I have to do so now. I adored you from the moment I first set eyes on you, and everything I have seen of you since only makes me love you more. I can't live without your love. I need you, I love you dearly and I want you to be my wife.'

Carlo tipped Lucy's chin up and smiled down at her. 'This may be the wrong way of going about things, but I'm afraid of risking another misunderstanding and another rejection, and I have managed both to move too slowly and too quickly, if you see what I mean. If you still want me, Lucy, the bans will go up on Sunday, and a little over two weeks from now we'll be married.'

'You've been unfailingly kind, Carlo, but you were so angry with me... I... I didn't know what to think.'

Lucy turned her face away. Her eyes were filling with tears and red patches of embarrassment had appeared on her cheeks.

'Well, Lucy darling, I'm telling you now. You're the most fascinating, beautiful, loveable, clever and wonderful girl in the world. You've enchanted everyone at Hatherleigh Farm and you've put me under the most binding spell imaginable.' Carlo took Lucy into his arms and held her close while covering her face with small kisses and swaying her slightly one way and another in his arms. 'You're the most gorgeous, talented and perfect girl. The best girl that ever walked the earth at any time in the past, present or the future. I want you with me forever, whatever life throws at us.'

Lucy thought this last comment slightly strange, but she had too much going through her mind just then to give it much thought. She was struggling to come to terms with the sudden shift in her situation and with the feelings that such close contact with Carlo's warm body were arousing in her.

Sensing that Lucy was relaxing a little, Carlo couldn't resist teasing the poor girl. He found her ear and breathed a message into it. 'So, now you must learn about *"The Duties of a Tudor Wife"*,' he said, 'even though the thought of it fills you with apprehension.'

Relaxing now that she realised Carlo really did love her and want her, Lucy joined in the joke. She decided to pretend to be put out. 'I feed the hens, Carlo, I dig the garden and I take care of Hazel. I will soon take over the bookkeeping for the farm, because we both know Jackson hates doing it and I would find it easy. I make supper when Bessie is out, I wash my smalls and I even make toast for breakfast. What other duties could there possibly be?'

'Keeping husbands happy, that's what,' said Carlo, standing away a little so he could look at Lucy's face and laugh at her imitation pout.

Now, though, Lucy decided to speak out about her fears. She told Carlo, 'I don't know much about that stuff... I really don't. Most girls of my era seem to have been shagging every boy they come across from the age of twelve, and know every trick in the sex manual, but I missed out on all that - and to be honest, slagging around with all and sundry really isn't my style.' She hesitated a moment, took a deep breath and went on, 'You're a sophisticated and experienced man, so you'll have to show me what it is that you want me to do for you.'

'Do for me!' Carlo was dumbfounded. 'I'm not talking about lovemaking as yet another chore, my sweet, I'm talking about ecstasy, passion and pleasure.' Carlo nuzzled his face into Lucy's hair. 'Oh, Lucy my love, you're in for a real treat - and so am I.'

Lucy said nothing, but a churning sensation was starting up somewhere beneath her new dress, and her breasts were tingling. It felt as though her body was reaching out for Carlo, so when he tipped up her face and gently kissed her, a raging fire started up and a white-hot firework shot upwards, encircling her heart before leaving her gasping for breath.

* * *

The cleaners had completed their work and were long gone, while Bessie had taken the rest of the day off, so the kitchen was unusually tidy and quiet. The fire was still alight, but it had died down, so Lucy added some more wood and swung the trivet into place before putting a small kettle of clean water on to boil. Meanwhile, she folded Bessie's old dress and left it on a sideboard for Bessie to find the next morning, before taking down a couple of mugs and a precious pack of PG Tips.

Carlo went across to the farm office to have a word with Jackson. It was obvious that the weather was changing and that they would be in for a storm. There was no point in the farm workers trying to do outdoor jobs in such bad weather, so Carlo wanted to check that Jackson had instructed the workers to carry on with such jobs as they could do inside the stables or barns. He suggested that once everything that needed to be done had been completed, they all take the rest of the day off.

When he returned, Carlo used one of the New London firelighters to start his bedroom fire, leaving it to catch while going in search of Lucy. He brought the mugs of tea through to his room, with Lucy following, and soon, they were sitting by the crackling fire and chatting comfortably about the day's events. Lucy was still trying to come to terms with the sudden change in her fortunes when Carlo took the empty mug from her hands and set it down by the hearth next to his.

He gently pulled Lucy up from her chair before untying the cross hatched lacing on the front of her new dress. Truth to tell, he was better at handling Tudor dresses than she was, having helped so many girls off with their clothes, but now he slowly undressed Lucy, kissing her all the while and telling her how much he loved her. Knowing she knew little about love making, he took things slowly, leaving the petticoat in place for a while, lying down on the big bed beside her and gently kissing her face, neck and arms. He quickly removed most of his own clothing before rejoining Lucy.

Carlo stroked Lucy's back and ran his hands through her hair. He was happily stroking the back of her neck and nibbling her ears and the corner of her mouth when her body took on a life of its own. Lucy gripped Carlo as though she was drowning, while the flames that had begun to run up and down her belly were causing a sensation that was fast becoming unbearable. He kissed her lips gently, her mouth opened and she found herself kissing him back fiercely while welcoming his exploring tongue.

Lucy's adoration for Carlo and her deep longing for affection were soon taking her over, to the point where the gentle and ladylike Lucy suddenly discovered that her body had a fervent nature all of its own. The years of famine and frustration soon gave way to a bombshell of innate passion as her body arched up towards Carlo and she whispered his name over and over.

Carlo leaned back and looked at her flushed and happy face; her hazel eyes sparkled up at him in the light of the fire, so now he untied the front of the petticoat and ran his fingers back and forth across the upper part of her left breast. He decided to leave clever love-making tricks alone for the time being while keeping things very gentle and very simple, so he stroked and kissed her breasts while she gripped him and writhed against him in her desperate need. When he gently entered her, he wasn't overly surprised to meet a little resistance, or to feel her buck when a short sharp pain hit her. He kept going, still stroking and kissing her, until their mutual need took them out of the real world and into the world of love, pure sensation and joy that only good lovemaking can bring. Especially when the lovers needed each other this much.

When he finally turned her onto her back so he could give himself the release he needed, he didn't expect an answering orgasm, because Lucy had already come a couple of times, but she met him with equal need and passion. When it was over, they were both tangled in each other, tired, relaxed and happy.

'You know, Carlo that actually hurt a bit – just for a moment' Lucy said.

Carlo whispered into her neck. 'Not surprising, my sweet. Your maidenhead couldn't have been completely busted.'

'You're saying I was still a virgin? Or partly a virgin?' Lucy was amazed. 'That's crackers, Carlo. I had sex three times with Chris, although to be fair, it didn't really work the third time because he couldn't quite get it up, if you know what I mean.'

'It didn't work the first or second times either, my love. It takes a clever chap like me to do the job properly.'

Lucy giggled, but it didn't take her long to work out what must have happened. She knew Chris hadn't been built right and she now knew that, while he'd liked her well enough as a person, and that the unaccustomed drink on those occasions had revved him up, he wasn't really attuned to sex with a woman. Carlo was a very different proposition. He was a passionate and experienced heterosexual man: and in the words of her friend Riva, he had the requisite "plumbing" for the job. And he loved her.

To her surprise, after a rest in the cosy, warm bed, Carlo came back for more, and this time, with more control over his own bodily responses, he took the time to drive his lovely Lucy completely potty. Later that night, she got up to use the loo and have a bit of a wash, and when she came back, she found Carlo awake, and holding his arms out to her. He cuddled her closely for a while, before kissing every part of her body and making her wait for what she needed, before taking her over that impossible rainbow time after time after time.

They finally fell into a deep sleep. They were unusually late for breakfast the following day, which made Bessie smile with joy in recognition of the welcome new development. However, unknown to both of them, one of Carlo's frisky sperms had taken the opportunity of jumping into what it considered to be an unbelievably alluring and attractive egg... and so, within hours of them first making love, a new life had begun.

Chapter Twenty Eight

ALL SOUL'S DAY

Happiness is like a kiss. You must share it to enjoy it.
BERNARD MELTZER

Sophie and Lucy fell into each other's arms while Thomas and Carlo hugged and patted each other.

'Thank God you're all right, Lucy. I've been so worried. I nearly came back for you more than once, but Tommy said I should stick to the arrangement.' Sophie stepped back and looked at Lucy. 'Hells bells, Loo, you look wonderful. I *love* the dress.'

Lucy was wearing a fine wool dress in layers of cream and magenta. The bodice was embroidered and gently laced at the front. Lucy twirled around and let Sophie admire her for a moment.

'This is nothing. You should see what I wore for our wedding.'

'Wedding!' shrieked Sophie. 'You're *married*? Oh, wow! I'm so *glad* for you, and for Carlo, too!'

Carlo asked Thomas to ride out with him after lunch because he had one or two things he wanted to talk over with him, but during lunch, Thomas had news for Lucy.

'You may remember we were setting up new offices on the two floors beneath ours, Lucy.'

Lucy nodded.

'Well, that's done now and it's made quite a change. The twelfth floor is still the same, although Baz, Jack and Kelly are now on the tenth, and their three offices that were on the twelfth have been knocked into one big one, which is now mine, and it overlooks the river of course, which I love. Ryan has my old office. On the other side of the reception area, we now have file and data storage, along with collators and people doing searches of all kinds here and around the world. Downstairs we have an amazing techie department and an ops room that NSA designed for us, and we've recruited loads of new agents.' Thomas smiled and said, 'However, what you'd *really* love is Sophie and Raj's new toy.'

'What's that, Tom?'

'They are putting a TUDOR communications satellite into orbit.'

'A satellite?' Lucy stared open mouthed at Sophie. 'You mean a space rocket and comsat - just for TUDOR?'

Sophie nodded.

'Jeez, Sophie, I'd give my right arm to help design that,' Lucy stopped for a moment, thought and then said, 'but I also love being here.'

Sophie smiled sympathetically, while Thomas went on.

'Exchequer has grown and Steven now also handles human resources and admin. We've discovered that Mrs Shulman has a soft spot for him, so if there's anything we want, we send him to talk her into it. He complains bitterly and says that I give him all the dirty work, but I tell him how important his contribution is and he trots along like a good boy.'

'Crafty bugger!' laughed Carlo.

'Baz runs the field agency with Jack and Kelly assisting him. We've ditched the police ranks and use ranks based on the American agencies. They make more sense to our operations these days, so the old guard have all been promoted and now they're paid more than ever. Interestingly, our new agents come from every part of the armed forces, the police and other security organisations. Not all of them are British though, and some of our spies are far from young, with a small number in their fifties and sixties.'

'Why would you employ old spies?' asked Lucy.

'Two reasons, really. They have contacts from the past that they can tap into, and when we send them out to scout around, nobody suspects them of anything other than of being past their use-by dates.'

Lucy shook her head in amusement.

'Here's an instance,' smiled Thomas. 'You might remember reading in the papers last year that Putin and Obama took a big dislike each other.'

Lucy nodded.

'A side effect of that made it politically incorrect for the Russkies to talk directly to us. Well, one of our old codgers is Douglas Kitteridge, who everyone calls "Smiley" after the character in John le Carré's books. It so happens that Smiley once occupied a high position in MI6, and he used to oppose a chap called General Andrei Balabolin at the KGB. Despite the fact that the two men were supposedly sworn enemies, they often quietly collaborated with each other to get things done. So when Balabolin realised we'd recruited Smiley, he flew over from Moscow and the two of them spent an evening drinking Smiley's local pub dry and crashing out at Smiley's flat. It happens that the General's son, General *Valeri* Balabolin is now the big cheese at the Russkie Commonwealth security office, so as a result of the family connection, we've had no more problems. As always, and in every sphere and every era, it's who you know rather than what you know, isn't it?'

Lucy and Carlo stared at Thomas in fascination.

'However, that's not all. General *Andrei*, as everyone calls him, spends so much time in London that he's rented a nice little flat in Pimlico. Smiley takes him round tourist sites and General Valeri pops in to Millbank unofficially whenever he comes to visit his dad.'

'Those two old geezers must be happy to feel appreciated,' said Lucy.

* * *

Bessie bustled in, gave Thomas and Sophie a hug and said how lovely it was to see them again, and asked them to take seats in the dining room because she was sending in soup and rolls for them start with, and cold meat and pickle to follow. She handed Lucy a pinafore because she didn't want to drop anything down her lovely dress. Lucy shook her head at the still unaccustomed joy of living in a world where people cared about her - and about her dresses.

When they were happily tucking in, Thomas told them his main news of the day.

'The government is setting up a massive organisation based on the FBI, to be called the *British Bureau of Investigation* - and it will be known as the BBI, of course. It will hold copies of everything and it will centralise every kind of data, but we will keep our own files at TUDOR as well. The new organisation will employ hundreds of field agents and have satellite offices in different parts of the country. When the PM asked Mrs Shulman to recommend someone to head it up, she said there was only one person she'd trust, and that was Sir David.'

'So if Sir David's leaving, who will run TUDOR?' asked Lucy.

'Well, this all happened just over two weeks ago, and as soon as Sir David heard the news he immediately put me up for the job, and Mrs Shulman phoned later the same day to ratify the decision.'

Carlo broke in, 'And you're taking the job?'

Thomas nodded.

Carlo thought for a moment. 'How many people are there above you, Tom?'

'Well, in theory, only the Home Secretary. The Cabinet makes the major political decisions, but Mrs Shulman is both a member of the Cabinet and a law in her own right as far as internal security is concerned. If we get involved in foreign adventures, we'll have MI6 and the Foreign Office to deal with, but she'll handle most of that for us anyway, so really it's just the Home Secretary I have to worry about.'

'Not the Queen?'

'No, the Queen doesn't wield any power. You see, in a Constitutional Monarchy, the monarch reigns, but she doesn't rule, so the Queen's role and that of the Royal Family is mainly ceremonial. She knows everything that goes on and she gives advice on occasion. She's a sensible woman who's been on the throne for six decades, so she knows the background to everyone and everything, and if she suggests something, it's usually worth hearing. The same goes for her son, the Prince, who is taking over more of the work for her these days.'

'So you've got your old job back - or something very much like it - and with only one person above you. Won't this make you even more visible than when you worked for Thomas Cromwell?' Carlo's expression was serious and concerned. 'Doesn't it bring back bad memories?'

Thomas drew his lips back and gritted his teeth for a moment. He brushed a hand through his unruly hair while thinking back to those dark days.

'I don't mind telling you that when I heard about the job, it kept me awake for a few nights. I kept dreaming that I was back working for Thomas Cromwell and watching him make all those stupid mistakes during his last year in office, when he was ill and no longer thinking straight. The worst thing he did was insisting that Norfolk dig up the bodies of his dead relatives and move them to a place of Cromwell's choosing. I think it was that kind of unnecessary cruelty as much as anything else that led to his downfall - and mine. One night, this got to me so badly that I gave up trying to sleep and went downstairs. Unsurprisingly, Sophie was also only sleeping fitfully, so she came down to comfort me.'

Sophie took up the story. 'It occurred to me that if Tommy refused to take the job, he would have to train up a new boss, and that would put the new guy in an impossible position. Can you honestly see Steven, Baz, Raj or anyone else taking orders from someone new if Tommy was still there?'

Carlo shook his head. 'Tom would be forced to give up a job he's made for.'

Sophie finished her soup and wiped her lips. 'I encouraged him to go for it, Carlo. After all, even if history repeats itself and Mrs Shulman makes some major cock-up - or if Tommy makes one himself - he could lose his job and maybe his pension, but he wouldn't lose his head.'

Sophie smiled proudly at her husband, and turning to Carlo and Lucy, said, 'When you think of it, what Tommy has achieved is absolutely astounding! We know he wouldn't have got the job in the first place without the existence of the Project, and without the recommendation from Baz; but he took it and ran with it, and he's made a tremendous success of it. Frances Shulman isn't much given to sentiment, and she wouldn't have handed Tommy the job on a plate if she'd had any doubts. Let's also remember that she trusts Steven "Exchequer" Byers to head up the finances and the admin side of things. All in all, I think congratulations are in order, don't you?'

'Definitely,' said Lucy firmly.

'Let's raise a glass to Tommy,' agreed Carlo. 'You're absolutely right, Sophie. What Tommy has done is way beyond the impossible. To become the third most powerful man in Tudorland, and then to reach the same position all over again in New London, is truly astonishing. Congratulations, cousin. You've proved yourself to be a real phenomenon!'

Chapter Twenty Nine

A NEW FUTURE BECKONS

One of the most beautiful qualities of true friendship is to understand and to be understood.

LUCIUS ANNAEUS SENECA

The lads went out for their ride, while Sophie and Lucy went back to the great room to enjoy a New London cuppa. Sophie asked Lucy about life in Tudorland, and Lucy told her about the harvest.

'It really is a case of all hands to the pump, Soph. Everyone gets stuck in, so all the farm hands and other workers in the area pitch in, as do their families. We pick peas and barley, there are old people, children and relatives from all over the area doing their bit, and I can tell you from personal experience that harvesting barley is very hard work. The barley is taken to the barn, where we spread a layer of it on pallets, followed by a layer of gorse, then another layer of barley, then more gorse, and so on. This technique discourages rats. Even before we reached the barn, Jackson let three young terriers loose and they killed loads of mice. They shake them to death, you see.'

Sophie sat rapt at this description of history coming alive, but then Lucy surprised her by telling her even more about Tudor farming methods.

'Amazingly, ploughing with oxen, scattering seed and scything are still done in the sixteenth century exactly as they were in Ancient Egypt in fifteen hundred BC, so it hasn't changed at all in three thousand years. And that's not all; I remember some of the old timers at the garden centre where I used to work during my school holidays telling me about their parents and grandparents who farmed during and after the Second World War. The lack of petrol meant that there were no tractors or combines in use, so they used horse drawn reapers, while land girls scythed wheat and other cereals just as we do here. The old geezers told me how their families used to reap the fields around the edges first, working inwards from the outside, so that rabbits and hares ran into the centre where they could be shot for food. The same thing happens here, Soph, because when the reapers get close in, they stop for a while, then Carlo and some of the others line up with bows and arrows and shoot the rabbits. Jolly good eating they are too.'

'Holy Morony, Loo! It sounds yucky to a city girl like me, but it's amazing how well you're adapting!'

'Carlo says that it's because I'm a Gemini, and he says it's one of the more adaptable signs. I wouldn't have thought so before all this happened, but it seems to be the case.'

Alice's young daughter brought in tea and cakes, along with some luscious plums and raspberries for Sophie, and while they sipped their tea, Sophie fixed her protégé with a gimlet eye.

'You're pregnant, aren't you, Lucy?'

'I guess I am. I haven't seen a period since I left New London, so I must be a couple of months gone.'

'But you've only *been* here two months!' laughed Sophie.

'Don't look at me in that way, Soph. I'm hardly the local bike! You didn't check whether I had any contraceptives in my handbag when you frog-marched me to the Mews and then dumped me here, straight into the lap of Sir Charles Shagalot, did you?'

'Sir Charles Shagalot!' shrieked Sophie. 'Oh dear. He sounds just like my Tommy.'

'Well if your Tommy gets withdrawal symptoms if he goes more than two days without a bonk, he *is* just like Carlo.'

'Yeah, that figures. He's like Tommy all right. That's partly why I only work part time, I have to preserve some of my strength for Tommy.' Sophie giggled at the thought. 'Tell me, Loo, what happened after I left?'

Lucy thought back to that fateful day, sipped some of her tea and started to reminisce, turning her mind back to the immediate aftermath of Sophie's departure.

'Well, we were all stunned at first, and we stood there like statues, but needless to say, Carlo was the first to come to life. The next thing I knew, I was in here, with a cup of milk in my hand. Carlo went to change out of his grubby clothes, but then came back in here wearing a gorgeous doublet, and he plonked himself down in front of me. He sprawled in a chair with one leg stuck out in front of him, leaning back as though he hadn't a care in the world. He just looked at me, Soph; didn't say a bloody word. Just looked.'

'Oh Christ, that reminds me of Tommy when he's interrogating some poor sod at TUDOR. One day, I sat on the suspect's side of the table and watched him at work, just to get an idea of what it felt like to be on the receiving end and I'm telling you, it was a chilling experience. Baz and Jack can interview, and so can Kelly, but when Thomas gets that look in his eyes, well, a whiff of his old Tudorland torture chamber seems to seep into the room and land up in everyone's aura. And those eyes of his just bore into one's soul. Sometimes the suspect takes one look at his face and sings like a canary.'

'I did the same, Soph. Carlo's eyes are grey of course, but they change colour with his mood, and on that day, they looked like thunder clouds just before the rain comes down. I asked him if he wanted to know why I had lost so much weight, and he just raised an eyebrow.'

'Oh my God! I know that one too. It means you're taking your life in your hands if you don't tell them everything: like *now*!'

'Yep. I got the message. In a way though, talking about it helped me get to grips what had happened to me. You see, after my flat-mate suddenly left for Canada, everything started going downhill, financially and in every other way, and apart from getting the job at TUDOR, nothing went right. Falling in love with Carlo was the last straw, and when he asked me to marry him and to come and live here, I couldn't see how I could throw away the independence I had worked so hard for; I couldn't see how I could gamble on life in a world where women have so few rights. After he left, I couldn't forgive myself for turning him down. I fell apart. I think I was in a downward spiral of depression and hopelessness.

'When those two bitches at Millbank started to bully me, I didn't have the strength to fight them, and in a weird way, I kind of agreed with their estimation of me as being a useless waste of space. My parents hadn't wanted me and they always made me feel as though I had no right to be on this earth, so I guess I've always been imbued with the sense of being in everyone's way, and they just emphasised that. I started to give up on life.'

'I thought it was something like that,' Sophie said quietly. 'You see, when Carlo came back to Tamerlane

Square that day, he had a face like a busted boot. He ordered me to fly him back here ASAP, without even stopping to say goodbye to anyone.'

'I'm sorry, Sophie. I'm sorry I caused you all so much trouble.'

Sophie waved her apology away. 'Don't be silly, Loo. You made a perfectly sensible decision on the face of it. The fact that your heart didn't agree with it was another matter. But what happened next?'

'Carlo pulled me up from the settee, took me outside and walked me around the home farm. Then he took me to the kitchen garden and I started talking with old Fred about lettuce or something, while Carlo just stood by and let us ramble on. When we came back for dinner, my emotions were churning so much that I didn't want to eat; my stomach had shrunk with all the weeks of not eating properly and I had no real appetite. That was when Carlo got really frightening.'

Lucy shucked off her shoes and tucked her feet up under her.

'You see, Sophie, when Carlo was fighting in France, he took part in a siege, so he knows the effects of starvation and severe mental stress. He'd asked Bessie to give me a very small plate of food, but I just pushed the stuff around and left it. Carlo was ready for that though, so he pushed the plate back at me and told me that I would eat it all, or he would have someone take me to Lydford jail and leave me there for the rats to finish off. Apparently, it's a horrific place.'

Sophie looked stricken. 'Christ, Loo, if I'd known he could be so hard, I would never have brought you here.'

Lucy sighed. 'Don't blame yourself, Sophie. You meant well. Anyway, he said that if I gave him any lip or if I ate the stuff and sicked it back up, he would have me stripped and flogged before leaving me to die. He said the rats would smell my blood and they'd make short work of me.'

'Oh my God! I had no idea he could be so ruthless. I'm so sorry, Lucy darling.'

'Well, needless to say, I ate the meal. It took a long time for me to get it down and I struggled to keep it down. Carlo sat over me the whole time with a face like thunder, and then I went into shock.'

'Whaaat!'

'Carlo called it "battle shock". I think it's been called shell-shock, battle fatigue or PTSD at different times by different armies. Anyway, I was shaking, I was ice cold and apparently, I was staring off into the distance - the Americans in the Viet Nam war used to call it "*the thousand-yard-stare*". My eyes went out of focus, my heart was slowing and I was on my way out.'

Sophie was appalled.

'Oh fuck-a-duck, Lucy. I feel so bad. If I had only known. Christ, Lucy, you needed *hospital* treatment, not torture!'

'Well Carlo didn't hang about. He gathered me into his arms, ran to his bedroom and pulled my clothes off, apart from my knickers. He pulled one of his old shirts over my head, piled up the pillows and slung me into the bed sitting upright so the food would stay down, then he made up a fire, got more pillows, pulled his own clothes off, climbed into the bed and took me onto his lap, held me tight and warmed me with his body until I fell asleep.'

'Bloody hell, Loo,' whispered Sophie shaking her head slowly.

'Later that night, I woke up and made my way to the garderobe. When I got back, Carlo made us mugs of hot chocolate and we started to talk properly for the first time. I told him about my childhood and about my strange relationship with Chris, and he told me about the loss of his mum and his gratitude to Bessie, who adopted him after losing her own husband.'

Lucy drank her tea and smiled at the memory. 'The next day I learned to ride my pony, and now I am chief chicken feeder and I work in the garden with Fred.'

'*Your* pony. You have your own pony?'

Lucy nodded. 'She's really gentle. I call her Hazel and now she won't come to anyone unless they use her name. She is independent, awkward and she has a habit of wandering off unless I tether her. If I let her loose down the road or something, she'll eat stuff that upsets her. Carlo says she's as much of a pain in the arse as I am, but he moans about everything, so I don't take him seriously.'

Sophie giggled and asked Lucy if she had ever ridden a pony before.

'Never even been near a pony or even a seaside donkey, but I ride Hazel all over the place now. Church and everywhere.'

'Church?'

'Yeah, I go to church on Sundays. Everyone does. I didn't think I'd enjoy it, but I do. I get to chat with Carlo's friends Sir John and Lady Isabel Foxley, and play with their kids after the service. I don't care much for Sir John or Lady Isabel; there's something about them that I don't trust, but their kids are nice.'

'Bloody 'ell, Loo. It's like listening to The Archers. You'll be telling me what to do about carrot fly and how to deal with chickens who are off their food in a minute!'

'Plant carrots in raised beds to prevent carrot fly infestation, and give chickens chopped cabbage, lettuce and grapes if you have them, because they're probably constipated.'

'Now I've heard it all!' Sophie searched frantically for a hanky to mop up her tears of laughter. When she got her breath back she asked Lucy what Carlo was like in bed.

'Well that's a whole story in itself, Sophie.'

'What do you mean?'

'Well, he's perfectly capable of making love for hours on end and in every way you can imagine. He can come, recover after a while, do it again and still look around for more - and then some. He also knows every erogenous zone, and a few that nobody's ever heard of, and he knows exactly how to stimulate what and when. He likes to take his time and he takes pleasure in driving me completely barmy. I start to lose my grip on reality the moment he takes me in his arms, and by the time he's finished, you could tell me I'm Justin Timberlake and I'd believe you.'

Tears of laughter were pouring down Sophie's face.

'Oh Loo, I always had the feeling you were naive, so being with Carlo must have been a revelation.'

Lucy nodded. 'Apart from Chris's fumbling when he was trying to convince himself he wasn't a shirt-lifter - or in his case, a shirt-liftee - I haven't had any contact with men. I was too busy trying to survive, and having Chris around tended to put them off. I was really ignorant, and that worried me, because it's obvious that Carlo's a sophisticated man. Do you know, Soph, there's been times when some fancy-pants mother has offered her daughter to Carlo in marriage due to his status and wealth, and she's offered herself as a by-product.'

'And did he take the mothers up on their offers?'

'As long as the women understood that he wasn't going to marry their daughters, and if he happened to fancy them, he certainly did! Then he bedded the daughters the next day for good measure. On one occasion there was a very lively mother, followed a day later by her twin daughters. He said it took him three days to regain the strength to make the ride back from Worcester after that escapade!'

By now, Sophie was howling with laughter. 'So he's all right then?' she said.

'It's fine. I was afraid he'd find me stupid or lacking whatever it takes, but he seems happy. I love his love-making, and I'm gradually learning - kinda how to take charge of things a little bit for a change - if you know what I mean.'

Sophie nodded in understanding. She'd been there in her early days with Thomas and she was still learning how to please him, even after several years of marriage.

'One day, just to make him laugh, I offered to spread honey on his tummy and lick it off. I didn't mean it of course, but the cheeky bugger raced down the passage to the kitchen, found the honey pot, ran back and spread it on *me*!'

'On your tummy?'

'Not my tummy actually... er. It was er... a bit to the south of that.'

Sophie was so doubled up with hysterics by now that she nearly fell off the sofa. It took the girls a while to regain their equilibrium.

Lucy gave Sophie a searching look. 'You seem to be putting on a bit of weight yourself, Soph.'

'I was going to tell you, but I was so concerned about you that I forgot. I'm a bit further down the road than you, because I'm nearly four months gone.'

'But I thought you couldn't *get* pregnant?'

'I was born with mangled fallopian tubes, but the doctors always said the better of the two tubes might unfurl itself just enough one day to allow an egg to pass down, and that must be what happened. I'm only going to have one child though, because the doctors say there's too many

273

potential dangers for me health wise, and my age is also against me. Tommy is more concerned about my health than he is about having more children. He knows what it's like to love a wife and a child - and to lose them.'

'That's understandable, but I'm still happy for you Sophie.' Lucy gripped Sophie's hands. 'I will pray that you to have a healthy baby and stay well.' Lucy went over to her friend and gave her a hug.

'By the way, do you know what sex it is?'

'It's a girl. I always wanted a daughter and I'm over the moon, but I am following the Jewish superstition of not giving her a name or buying anything until she's here. Kate and Margie will have to rush around and get stuff for us when that happens, please God, but I can see them loving that!'

Before the men came back, Sophie handed Lucy a spare set of keys to her flat and told her she was still being paid her TUDOR wages, so the direct debits on the flat would be more than covered. She also handed her a car key and a velvet roll containing safety rings and a safety locket.

'This locket is new. It works like the safety rings in that you open it and press the button. It might be easier to use in an emergency because the button is a bit bigger. We came over in two projects, one being a van full of groceries and bottled water for you, and the other a Corsa that we're leaving here for you and Carlo. So now you can come back to visit, come back to have the baby, or come back for good or whatever.'

Lucy was just thanking Sophie when the cousins strode purposefully into the sitting room, and it was obvious from their faces that something was wrong.

Chapter Thirty

THE GRIBBONS ATTACK

*The moving finger writes, and having writ, moves on. Nor
all thy piety nor all thy wit, can cancel half a line of it.
Nor all thy tears wash out a word of it.*

OMAR KHAYYAM

When Sophie and Thomas were back in their
Tamerlane Square house, Thomas told his wife
about his ride out with Carlo.

'We rode north to the edge of Carlo's land. A small
corridor of his land reaches the sea, but most of the land
to the north is owned by a family called Gribbons. They
moved in about a year ago. The family consists of a man
and five grown sons, and local gossip says they have
plenty of money on hand from robberies that they've
carried out elsewhere.

Anyway, they're set on taking control of as much of the
area as they can, so they started by buying up some of the
farms surrounding Carlo's, and later helping themselves to
others without actually bothering to pay for them. They've
pushed one widow off her land and terrorised several
elderly smallholders into leaving, so now the only sizeable
land areas left are Carlo's and the Foxley lands, which lie
to the north east of Hatherleigh village. Until a few days

ago, Carlo still felt that he could keep the Gribbons off his back by joining forces with Sir John Foxley.'

Thomas poured himself a glass of wine. He didn't offer any to Sophie, because she was avoiding alcohol until the baby was born. Thomas carried his wine over to his armchair and sat down before continuing.

'Last week after church, Sir John told Carlo that his older brother had recently died without leaving any heirs, so now Sir John has inherited a massive estate and several business enterprises in Yorkshire, so of course, he wants to move up there as soon as possible. Amazingly, he didn't offer his land to Carlo, but sold it off very quickly to the Gribbons. He admitted he didn't get the full market price, but the elder Gribbons told him they had ready money on hand while Carlo would doubtless need to raise the funds, and that would have taken too long. So in short, the rotten bastard took the Gribbons' offer without even stopping to consult Carlo.'

'Jesus Christ, Tommy!' Sophie was horrified. 'What a backstabbing shit-pot! Poor Carlo.'

Thomas nodded. 'Carlo is hopping mad. He said that he probably did have most of the money on hand, and he could have borrowed the rest. However, while I see his point, I can also see that it would be the devil of a job controlling two territories, several miles apart with a small town between. Worse still, the old sheriff can no longer stand up to the Gribbons family, and his troopers have all melted away.'

'We've got to help them,' urged Sophie. 'Can't we get Baz, Jack and the others to help? I mean, how hard would it be for modern troops to take out these Gribbons?'

'Well, that's the obvious idea and I did suggest it, but Carlo can see several problems. Firstly, he feels that going after the Gribbons *before* they made an actual attack on his land would make him no better than them. That's a moral reason, but a more practical one is that sitting men around on his lands, possibly for months on end while waiting for an attack to come to him would be unworkable.'

'That's probably true.' Sophie couldn't help but agree.

'Worse still, there is another issue - and in its way, it's far more dangerous.'

'Like what?'

'When Baz and I first went to Hatherleigh Hall to ask Carlo whether he could accommodate our dry run, a surly maid answered the door. It seems that the woman had wormed her way into the household while Bessie was off sick, and while she was a good cook and housekeeper, Carlo never felt comfortable with her, and Bessie loathed her. When we came along with our request for the dry run, Carlo decided to get her out of the house. He wrote her a letter of reference, and the next morning Jackson put her in the pony trap and ran her down to a big house near Ivybridge that he knew was taking on staff.'

'And?' asked Sophie.

'Well, it appears that the woman is *related* to the Gribbons, and she had taken the job at Carlo's to spy on Hatherleigh Farm and see how much protection Carlo had - or lack thereof.'

'Oh my God,' gasped Sophie.

'Do you remember the night we were attacked? The night Raj got that arrow in his back?'

'Of course.'

'Well, it wasn't pirates, but a group of rather stupid goons that the Gribbons had hired to watch the comings and goings on Carlo's land. They heard our shooting practice and had seen what looked like buildings suddenly arrive and just as suddenly disappear, and they reported this back to the Gribbons. The bloody maid has now put it about that Carlo's new wife is a witch, as are their new friends.'

'Oh shit.' Sophie knew this would be a serious accusation in Tudorland.

'My sentiments exactly.' Thomas put his empty glass back on the wine tray and sat down again. 'You see Sophie love, once that kind of rumour takes hold, even friends and neighbours will denounce Carlo and Lucy. It seems crazy to us, but in Tudorland, an accusation of witchcraft is akin to being caught with a paid up membership card for Al Qaeda in your pocket. Worse still, there would be no trial as we know it, just torture and the stake.'

'We've got to get them *out*!' yelled Sophie. 'I know they've a Project there now, but we need to help them. I think we should go back there, like right *now*?'

'I think they'll land up here quite soon, because Carlo is dismantling the household and the farm in as unobtrusive a way as he can. He sold the sheep and the harvested crops to a couple of Cornish farmers, and Bessie has already gone, taking Jackson, Billy and their families, along with the horses.' Thomas shook his head and smiled gently. 'They packed the dogs, cats and chickens into carts, along with the kitchen tools, because Bessie didn't want to leave the bloody Gribbons anything they could use. Alice, her daughters and the maid have gone to their own families, and Fred very reluctantly went to his widowed sister in Cornwall. Meanwhile Lucy and Carlo are finishing up and they will come to New London in the next day or so.

'They could use Carlo's gold supply to get their hands on a piece of land near to Bessie's holdings, and maybe enlarge her lands and share them with her. However, Carlo said it may not be possible to buy what they want, and having something small in some other place would put them in poverty, so all in all, it looks as if they'll be coming back to New London for good.'

278

'I saw you carting a few heavy boxes back here and putting them into the Mews safe. I take it that was gold?'

Thomas nodded. 'Carlo told me he knew in his heart of hearts that when push came to shove, he wouldn't be able to rely on either the old sheriff or Sir John Foxley, but he had kept that information from Lucy. Fred had picked up the news on the grapevine, but Carlo told him to keep quiet and let Lucy carry on working in the garden for the time being because it made her so happy.'

Thomas rubbed his hands over his face.

'Carlo said that if I was still in Austin Friars and working for Thomas Cromwell, he might have come to me for help, but now he doesn't know what to do for the best. He doesn't want be a burden to us, but I told him to come here and not to worry about that.'

'Look Tommy, we'll do the same for them as we did for Kate and Steven when we pulled them out of Tudorland during that plague outbreak.' Sophie couldn't help feeling that they needed to do something immediately, so she spoke her mind. 'Let's not muck around. Let's ring Baz, Jack and Kelly, and get ourselves over to the Mews and gear up. I can't sit here worrying myself sick, and I can't see either of us getting a night's sleep knowing Lucy and Carlo could be in danger.'

Thomas pushed a rogue lock out of his eyes, got out of the chair, walked swiftly to a side table and picked up the phone.

* * *

'This isn't the end of Tudorland, Lucy darling. We can fly back and visit Bessie and the lads, and you can still ride Hazel.'

'It won't be the same. She won't be my pony any longer and she might not want to know me. You know how capricious she can be.'

Carlo smiled into Lucy's hair. 'I know, darling, I know.' He kissed her forehead gently. 'You've been happy here and I realise how that bloody stupid pony of yours helped you heal, but we have to move on. After all, we've the baby to think of, haven't we? We'll be happy again soon, I'm sure of it.'

'Yeah, you're right,' sighed Lucy. 'But it's heart-breaking to see all that you've worked so hard to create being dismantled in this way. I'm upset enough about leaving the kitchen garden where Fred and I did so much good work, but when I think of the years you've spent building up these lands, managing the woods, the fields, the sheep and everything...'

Lucy turned away, too choked to go on.

Carlo bundled up the sheet containing Lucy's precious wedding dress and stuck a New London torch into his mouth to help him find the way across the yard in the dark. When he came back, he asked Lucy if she wanted to spend another night at the farm and make a fresh start in the morning.

Lucy shook her head. 'I don't think I can bear it.'

She picked up a small leather bag that held her wedding jewellery and the last pieces of gold from the sale of farm implements. She stuffed it into her handbag and pulled out the velvet roll with the safety rings and lockets. They were already dressed in their New London clothes.

Lucy reached up and stroked Carlo's face. 'If you want to pack your decent doublet and sword in a sheet and take it along, I'd understand. I'd even understand taking the groceries rather than leaving them for those thieves, but I would rather get going. It's just too sad to hang on. It's unbearable to stay here in this room where I started coming back to life, and where we first made love. Oh Carlo, I just want to go.'

Carlo cocked an ear. Despite the fact that the farm was supposedly deserted, he could hear shouts and men running around. Worse still, there was something going on above their heads and it didn't feel right.

'Is it my imagination or can I hear a crackling noise,' asked Carlo.

'Carlo, there's someone on the roof - and I can smell fire!'

'Christ, Lucy, this building is really old and the roof isn't strong. If they muck about up there, the whole lot could come down on us!'

The next moment, the roof did just that. Ancient beams and tons of dusty old reeds fell into the room, knocking them to the ground. A beam crashed down onto Lucy's head and she collapsed in Carlo's arms. The vast quantity of dust and debris falling onto them was making it hard for Carlo to breath. It was pitch black, but he heard the remainder of the roof falling in on top of the tons of stuff that was already knocking the life out of him.

Holding his dying wife in his arms, Carlo's last thoughts were that he and Lucy would now be together in paradise, and he knew exactly what it would be like. It would be just like that day his horse ambled into the TUDOR village and he saw Sophie's backside waving in the air on top of the lodge. Once again, he would meet the tall and capable Baz, help a swearing and sweating Thomas build desks and finally spot Lucy strolling out of the Command Centre, turn her face to the sun and squint slightly, while she took a deep breath of clean Devon air. To him, Lucy would be forever young and beautiful, and she would forever be wearing her navy shorts and yellow tee shirt. And he would love her through all eternity.

Carlo knew that something was wrong with his left arm and he realised that it was trapped between Lucy and the edge of a beam. His right arm was also tucked beneath Lucy, but it was fairly free, so he worked it further round his darling's body while he buried his face in her neck. As he did so, his hand connected with the safety ring on the middle finger of his left hand. He didn't think anything useful would come of it, but he flipped the top of the ring open anyway, and pressed down hard on the button.

Chapter Thirty One

THE OTHER SIDE

Being deeply loved by someone gives you strength, while
loving someone deeply gives you courage.

LAO TZU

Under normal circumstances, the first thing we notice when waking from a deep sleep is pressure on the bladder, but Lucy's first sensation was the sound of voices somewhere off to her right. She had expected to travel down a tunnel, move towards a bright light, feel the wings of an angel folding around her and to wander into the Garden of Eden. *That* she was really looking forward to - along with finding Carlo. However, when she opened her eyes just a little, nothing she saw resembled any of the descriptions she'd read about the journey to heaven.

There was a bright light for sure, but it came from a window to her left. She also became aware of a crashing headache and of holding something in her right hand. As her mind started to function, she realised she must be in a hospital, and that pressing the thing in her hand would bring help.

* * *

'You're awake, Mrs Hatherleigh. Good.'

'Who the hell was Mrs Hatherleigh?' thought Lucy.

'Carlo. Where's Carlo?' she croaked.

'Carlo? Do you mean Mr. Charles Hatherleigh, perhaps?'

Lucy tried nodding, but gave it up as too painful, but the nurse got the message.

'Mr Hatherleigh is asleep in the next room. He lost some skin from the back of his right shoulder and his ribs are badly bruised, but fortunately not broken, and his spine wasn't damaged at all, thank God. He broke his left arm though, and that's been set. Other than that, he's fine, although very tired and still somewhat shocked. He was very glad to know you're here though, Mrs Hatherleigh.'

'Lucy. It's Lucy, nurse. And Mr Hatherleigh is Carlo,' said Lucy, falling back to sleep.

* * *

She woke that afternoon feeling brighter. The nurse came in, detached an IV from her left arm and the catheter from her bladder. She held a plastic glass to Lucy's lips and let her drink a few sips of water. It felt like ambrosia in Lucy's parched mouth.

'We've got good news,' the nurse said. 'Carlo is coming along nicely and as soon as we've cleaned you up, he'll be in to see you. Also, your baby is safe and it's doing well.

'Baby? What baby?' thought Lucy. 'The woman's mad. I haven't got a baby.' Then it came back to her. She was *pregnant*!

The nurse walked Lucy into the ensuite, where she helped her take a proper leak and sat her on a stool under the shower while she gently cleaned and washed the soot and mess out of Lucy's hair. It took several washes before it came clean.

After drying her gently and using a hairdryer on her long, wavy hair, the nurse dressed Lucy in a clean gown and stood her by the sink to take a look in a mirror. She looked horrific. Her forehead was completely black, as were both eyes. Her forehead bulged so far forward that she resembled Dr Frankenstein's monster, and the black mess actually wobbled as she moved. Her headache was fierce.

'Your face will recover,' said the nurse gently while she tucked Lucy back into a freshly made up bed. 'It's called a haematoma, which is really just a massive bruise. It looks terrible now, but it will clear up in a couple of weeks. You've had an MRI, and despite being badly concussed, there doesn't seem to be any permanent damage, although a brain can swell and damage can show up some hours *after* an accident, so the surgeon has recommended that you stay here for observation, stay quietly in bed and have another MRI tomorrow. Tomorrow is Saturday, and if you're still fine by Monday, you'll be able to leave. The surgeon says that you may never remember exactly what happened, though.'

The nurse smiled gently at her. 'There's more good news. The obstetrician examined you while you were unconscious and the results were fine. The baby has a strong heartbeat and seems to be developing well. The obstetrician will come in to chat to you later today and she suggests you come in next week for a fuller examination and an ultrasound.'

Plumping up pillows, the nurse said she would send Carlo in to her, and a few moments later, Carlo was hugging her with his good arm and nuzzling his face into her neck. That was the best tonic Lucy could have asked for.

'I was sure I'd lost you, Lucy, and I just couldn't bear it. When they told me you were here, I wanted to get down on my knees and thank God, but I couldn't because my back and arm are so painful. I love you so much, my darling, and I thank God you're alive.'

'Carlo, I hate to think of you in pain.' Lucy was truly anguished.

'It's fine, darling. I'll mend. We're both alive and we're here in New London with the family. What could be better?'

* * *

Later that day Carlo filled Lucy in on all that had happened, because the last vague memory she had was of wrapping her precious wedding dress in a sheet and of Carlo taking it across to the barn to pack into the Corsa.

'The Gribbons decided to destroy the house with us inside it rather than try and buy the land from us. They set fire to the roof and a beam came down, giving you a glancing clout on the forehead. You were dying and I wouldn't have been far behind, because the air was filling with dust and soot, and there was no way I could dig us out from under tons of old thatch and ancient ceiling beams.'

Carlo gave Lucy's cheek a gentle kiss. 'My left arm was broken, but I wanted to hold you close as we died, so I worked my right arm further round you and it met my left hand and landed on the safety ring. I'd forgotten about that, but on the off chance that something useful might happen, I opened it and pressed the button.'

'Thank God you did,' breathed Lucy.

'You see, the Gribbons set the barn on fire *before* they'd started on the house, and a load of burning thatch had landed on top of the Project, but the car itself was all right. When I found myself by the side of it with you in my arms, I opened the door and shoved you into the driver's seat, then I climbed into the passenger side. The system worked exactly as Sophie and Raj had said it would, because the Project came straight through to the Mews. I guess I must have passed out then, because the next thing I knew was Baz dragging me out while Jack was using some kind of machine to pour water all over the car, and all over us.'

Lucy was licking her dry lips, so Carlo managed to pour a little water into a plastic cup for her and he held it to her lips. She sipped gratefully while he told her the rest of it.

'Tom brought us here to the *Winston Churchill Hospital*, the private one that TUDOR uses. The hospital is keeping Tom in the picture and he and Sophie will pass on news to everyone else. The doctors have said that if you're still all right tomorrow, Tom, Sophie, Kate and Steven can come in for a few moments, but you must stay in bed for the time being.'

When the family came in the next day, they spoke to Lucy for a minute or two, but Steven took Carlo aside and said he should leave decisions about the future for now and just focus on both of them getting better.

Chapter Thirty Two

ROSIE

*The only rock I know that stays steady, the only institution
I know that works, is the family.*

LEE IACOCCA

Sophie's pregnancy was tricky. She needed medication
for her diabetes and she watched her diet even more
carefully than usual to prevent the baby from growing too
large, because the babies of diabetics are often oversized
due to absorbing too much glucose while in the womb. She
went swimming a couple of times a week and she walked a
lot, but towards the end of the pregnancy, she developed
problems with anaemia, which meant that she had to endure
painful iron injections. When her time got closer, the doctor
suggested that Sophie consider sterilisation as soon as possible after the birth, because her age, her family history of
heart trouble and her general health could make a second
pregnancy dangerous.

One April day, Sophie was pottering around indoors
when she suddenly felt as though she was starting a period,
and when she waddled to the loo to see what was going on,
her waters broke. She rang Thomas and he rang Kate, who
was closer to home, asking her to take Sophie to the hospital and to stay with her. Kate parked Robbie and Harry with
her neighbour and stayed with Sophie, rubbing her back

and talking gently to her until Thomas arrived. He sat with her, holding her hand, encouraging her when the pains came, and telling her how much he loved her. He also gave her a piece of amber to hold, because Tudorlanders swore by it to ensure a safe delivery. One o'clock the following morning, Margie walked in.

'I couldn't sleep, Tommy love. Why don't you go down to the car and have a lie down. I'll stay with Soph and give her a bit of healing. It'll give her extra strength.'

A very wrung out Thomas took Margie's advice, and he was soon fast asleep on the back seat of his Beamer. The baby was determined to take its time and Sophie was getting tired, but Margie was as good as her word. She stayed with Sophie through the night and gave her many bouts of spiritual healing. Even the doctors were impressed, agreeing that Margie's ministrations had given Sophie the strength she needed to let the labour take its course rather than risk a caesarean.

Dawn broke and Thomas wandered back into the room looking grimy and dishevelled, but another twelve hours was to go by before Sophie was trundled into the delivery room. The doctor kept Thomas out of the room in case of complications, so the poor man paced the corridor with his ears practically standing out on stalks. Margie came back just then, so the two friends paced up and down the passage for the better part of an hour, until they were rewarded with a thin cry. A few moments later, a nurse came out to tell them that Sophie had given birth to a healthy baby girl, and that Sophie would be just fine, although she was very weak and very tired.

A few days later, Sophie was back in the delivery room to have her tubes ligated. Thomas had offered to have a vasectomy, but Sophie said she was happy to be sterilised and to get over the operation and the birth in one go. She also said that being sterilised wouldn't bother her, as it would simply put her back to where she'd been before.

Kate and Steven got in touch with an agency and recruited a nurse to move into the Tamerlane Square house for a few weeks to take care of Sophie and the baby until Sophie felt well enough to cope. They arranged for a cleaner to come in three days a week, and she was such a godsend that Sophie kept her on afterwards as house-keeper. The girls had a grand time buying cots, prams, strollers, baby clothes, toys and all manner of equipment. Knowing that Thomas couldn't cook, they popped in with homemade stews for him to put into the microwave, take-aways and extra bottles of milk for Sophie. Riccardo and Marco, who ran their favourite trattoria, sent round excellent pizzas and plates of their home made *ravioli al sugo*, because in their opinion, a good *ravioli* was guaranteed to make Sophie strong.

Even if Sophie had *wanted* to object to all the help everyone was giving her, they made it clear they weren't listening. Surprisingly, Sophie was able to breast-feed the baby, but she really was glad to have everything else done for her for a while.

* * *

Rosie grew into a gorgeous toddler, with Thomas's dark wavy hair, classic features and huge blue eyes. Thomas was potty about her and had to hold himself back from spoiling her. Baz and Margie's children, Shelley and Taylor now had a dog in the shape of Jimmy the Golden Labrador, while Kate and Steven had become inadvertent cat owners when a large ginger tom decided to move in with them. They called the cat Wolsey on account of its habit of walking around with its nose in the air, along with its other habit of helping itself to anything that it fancied. Even patient, stoical Steven sometimes lost his temper with the crafty animal, yelling at it and throwing it bodily out into the garden, locking the cat-door shut for an hour or so to teach the great thief a lesson. Wolsey did eventually learn to keep out of the kitchen when Steven was around, but at other times, he stole food with impunity.

Needless to say, Rosie now also wanted a dog. Sophie had never had a pet so she was unsure about the idea, but one day Thomas came home with a miniature Yorkshire terrier that was hardly larger than a kitten, and Rosie promptly called it Betsy. Sophie couldn't bear to leave the tiny creature shut up alone all day, so she took Betsy to the Mews on her working days, where Betsy greeted everyone who came in by running up to them and begging to be picked up, and of course, nobody could resist the little creature. Like Thomas, Sophie and Rosie, Betsy had an endless need for love and affection. Rosie adored Betsy, and when she was at home, she carted the little dog around everywhere with her, often pushing Betsy round the garden in her toy pushchair. Betsy didn't mind. As long as she was in the middle of everything, she was happy.

Along with her parents and Betsy, Rosie loved her many uncles, aunts and cousins, but she took a special delight in "Uncle" Jack Duquesne. Whenever Jack came around, he would play with Rosie and talk to her in French, and soon the little girl was answering him in his own language. One sunny day, Sophie and Thomas were relaxing in the garden with their friends, with Thomas half asleep in a garden chair, when he clearly heard Rosie say, *'Je t'aime, Oncle Jacques, je t'aime beaucoup.'*

Thomas sat up. 'Did you hear that!' he looked at Sophie in disgust. 'Even Rosie's fallen under that bloody reprobate's spell. What the hell's he *got*?'

'He's fun to be with and he listens to what people say, whatever age they are or whoever they are, he's good looking, capable and bright, but he isn't arrogant. It's a powerful focus, even for a three-year-old, and more to the point, he loves Rosie to bits and she loves him. It's good for both of them.'

Thomas watched Rosie and Jack, who were playing tennis with child-sized racquets and a sponge ball. He said, 'I guess it's good for her to be with people she loves. She doesn't have grandparents and there'll never be any siblings. And Jack seems to be growing up somewhat at long last. He and Ryan often play golf at the weekends now. They flirt with girls in the other Millbank offices and they sometimes go clubbing and come in the worse for wear on a Monday morning, but even that's less often these days.'

'You know, Tommy, you have just as much charisma as Jack and Carlo, although yours is different. You're a more serious personality than either of them, but there can't be a woman of any era or any age who doesn't like you, talk to you and respond to you. I bet even Joan of Arc would have fancied you!'

'Perhaps I ought to jump in the Project and see how I get on with her,' he said. 'Maybe those dreams she had about swords entering her body weren't as godly as she persuaded her followers to believe. It could have been nothing more than the lack of a good man.'

'Well it won't be *you*, my love! Not this time,' smiled Sophie.

As the sun went down on the hot summer evening, Jack picked up a tired Rosie and made himself comfortable on a garden chair, lulling the little girl to sleep in his arms. Sophie handed Jack a bottle of Coors, and Thomas smiled at the contented face of his sleeping daughter, curled up in the warm security of her beloved uncle's embrace.

Sophie also looked at her daughter. 'She's going to be clever and beautiful, and the boys will buzz like bees round a honey-pot when she reaches her teens.'

'I'll *kill* them!' hissed Thomas. 'I won't have their grubby hands anywhere *near* my precious daughter!'

Chapter Thirty Three

TUDOR WEST

*The only way to make sense out of change is to plunge
into it, move with it, and join the dance.*

ALAN WATTS

Carlo followed the lead set by Thomas, Steven and Kate
by taking courses in English as a foreign language and
several more on different aspects of computing, while
taking on work at TUDOR. He started with mundane jobs
for Jack and Kelly, such as surveillance and checking
CCTV footage, while he gradually learned about modern
security work. Over time, he resurrected his interrogation
skills and the investigation methods he'd developed while
working for the sheriff in Tudorland, eventually becoming
a full time operative under Jack Duquesne. He learned from
Jack how to look half asleep while actually being very alert
indeed and he made friends with a new chap who'd spent a
few years in the army. Michael was a black guy from
Martinique and he spoke excellent French, so they both
used French on occasion to sharpen their linguistic skills.

Sir David Cromwell now headed up BBI, working out
of offices in Maida Vale, while Thomas had taken over as
Director of TUDOR with Baz as his second in command.
Baz had always considered himself a copper rather than a

potential Director, but age and experience had broadened his abilities, so now he was happy to be Deputy Director.

* * *

Lucy's pregnancy and birth had been much easier than Sophie's, and now she and Carlo were the parents of a gorgeous baby boy who they called Daniel. Needless to say, Danny had inherited the Hatherleigh looks, and apparently also the Hatherleigh nature, because no female on earth could resist his smile, and Lucy had to take care he wasn't spoiled rotten. The only apparent blot on their happiness was that, while he never said anything, it was clear that Carlo badly missed the outdoor life. He bought magazines on farming and spent as much time as he could researching the subject on the Net, or taking the family out into the countryside.

* * *

One day in June, Thomas called Carlo into his office. Baz was already there and Thomas was gazing out at the traffic on the Thames. It always calmed him and helped him to think.

Thomas sat down, picked up a cup of coffee and opened the mini-meeting.

'TUDOR is growing, Carlo, and we feel the need to open branches in two other locations.'

Carlo couldn't see where this was going.

'Baz is sending Mike and a few others to open an office in the north because that's where the large ethnic populations are, and where a certain amount of mischief gets brewed up for us. However, a less obvious, but equally difficult area, is the West Country.'

'The West Country? Why's that?'

'Well, there is every kind of military activity you can imagine down there, including nuclear submarines in Plymouth and nuclear attack installations in hidden locations. There are civilian and military ports in Bristol, Plymouth, and Falmouth and plenty of other places that could be vulnerable. There's GCHQ, Yeovilton, Culdrose, the Navy and much else. During World War Two, there used to be what were called "listening posts" near Exeter, and we want to open a modern version of those, with a potential for taking action if needed. We want to site the office somewhere in Devon, and the new outpost will liaise with the military and with GCHQ.

'We think that a farm, an equestrian centre, a garden centre or any combination thereof would make a great cover for a sub-branch that we want to call TUDOR WEST, although it will probably end up being named T-West with the Northern branch being T-North. Anyway, TUDOR will finance the purchase of land and a farm, and we'll provide everything that might be needed, from combine harvesters to the sheep, horses, tomato seeds or whatever. Lucy could even go back in time and get her pony.'

Carlo looked at Thomas in astonishment. He wondered if his cousin had lost his marbles. Truth to tell, he felt that he was losing his own, and he began to wonder if he was taking part in an episode of *"Allo 'Allo"*.

'Let me get this right, Tom. You want Lucy and me to start a farm in Devon and run a satellite listening post as a sub-branch of TUDOR out of our second best barn or something.'

'Your first best barn would be better,' laughed Baz.

'Okay. I'll check with Lucy, but I know what she'll say.'

'What's that?' asked Thomas.

'When do we leave and when can I get Hazel?' Carlo pulled a face. 'That bloody animal is useless. It's too weak to pull a plough. It refuses point blank to be clipped into a trap. It only comes when called by its name. It has to be tied up or it wanders off and eats stuff that makes it sick. You can't use the bloody mare for breeding and she's a fussy feeder.' Carlo looked at his grinning companions while he sighed deeply. 'What that animal really needs is to be put down, but Lucy loves her and truth to tell, Hazel's gentle with women and children, so she might come in handy for Danny to learn on.'

Carlo looked into some far distance and very quietly said, 'She'll be planning her kitchen garden a moment after I tell her, and she'll work at whatever you want her to. I guess Raj and the rest of you will fly up and down, so we'll need a really big house to accommodate you all, and a sodding great kitchen that will become a substitute boardroom.'

* * *

A visit to an estate agent in Hatherleigh showed Carlo and Lucy that a house and a quantity of land to the west of the little town were for sale. The agent told them it was called *Gribbons Farm*, although the farm had fallen into disuse and the original Gribbons family must have died out centuries ago. There was a very large farmhouse made of local stone, and a small stable block nearby, although it all needed updating.

When they got back to Hatherleigh village, they took themselves to a pub for a drink and a think. The place was clearly part of Carlo's original farm, although the landholding was now far smaller. Nevertheless, it was big enough for their purposes, so there was no question that they wanted it. That being so, they knew that TUDOR wouldn't even try to negotiate the price down, as Thomas would just go ahead and buy the place.

'The first thing I'm doing is changing that name, Lucy. I can't live in a place called "Gribbons Farm".'

'What about reverting to "Hatherleigh Farm"?'

Carlo nodded, but then he decided to tease his wife. 'You know darling, one real benefit of living in New London was not having to put up with that bloody pony of yours.'

Lucy looked daggers at her husband.

'Well,' sighed Carlo, pretending to be mightily put out, 'I suppose we'd better get on with buying the farm, then we can fly back to Bessie and pick up Hazel, can't we?'

Carlo's wonderful light grey eyes twinkled and turned silver as he gazed deeply into Lucy's.

'That's going to cost you, my girl - *big time*! You're going to have to do *"Duties of a Tudor Wife"* every night for a month - *and* you're going to spread honey on…'

His loving wife gave him a small thump.

'And lick it all off again.'

Lucy giggled and said, 'I'll be pregnant again in the blink of an eye if we're not careful.'

'Good job, too. I want you barefoot, pregnant and tied to the kitchen sink.'

'That'll be the day. I'll have an allotment and a home to run, Danny to look after and most probably a highly techie job with TUDOR.'

'You could be right,' said Carlo smiling, 'but "keeping husbands happy" is your most important job of all.'

'Always – as is "keeping *wives* happy"!

'Trollop!'

* * *

As head of TUDOR West, Carlo ran his farm using modern systems with the help of a really good manager. Lucy didn't bother with a full garden centre because she knew she would be too busy to cope with it, but she enjoyed her vegetable allotment and she grew plenty of flowers in their garden.

Carlo bought several more horses, which he rode and sometimes loaned out to a few selected locals. Thomas and Sir David also enjoyed a good ride out from time to time. Hazel was soon joined by a tiny pony that became Danny's mount, and the little lad soon got the hang of it.

The family visited Bessie, Jackson and Fred on occasion, and were made very welcome by the Tudorlanders. Fred had left his sister's Cornwall farm and had taken himself off to Bessie's farm, where he knew he'd be happier. He was getting very frail and sat around more than he used to, but he was happy to spend his last years with his beloved friends, and he was philosophical about reaching the end of his life. As he told Lucy, his lovely young wife and child were waiting for him in heaven, where he would be young and fit again and able to grow vegetables in the Garden of Eden to his heart's content.

TUDOR West became a communications centre, but the increasing threat of terrorism in the area meant that Carlo had to do more than simply run an office, so he often had his hands full. Lucy took on a very good nanny and worked part time in the TUDOR office. When Raj and Sophie became involved with developing and putting a dedicated TUDOR communications satellite into orbit, Lucy immediately got on board. Indeed, they all agreed that details of the job would be less likely to leak if they ran it out of T-West rather than Millbank or The Mews.

It wasn't long before they also moved the Projects to T-West, leaving only a couple of smaller shuttles at the Mews.

* * *

So, for the time being, everything was running like a well-oiled machine, but not for long...

You've finished "Lucy's Dilemma", but that isn't the end of Sophie, Thomas and their friends; more tales of the team's adventures and romance continue in "Emily's Mistake". Here is the first chapter from the latest book in the Tudorland series:

Emily Borrows the Project

We travel, some of us forever, to seek other states, other lives, other souls.

ANAÏS NIN

The Project shuddered, gave a little jiggle and came to a halt. Emily peered out through the window, but it was too dark to see anything. This puzzled her because she'd timed her arrival for ten in the morning, so unless she'd made a major error when she keyed in the data, the Project must have landed inside some kind of building. Wondering whether she'd bitten off more than she could chew, Emily briefly considered abandoning the whole potty idea and going home.

'Don't be such a wimp,' she told herself 'you're here now, so you might as well take a look.'

Grabbing a small torch from the cubbyhole, Emily stepped out of the car and immediately saw why it was so dark – the Project had landed in a cave. She could see light in the distance though, so she decided to make her way towards it. The air in the cave was warm and dry, and she noticed the temperature rising as she walked towards the light, but she was so busy focusing on reaching the light that she tripped over a rock that jutted up from the cave's floor. She swore to herself as she bashed her shin on the rock, and again when she realised she'd torn a hole in her new trousers, but apart from the trouser damage, there didn't seem to be anything else wrong, so she decided to carry on with her mission.

There were several blue-painted metal barrels stacked by the side of the cave's entrance, and once she'd passed by them, she found herself out in the open air. The landscape was just like that shown in television programmes about the Middle East, as it was rocky desert, with a few scrubby bits of brush, and a ridge of beautiful golden hills in the distance. However, the sun was so fierce that she wished she'd thought to bring her sunglasses.

Outside the cave, there were several more barrels stacked in the shade of a nearby rocky outcrop, but as Emily walked away from the cave, a loud 'whump' was immediately followed by a sensation of the ground shaking beneath her feet. For a moment, Emily was too stunned to work out what was going on, but before she could make sense of anything, a pair of strong arms grabbed her from behind and lifted her bodily before dropping her none too gently face down in a slit trench. Then the owner of the arms climbed in and settled himself on top of her.

Emily registered the smell of warm man, along with the slightly spicy aroma of an unfamiliar make of soap. She gasped and tried to push the man off her but he stayed put, while speaking to her in an urgent and somewhat angry tone. Emily had no idea what he was saying, so in the absence of any better ideas, she asked the guy if he spoke English – and to her relief, he did.

'Stay down, woman. They're tossing mortars over!' he said.

Emily tried to twist around and get a look at the man, but he hooked his chin over her shoulder and pushed her back down. Emily was so frightened that she could hardly

301

speak, but she managed to find enough energy to wriggle her right hip out of the way of a particularly sharp stone that was sticking into it. Meanwhile her captor held her down even more firmly, while shouting at her as though she was a stupid child.

'Keep your head down if you don't want to get us both killed! Those barrels contain gasoline and if a mortar hits them the fuel should flow along into the dip by the cave, so our only chance of survival is to stay here and hope that it does.'

'Who are you?' cried Emily. 'Where am I? What's going on?' She realised that she must sound positively demented.

The man would have agreed with her self-assessment, because she certainly did sound confused, but he decided to give her the benefit of the doubt.

'To answer your questions in the order given, I am sergeant Shimon Sobieski of the Israeli Regular Army, and in case you hadn't noticed, there's a war on.'

'The Six-Day War, I take it?'

'The what war?'

'What year is this?' asked Emily.

'1967, of course. What year did you think it was?'

'June 1967, is that?'

'Yes, of course.'

'What's the actual date today?'

'The ninth.' Shimon wondered whether the mortar blast had given the girl concussion. She was clearly disoriented.

'Poo!' exclaimed Emily. 'Double poo!' She realised that she'd misfired and arrived in Israel during the Six-Day War rather than after it. Christ, she could be killed here! She wished she'd had the sense to double-check the date before pressing enter on the Project's computer. This could easily be a costly mistake.

Another mortar fell, but it seemed a little further away. Emily was shaking so hard now that she wondered how her captor managed to stay on top of her, but he merely repeated his instruction to stay down and he didn't shift one inch from his position. Emily noticed that the guy's voice was lightly accented, so she supposed his first language must be Hebrew, but with a name like Sobieski, it could just as easily have been Russian or Polish. He'd pronounced his first name 'Shimon' with the emphasis on the 'on'. Was that Russian, or was it Hebrew? Also, he'd pronounced the 'o' in Sobieski like the 'o' in 'hot' rather than the 'o' in 'go'.

Another mortal fell, but it sounded further away. Even so, the sergeant continued to press her firmly into the bottom of the trench with her nose now digging into the sand. His right arm was curled around her body and his hand happened to be cupping her right breast, but she nearly jumped out of her skin when his thumb gave her nipple a speculative brush. Now, in addition to being so terrified that her teeth were actually chattering, and furious with herself for her mistaken data-entry, she was also getting seriously irritated with sergeant Sobieski.

'Saucy monkey,' she spat, but even those two words were an achievement with a mouth that was bone dry from shock, and not helped by the sand that was trying to edge it's way in.

Shimon raised his head and looked around, while listening hard. 'It looks as though they've moved off, so I'll have to get back to my men now. Before you go though, I need you to tell me who you are and what you're doing here.'

Emily had to think quickly; and on balance, she was rather pleased with the story she came up with.

'My name is Emily Cromwell and I came from England to visit a friend who lives in the next village, but I hadn't realised there would be fighting in this area, so I guess I became a bit disorientated with the shock of it all.'

'I suppose that makes some sense,' replied Shimon, not commenting on the fact that the only habitation within miles was an ancient monastery.

He climbed out and sat on the edge of the trench, while taking a good look at Emily. Scruffy and sandy as she was, he saw a pretty girl in her early twenties with a mass of dark blond hair, eyes of an unusual golden shade and a really decent figure. She was wearing a pale blue tee shirt, tightly fitting navy cotton trousers with a rip in the front and grubby white sandals. Shimon decided he wanted to know more about her, partly because he found all pretty girls interesting, but also because her story just didn't hang together. He contemplated taking her with him, but he knew he'd soon be in the thick of it again, and he wouldn't be able to take care of a passenger. He figured that even if Emily was some kind of spy, there wasn't much she could see here other than a few fuel drums, and anyway the war was clearly working its way to an end, so he decided to leave her to her own devices for the time being.

'Look, Emily,' said Shimon with a smile. 'I have to go now, but when the fighting is over, you can find me in the "Whisky a Go-Go" nightclub in Jerusalem late on any Saturday night. It's near the King David Hotel, so meet me there and we'll get properly acquainted. You can buy me a beer as an act of immense gratitude for saving your life.'

Looking at Shimon properly for the first time, Emily saw a tall, slim soldier with very blond hair and a pair of sparkling blue eyes in a lightly tanned face. His dimpled smile told her he was a cheeky one and he looked like fun, but soon Emily would be back in her own time and place, and she would have neither the desire nor the opportunity to search out Sergeant Shimon Sobieski in his Jerusalem night club. She merely nodded though, and watched him gather up his rifle from the lip of the trench and stride away.

Staggering back into the cave, it occurred to Emily that she'd completely forgotten the existence of the roll of safety rings in the glove compartment of the old car. If she'd thought to put one on, all she would have needed to do once the first mortar stuck, was flip open the decorative stone and press the little button inside the ring. That would have brought her safely back to the Project and thence back to its hiding place in The Mews, which was in present day London.

'I can see the safety ring's a great idea, and it would have been even better if I had actually thought of wearing the blinking thing!' said Emily in self-admonishment.

Stellium Ltd

We hope that you enjoyed this book. The intrepid TUDOR team continue their adventures, along with a few new friends, in the third volume, due out shortly. Search for "Tudorland" or "Sasha Fenton" on any Amazon site, or visit our website at www.stelliumpub.com for details.

It would be helpful to other prospective readers if you would kindly leave a review of this book on Amazon.

We also welcome your direct comments about this book (use stelliumpub@gmail.com), so let us know your thoughts about the Tudorland series, or let us know what you'd like to see in future books from Stellium.

Lightning Source UK Ltd.
Milton Keynes UK
UKOW01f1812071017
310545UK00006B/377/P